Feb. 23-1923.

Kathryn Jackson

From -

Grandma Boganwright -

THE RE-CREATION
OF BRIAN KENT

With love to Auntie Sue from Betty Jo.

THE RE-CREATION OF BRIAN KENT

A NOVEL BY
HAROLD BELL WRIGHT

Author of
"The Shepherd of the Hills"
"When A Man's A Man" etc.

WITH FRONTISPIECE IN COLOR BY
J. ALLEN ST. JOHN

A. L. BURT COMPANY

Publishers   New York

Published by arrangement with The Book Supply Company

DEAR AUNTIE SUE:

I have wondered many times, while writing this simple story of life and love, if you would ever forgive me for putting you in a book. I hope you will, because if you do not, I shall be heartbroken, and you wouldn't want me that way, would you, Auntie Sue?

I fancy I can hear you say: "But, Harold, how *could* you! You know I never did the things you have made me do in your story. You know I never lived in a little log house by the river in the Ozark Mountains! What in the world will people think!"

Well, to tell the truth, dear, I don't care so very much what people think if only they will love you; and that they are sure to do, because,—well, just because— You must remember, too, that you will be eighty-seven years old the eighteenth of next November, and it is therefore quite time that someone put you in a book.

And, after all, Auntie Sue, are you very sure that you have never lived in a little log house by the river,—are you very sure, Auntie Sue?

Forgive my impertinence, as you have always forgiven me everything; and love me just the same, because I have written only in love of the dearest Auntie Sue in the world!

Harold.

The Glenwood Mission Inn,
Riverside, California,
April 30, 1919.

5

"And see the rivers, how they run
  Through woods and meads, in shade and sun,
  Sometimes swift, sometimes slow,—
  Wave succeeding wave, they go
  A various journey to the deep
  Like human life to endless sleep!"
         John Dyer—"Grongar Hill."

CONTENTS

CONTENTS

THE RE-CREATION
OF BRIAN KENT

The Re-Creation of Brian Kent

CHAPTER I.

A REMARKABLE WOMAN.

REMEMBER as well as though it were yesterday the first time I met Auntie Sue.

It happened during my first roaming visit to the Ozarks, when I had wandered by chance, one day, into the Elbow Rock neighborhood. Twenty years it was, at least, before the time of this story. She was standing in the door of her little schoolhouse, the ruins of which you may still see, halfway up the long hill from the log house by the river, where the most of this story was lived.

It was that season of the year when the gold and brown of our Ozark Hills is overlaid with a filmy veil of delicate blue haze and the world is hushed with the solemn sweetness of the passing of the summer. And as the old gentlewoman stood there in the open door of that rustic temple of learning, with the deep-shadowed, wooded hillside in the background, and, in front, the rude clearing with its crooked rail fence along which the scarlet sumac flamed, I thought,— as I still think, after all these years,—that I had never before seen such a woman.

Fifty years had gone into the making of that sterling character which was builded upon a foundation of many generations of noble ancestors. Without home or children of her own, the life strength of her splendid womanhood had been given to the teaching of boys and girls. An old-maid school-teacher? Yes,—if you will. But, as I saw her standing there that day,—tall and slender, dressed in a simple gown that was fitting to her work,—there was a queenly dignity, a stately sweetness, in her bearing that made me feel, somehow, as if I had come unexpectedly into the presence of royalty. Not the royalty of caste and court and station with their glittering pretenses of superiority and their superficial claims to distinction,—I do not mean that; I mean that true royalty which needs no caste or court or station but makes itself felt because it *is*.

She did not notice me at first, for the noise of the children at play in the yard covered the sound of my approach, and she was looking far, far away, over the river which lay below at the foot of the hill; over the forest-clad mountains in the glory of their brown and gold; over the vast sweep of the tree-crowned Ozark ridges that receded wave after wave into the blue haze until, in the vastness of the distant sky, they were lost. And something made me know that, in the moment's respite from her task, the woman was looking even beyond the sky itself.

Her profile, clean-chiselled, but daintily formed, was beautiful in its gentle strength. Her hair was soft and silvery like the gray mist of the river in the morning. Then she turned to greet me, and I saw her eyes. Boy that I was then, and not given overmuch to serious thought, I knew that the high, unwavering purpose, the loving sympathy, and tender understanding that shone in the calm depth of those eyes could belong only to one who habitually looks unafraid beyond all earthly scenes. Only those who have learned thus to look beyond the material horizon of our little day have that beautiful inner light which shone in the eyes of Auntie Sue—the teacher of a backwoods school.

Auntie Sue had come to the Elbow Rock neighborhood the summer preceding that fall when I first met her. She had grown too old, she said, with her delightful little laugh, to be of much use in the larger schools of the more thickly populated sections of the country. But she was still far too young, she stoutly maintained, to be altogether useless.

Tom Warden, who lived just over the ridge from the schoolhouse, and who was blessed with the largest wife, the largest family, and the most pretentious farm in the county, had kinsfolk somewhere in Illinois. Through these relatives of the Ozark farmer Miss Susan Wakefield had learned of the needs of the Elbow Rock school, and so, finally, had come into the hills. It was the influential Tom who secured for her the modest position. It was the motherly Mrs. Tom who made her at home in the Warden household. It was the Warden boys and girls who first called her "Auntie Sue." But it was Auntie Sue herself who won so large a place in the hearts of the simple mountain folk of the district that she held her position year after year, until she finally gave up teaching altogether.

Not one of her Ozark friends ever came to know

16

in detail the history of this remarkable woman's life. It was known in a general way that she was born in Connecticut; that she had a brother somewhere in some South-American country; that two other brothers had been killed in the Civil War; that she had taught in the lower and intermediate grades of public schools in various places all the years of her womanhood. Also, it was known that she had never married.

"And that," said Uncle Lige Potter, voicing the unanimous opinion of the countryside, "is a doggone funny thing and plumb unnatural, considerin' the kind of woman she is."

To which Lem Jordan,—who was then living with his fourth wife, and might therefore be held to speak with a degree of authority,—added: "Hit sure is a dad burned shame, an' a plumb disgrace to the men of this here country, when you come to look at the sort of wimmen most of 'em are a marryin' most of the time."

Another matter of universal and never-failing interest to the mountain folk was the unprecedented number of letters that Auntie Sue received and wrote. That some of these letters written by their

17

backwoods teacher were addressed to men and women of such prominence in the world that their names were known even to that remote Ozark district was a source of no little pride to Auntie Sue's immediate neighbors, and served to mark her in their eyes with no small distinction.

It was during the fourth year of her life amid the scenes of this story,—as I recall time,—that Auntie Sue invested the small savings of her working years in the little log house by the river and the eighty acres of land known as the "Old Bill Wilson place."

The house was a substantial building of three rooms, a lean-to kitchen, and a porch overlooking the river. The log barn, with "Prince," a gentle old horse, and "Bess," a mild-mannered, brindle cow, completed the modest establishment. About thirty acres of the land were cleared and under cultivation of a sort. The remaining acreage was in timber. The price, under the kindly and expert supervision of Tom Warden, was fifteen dollars an acre. But Auntie Sue always laughingly insisted that she really paid fifty cents an acre for the land and fourteen dollars and a half an acre for the sunsets.

18

The tillable land, except for the garden, she "let out on shares," always under the friendly guardianship of neighbor Tom; while Tom's boys cared for the little garden in season, and saw to it that the woodpile was always ample and ready for the stove. And, in addition to these fixed and regular homely services, there were many offerings of helpful hands whenever other needs arose; for, as time passed, there came to be in all the Elbow Rock district scarce a man, young or old, who did not now and then honor himself by doing some little job for Auntie Sue; while the women and girls, in the same neighborly spirit, brought from their own humble households many tokens of their loving thoughtfulness. And never did one visit that little log house by the river without the consciousness of something received from the silvery-haired old teacher—a something intangible, perhaps, which they could not have expressed in words, but which, nevertheless, enriched the lives of those simple mountain people with a very real joy and a very tangible happiness.

For six years, Auntie Sue continued teaching the Elbow Rock school;—climbing the hill in the morning from her log house by the river to the cabin schoolhouse in the clearing on the mountain-side above; returning in the late afternoon, when her day's work was over, down the winding road to her little home, there to watch, from the porch that overlooked the river, the sunset in the evening. And every year the daily climb grew a little harder; the days of work grew a little longer; she went down the hill in the afternoon a little slower. And every year the sunsets were to her eyes more beautiful; the evening skies to her understanding glowed with richer meaning; the twilight hours filled her heart with a deeper peace.

And so, at last, her teaching days were over; that is, she taught no more in the log schoolhouse in the clearing on the mountain-side. But in her little home beside the river she continued her work; not from text-books, indeed, but as all such souls must continue to teach, until the sun sets for the last time upon their mortal days.

Work-worn, toil-hardened mountaineer mothers, whose narrow world denied them so many of the finer thoughts and things, came to counsel with this childless woman, and to learn from her a little of the art of contentment and happiness. Strong men, of rude dress and speech, whose lives were as rough as the hills in which they were reared, and whose thoughts were often as crude as their half-savage and sometimes lawless customs, came to sit at the feet of this gentle one, who received them all with such kindly interest and instinctive understanding. And young men and girls came, drawn by the magic that was hers, to confide in this woman who listened with such rare tact and loving sympathy to their troubles and their dreams, and who, in the deepest things of their young lives, was mother to them all.

Nor were the mountain folk her only disciples. Always there were the letters she continued to write, addressed to almost every corner of the land. And every year there would come, for a week or a month, at different times during the summer, men and women from the great world of larger affairs who had need of the strength and courage and patience and hope they never failed to find in that little log house by the river. And so, in time, it came to be known that those letters written by Auntie Sue went to men and women who, in their childhood school days, had received from her their first lessons in writing; and that her visitors, many of them distinguished in the world of railroads and cities, were of that large circle of busy souls who had never ceased to be her pupils.

Thus it came that the garden was made a little larger, and two rooms were added to the house, with other modest improvements, to accommodate Auntie Sue's grown-up boys and girls when they came to visit her. But never was there a hired servant, so that her guests must do their own household tasks, because, Auntie Sue said, that was good for them and mostly what they needed.

It should also be said here that among her many pupils who lived beyond the sky-line of the far, blue hills, not one knew more of the real secret of Auntie Sue's life and character than did the Ozark mountaineers of the Elbow Rock district, among whom she had chosen to pass the evening of her day.

Then came one who learned the secret. He learned —but that is my story. I must not tell the secret here.

CHAPTER II.

THE MAN IN THE DARK.

 MAN stood at a window, looking out into the night. There was no light in the room. The stars were hidden behind a thick curtain of sullen clouds.

The house was a wretchedly constructed, long-neglected building of a type common to those old river towns that in their many years of uselessness have lost all civic pride, and in their own resultant squalor and filth have buried their self-respect. A dingy, scarcely legible sign over the treacherous board walk, in front, by the sickly light of a smoke-grimed kerosene lantern, announced that the place was a hotel.

Dark as it was, the man at the window could see the river. The trees that lined the bank opposite the town were mere ghostly shadows against the gloomy masses of the low hills that rose from the water's edge, indistinct, mysterious, and unreal, into the threatening sky. The higher mountains that reared

23

their crests beyond the hills were invisible. The stream itself swept sullenly through the night,—a resistless flood of dismal power, as if, turbid with wrecked souls, with the lost hopes and ruined dreams of men, it was fit only to bear vessels freighted with sorrow, misfortune, and despair.

The manner of the man at the window was as if some woeful spirit of the melancholy scene were calling him. With head bowed, and face turned a little to one side, he listened intently as one listens to voices that are muffled and indistinct. He pressed his face close to the glass, and with straining eyes tried to see more clearly the ghostly trees, the sombre hills, and the gloomy river. Three times he turned from the window to pace to and fro in the darkened room, and every time his steps brought him again to the casement, as if in obedience to some insistent voice that summoned him. The fourth time, he turned from the window more quickly, with a gesture of assenting decision.

The crackling snap of a match broke the dead stillness. The sudden flare of light stabbed the darkness. As he applied the tiny, wavering flame to the wick of a lamp that stood on the cheap, old-fashioned

bureau, the man's hand shook until the chimney rat-
tled against the wire standards of the burner. Turning quickly from the lighted lamp, the man sprang
again to the window to jerk down the tattered, old
shade. Facing about, he stood with his back to the
wall, searching the room with wide, fearful eyes.
His fists were clenched. His chest rose and fell
heavily with his labored breathing. His face worked
with emotion. With trembling limbs and twitching
muscles, he crouched like some desperate creature at
bay.

But, save for the wretched man himself, there was
in that shabby, dingy-papered, dirty-carpeted, poorly
furnished apartment no living thing.

Suddenly, the man laughed;—and it was the reckless, despairing laughter of a soul that feels itself
slipping over the brink of an abyss.

With hurried step and outstretched hands, he
crossed the room to snatch a bottle of whisky from its
place beside the lamp on the bureau. With trembling
eagerness, he poured a water tumbler half-full of the
red liquor. As one dying of thirst, he drank. Drawing a deep breath, and shaking his head with a wry
smile, he spoke in hoarse confidence to the image of

himself in the dingy mirror: "They nearly had me, that time." Again, he poured, and drank.

The whisky steadied him for the moment, and with bottle and glass still in hand, he regarded himself in the mirror with critical interest.

Had he stood erect, with the vigor that should have been his by right of his years, the man would have measured just short of six feet; but his shoulders—naturally well set—sagged with the weariness of excessive physical indulgence; while the sunken chest, the emaciated limbs, and the dejected posture of his misused body made him in appearance, at least, a wretched weakling. His clothing—of good material and well tailored—was disgustingly soiled and neglected;—the shoes thickly coated with dried mud, and the once-white shirt, slovenly unfastened at the throat, without collar or tie. The face which looked back from the mirror to the man was, without question, the countenance of a gentleman; but the broad forehead under the unkempt red-brown hair was furrowed with anxiety; the unshaven cheeks were lined and sunken; the finely shaped, sensitive mouth drooped with nervous weakness; and the blue, well-placed eyes were bloodshot and glittering with the light of near-insanity.

The poor creature looked at the hideous image of his ruined self as if fascinated with the horror of that which had been somehow wrought. Slowly, as one in a trance, he went closer, and, without moving his gaze from the mirror, placed the bottle and tumbler upon the bureau. As if compelled by those burning eyes that stared so fixedly at him, he leaned forward still closer to the glass. Then, as he looked, the distorted features twitched and worked grotesquely with uncontrollable emotions, while the quivering lips formed words that were not even whispered. With trembling fingers he felt the unshaven cheeks and touched the unkempt hair questioningly. Suddenly, as if to shut out the horror of that which he saw in the mirror, the man hid his face in his hands, and with a sobbing, inarticulate cry sank to the floor.

Silently, with pitiless force, the river swept onward through the night, following its ordained way to the mighty sea.

As if summoned again by some dark spirit that brooded over the sombre, rushing flood, the man rose heavily to his feet. His face turned once more toward the window. A moment he stood there, listening, listening; then wheeling back to the whisky bottle and the glass on the bureau, he quickly poured, and drank again.

Nodding his head in the manner of one reaching a conclusion, he looked slowly about the room, while a frightful grin of hopeless, despairing triumph twisted his features, and his lips moved as if he breathed reckless defiance to an invisible ghostly company.

Moving, now, with a decision and purpose that suggested a native strength of character, the man quickly packed a suit-case with various articles of clothing from the bureau drawers and the closet. He was in the act of closing the suit-case when he stopped suddenly, and, with a shrug of his shoulders, turned away. Then, as if struck by another thought, he stooped again over his baggage, and drew forth a fresh, untouched bottle of whisky.

"I guess you are the only baggage I'll need where I am going," he said, whimsically; and, leaving the open suit-case where it lay, he crossed the room, and extinguished the light. Cautiously, he unlocked and opened the door. For a moment, he stood listening. Then, with the bottle hidden under his coat, he stole softly from the room.

A few minutes later, the man stood out there in the night, on the bank of the river. Behind him the outlines of the scattered houses that made the little town were lost against the dusk of the hillside. From the ghostly tree-shadows that marked the opposite bank, the solemn hills rose out of the deeper darkness of the lowlands that edged the stream in sombre mystery. There was no break in the heavy clouds to permit the gleam of a friendly star. There was no sound save the soft swish of the water against the bank where he stood, the chirping of a bird in the near-by willows, and the occasional splash of a leaping fish or water animal. But to the man there was a feeling of sound. To the lonely human wreck standing there in the darkness, the river called—called with fearful, insistent power.

From under the black wall of the night the dreadful flood swept out of the Somewhere of its beginning. Past the man the river poured its mighty strength with resistless, smoothly flowing, terrible force. Into the darkness it swept on its awful way to the Nowhere of its ending. For uncounted ages, the river had poured itself thus between those walls of hills. For untold ages to come, until the end of time itself, the stream would continue to pour its strength past that spot where the man stood.

Out of the night, the voice of the river had called to the man, as he stood at the window of his darkened room. And the man had come, now, to answer the call. Cautiously, he went down the bank toward the edge of the dark, swirling water. His purpose was unmistakable. Nor was there any hint of faltering, now, in his manner. He had reached his decision. He knew what he had come to do.

The man's feet were feeling the mud at the margin of the stream when his legs touched something, and a low, rattling sound startled him. Then he remembered. A skiff was moored there, and he had brushed against the chain that led from the bow of the boat to the stump of a willow higher up on the bank. The man had seen the skiff,—a rude, flat-bottomed little craft, known to the Ozark natives as a John-boat,— just before sunset that evening. But there had been no boat in his thoughts when he had come to answer the call of the river, and in the preoccupation of his mind, as he stood there in the night beside the stream, he had not noticed it, as it lay so nearly invisible in the darkness. Mechanically, he stooped to feel the chain with his free hand. A moment later, he had placed his bottle of whisky carefully in the boat, and was loosing the chain painter from the willow stump.

"Why not?" he said to himself. "It will be easier in midstream,—and more certain."

Carefully, so that no sound should break the stillness, he stowed the chain in the bow, and then worked the skiff around until it pointed out into the stream. Then, with his hands grasping the sides of the little craft, and the weight of his body on one knee in the stern, he pushed vigorously with his free foot against the bank and so was carried well out from the shore. As the boat lost its momentum, the strong current caught it and whirled it away down the river.

Groping in the darkness, the man found his bottle of whisky, and working the cork out with his pocket-knife, drank long and deep.

Already, save for a single light, the town was lost in the night. As the man watched that red spot on the black wall, the stream swung his drifting boat around a bend, and the light vanished. The dreadful mystery of the river drew close. The world of men was far, very far away. Centuries ago, the man had faced himself in the mirror, and had obeyed the voice that summoned him into the darkness. In fancy, now, he saw his empty boat swept on and on. Through what varied scenes would it drift? To what port would the mysterious will of the river carry it? To what end would it at last come in its helplessness?

And the man himself,—the human soul-craft,—what of him? As he had pushed his material boat out into the stream to drift, unguided and helpless, so, presently, he would push himself out from the shore of all that men call life. Through what scenes would he drift? To what port would the will of an awful invisible stream carry him? To what end would he finally come, in his helplessness?

Again the man drank—and again.

And then, with face upturned to the leaden clouds, he laughed aloud—laughed until the ghostly shores gave back his laughter, and the voices of the night were hushed and still.

The laughter ended with a wild, reckless, defiant yell.

Springing to his feet in the drifting boat, the man

32

shook his clenched fist at the darkness, and with insane fury cursed the life he had left behind.

The current whirled the boat around, and the man faced down the stream. He laughed again; and, lifting his bottle high, uttered a reckless, profane toast to the unknown toward which he was being carried by the river in the night.

CHAPTER III.

A MISSING LETTER.

AUNTIE SUE'S little log house by the river was placed some five hundred yards back from the stream, on a bench of land at the foot of Schoolhouse Hill. From this bench, the ground slopes gently to the river-bank, which, at this point, is sheer and high enough to be well above the water at flood periods. The road, winding down the hill, turns to the right at the foot of the steep grade, and leads away up the river; and between the road and the river, on the up-stream side of the house, was the garden.

At the lower corner of the garden, farthest from the house, the strong current had cut a deep inward curve in the high shore-line, forming thus an eddy, which was margined on one side, at a normal stage of water, by a narrow shelf of land between the water's edge and the foot of the main bank. A flight of rude steps led down from the garden above to this natural landing, which, for three miles up and down the river,

34

was the only point, on Auntie Sue's side of the stream, where one could go ashore from a skiff.

From the porch of the house, one, facing up the river, looked over the gently sloping garden, over the eddy lying under the high bank, and away over a beautiful reach of water known as The Bend,—a wide, sweeping curve which, a mile distant, is lost behind a wooded bluff where, at times, during the vacation or hunting season, one might see the smoke from the stone chimney of a clubhouse which was built and used by people who lived in the big, noisy city many miles from the peaceful Ozark scene. From the shore of The Bend, opposite and above Auntie Sue's place, beyond the willows that fringe the water's edge, the low bottom-lands extend back three-quarters of a mile to the foot of a heavily timbered ridge, beyond which rise the higher hills. But directly across from Auntie Sue's house, this ridge curves sharply toward the stream; while less than a quarter of a mile below, a mighty mountain-arm is thrust out from a shoulder of Schoolhouse Hill, as if to bar the river's way. The high bluff thus formed is known to the natives throughout all that region as Elbow Rock.

THE RE-CREATION OF BRIAN KENT

The quiet waters of The Bend move so gently on their broad course that from the porch, looking up the stream, the eye could scarcely mark the current. But in front of the little log house, where the restraining banks of the river draw closer together, the lazy current awakens to quickening movement. Looking down the stream, one could see the waters leaving the broad and quiet reaches of The Bend above and rushing away with fast increasing speed between the narrowing banks until, in all their vicious might, they dashed full against the Elbow Rock cliff, where, boiling and tossing in mad fury, they roared away at a right angle and so around the point and on to another quiet stretch below. And many were the tales of stirring adventure and tragic accident at this dangerous point of the river's journey to the far-away sea. Skilled rivermen, by holding their John-boats and canoes close to the far shore, might run the rapids with safety. But no boat, once caught in the vicious grip of the main current between the comparatively still waters of The Bend and that wild, roaring tumult at Elbow Rock, had ever survived.

It was nearing the close of a late summer day, and Auntie Sue, as was her custom, stood on the porch watching the sunset. In the vast field of sky that arched above the softly rounded hills there was not a cloud. No wind stirred the leaves of the far-reaching forests, or marred the bright waters of the quiet Bend that mirrored back the green, tree-fringed banks and blue-shadowed mountains. Faintly, through the hush, from beyond the bottom-lands on the other side of the stream, came the long-drawn "Wh-o-e-e! Wh-o-e-e!" of farmer Jackson calling his hogs. From the hillside, back of the house, sounded the deep, mellow tones of a cowbell, telling Auntie Sue that neighbor Tom's cattle were going home from their woodland pastures. A company of crows crossed the river on leisure wing, toward some evening rendezvous. A waterfowl flapped slowly up the stream. And here and there the swallows wheeled in graceful circles above the gleaming Bend, or dipped, flashlike, to break the silvery surface. As the blue of the mountains deepened to purple, and the rosy light from below the western hills flushed the sky, the silver sheen of the quiet water changed with the changing tints above, and the shadows of the trees along the bank deepened until the shore-line was lost in the dusk of the coming night.

And even as the river gave back the light of the sky and the color of the mountains, so the gentle face of the gray-haired woman, who watched with such loving reverence, reflected the beauty of the scene. The peace and quiet of the evening of her life was as the still loveliness of that twilight hour.

And, yet, there was a suggestion of pathos in the loneliness of the slender figure standing there. Now and again, she clasped her delicate hands to her breast as if moved by emotions of a too-poignant sweetness, while in her eyes shone the soft light of fondest memories and dearest dreams. Several times she turned her head to look about, as if wishing for some one to share with her the beauty that moved her so. At last, she called; and her voice, low and pure-toned, had in it the quality that was in the light of her eyes.

"Judy! Judy, dear! Do come and see this wonderful, wonderful sky!"

From within the house, a shrill, querulous, drawling voice, so characteristic of the Southern "poor-white" mountaineer, answered: "Wha-a-t?"

A quick little smile deepened the crows'-feet at the corners of Auntie Sue's eyes, as she called again with gentle patience: "Do come and see the sunset, Judy, dear! It is so beautiful!" And, this time, in answer, Judy appeared in the doorway.

From appearances, the poor creature's age might have been anywhere from fifteen to thirty-five; for the twisted and misshapen body, angular and hard; the scrawny, wry neck; the old-young face, thin and sallow, with furtive, beady-black eyes, gave no hint of her years. As a matter of fact, I happened to know that Judith Taylor, daughter of the notorious Ozark moonshiner, Jap Taylor, was just past twenty the year she went to live with Auntie Sue.

Looking obliquely at the old gentlewoman, with a curious expression of mingled defiance, suspicion, and affection on her almost vicious face, Judy drawled, "Was you-all a-yellin' for me?"

"Yes, Judy; I want you to help me watch the sunset," Auntie Sue answered, with bright animation; and, turning, she pointed toward the glowing west,— "Look!"

Judy's sly, evasive eyes did not cease to regard the illumined face of her old companion as she returned, in her dry, high-pitched monotone: "I don't reckon as how you-all are a-needin' much help, seein' as how

39

you are allus a-watchin' hit. A body'd think you-all was mighty nigh old 'nough, by now, ter look at hit alone."

Auntie Sue laughed, a low, musical, chuckling laugh, and, with a hint of loving impatience in her gentle voice, replied to Judy's observation: "But, don't you understand, child? It adds so to one's happiness to share lovely scenes like this. It makes it all so much—so much—well,—*bigger,* to have some one enjoy it with you. Come, dear!" And she held out her hand with a gesture of entreaty, and a look of yearning upon her dear old face that no human being could have withstood.

Judy, still slyly watchful, went cautiously nearer; and Auntie Sue, putting an arm lovingly about the crooked shoulders of the mountain girl, pointed again toward the west as she said, in a low voice that vibrated with emotion, "Look, Judy! Look!"

The black eyes shifted, and the old-young, expressionless face turned toward the landscape, which lay before them in all its wondrous beauty of glowing sky and tinted mountain and gleaming river. And there might have been a faint touch of softness, now, in the querulous monotone as Judy said: "I can't see as how hit could be ary bigger. Hain't ary reason, as I kin see, why hit should be ary bigger if hit could. Lord knows there's 'nough of hit as 't is; rough 'nough, too, as you-all 'd sure know if you-all had ter trapse over them there hills all yer life like I've had ter."

"But, isn't it wonderful to-night, Judy? It seems to me I have never seen it so perfect."

"Hit's just like hit's allus been, so far as I kin see, 'ceptin' that the river's higher in the spring an' more muddier," returned the mountain girl. "I was borned over there on yon side that there flat-topped mountain, nigh the mouth of Red Creek. I growed up on the river, mostly;—learned ter swim an' paddle er John-boat 'fore I kin remember. Red Creek, hit heads over there behind that there long ridge, in Injin Holler. There's a still—"

She checked herself suddenly, and shot a fearful sidewise look at Auntie Sue; then turned and pointed in the opposite direction with a pretense of excited interest. "Look down there, ma'm! See how black the old river is where she smashes inter Elbow Rock, an' how white them waves be where the water biles an' throws hitself. Hit'd sure git you if you was ter

41

git ketched in there with er John-boat, wouldn't hit ? Listen, ma'm ! You kin hear hit a-roarin' like hit was mad, can't you ?"

But the older woman turned to face, again, the quiet reaches of The Bend.

"I think I like The Bend best, though, Judy. See how perfectly those trees and hills are mirrored in the river; and how the water holds the color of the sky. Don't you think God is good to make the world so beautiful for us, child ?"

" 'Beautiful' !" cried poor, deformed Judy, in a voice that shrilled in vicious protest. "If there is a God, like you-all are allus a-talkin' 'bout, an' if He sure 'nough made them things, like you-all sees 'em, He sure hain't toted fair with me."

"Hush, Judy !" pleaded Auntie Sue. "Please don't, child !"

But the mountain girl rebelliously continued: "Look at me ! Just look at me ! If that there God of your'n is so all-fired good, what did He go an' let my pap git drunk for, an' beat me like he done when I was a baby, an' make me grow up all crooked like what I be ? 'Good' ? Hell ! A dad burned ornery kind of a God I call Him !"

For some time, Auntie Sue did not speak, but stood with her face upturned to the sky. Then the low, gentle voice again broke the silence: "See, Judy, dear; the light is almost gone now, and there is not a cloud anywhere. Yesterday evening, you remember, we could not see the sunset at all, the clouds were so heavy and solid. The moon will be lovely to-night. I think I shall wait for it."

"You-all best set down then," said Judy, speaking again in her querulous, drawling monotone. "I'll fetch a chair." She brought a comfortable rustic rocking-chair from the farther end of the porch; then disappeared into the house, to return a moment later with a heavy shawl. "Hit'll be a-turnin' cold directly, now the sun's plumb down," she said, "an' you-all mustn't get to chillin', nohow."

Auntie Sue thanked her with gentle courtesy, and, reaching up, caught the girl's hand as Judy was awkwardly arranging the wrap about the thin old shoulders. "Won't you bring a chair for yourself, and sit with me awhile, dear?" As she spoke, Auntie Sue patted the hard, bony hand caressingly.

But Judy pulled her hand away roughly, saying: "You-all ain't got no call ter do sich as that ter me.

43

I'll set awhile with you but I ain't a-needin' no chair." And with that, she seated herself on the floor, her back against the wall of the house.

The last of the evening was gone from the sky, now. The soft darkness of a clear, star-light night lay over the land. A gentle breeze stole over the mountains, rustled softly through the forest, and, drifting across the river, touched Auntie Sue's silvery hair.

Judy was first to break the silence: "I took notice neighbor Tom brung you-all a right smart bunch of letter mail this evenin'," she said, curiously.

There was a troubled note in Auntie Sue's gentle voice as she returned, "The letter from the bank did not come, Judy."

"Hit didn't?"

"No; and, Judy, it is nearly four weeks, now, since I sent them that money. I can't understand it."

"I was plumb scared at the time, you oughten ter sent hit just in er letter that a-way. Hit sure looked like a heap of money ter be a-trustin' them there ornery post-office fellers with, even if hit was funny, new-fangled money like that there was. Why, ma'm,

you take old Tod Stimson, down at the Ferry, now,
an' that old devil'd steal anythin' what warn't too
much trouble for him ter lift."

"Argentine notes the money was, Judy. I felt sure
that it would be all right because, you know, Brother
John sent it just in a letter all the way from Buenos
Aires. And, you remember, I folded it up in extra
heavy paper, and put it in two envelopes, one over
the other, and mailed it at Thompsonville with my
own hands."

"Hit sure looks like hit ought ter be safe er nough,
so long as hit warn't mailed at the Ferry where old
Stimson could git his hands on hit," agreed Judy.

Then, after a silence of several minutes, she added,
in a more reassuring voice: "I reckon as how hit'll
be all right, ma'm. I wouldn't worry myself, if I
was you. That there bank-place, like as not, gits er
right smart lot of letters, an' hit stands ter reason the
feller just naturally can't write back ter ev'rybody at
once."

"Of course," agreed Auntie Sue. "It is just some
delay in their acknowledgment, that is all. Perhaps they are waiting to find out if the notes are

45

genuine; or it may be that their letter to me went astray, and will have to be returned to them, and then remailed all over again. I feel sure I shall hear from them in a few days."

So they talked until the moon appeared from behind the dark mountains that, against her light, were silhouetted on the sky. And, as the old gentlewoman watched the queen of the night rising higher and higher on her royal course, and saw the dusky landscape transformed to a fairy-scene of ethereal loveliness, Auntie Sue forgot the letter that had not come.

With the enthusiasm that never failed her, the silvery-haired teacher tried to give the backwoods girl a little of her wealth of vision. But though they looked at the same landscape, the eyes of twenty could not see that which was so clear to the eyes of seventy. Poor Judy! The river, sweeping on its winding way through the hills, from the springs of its far-away beginnings to the ocean of its final endeavor,—in all its varied moods and changes,—in all its beauty and its irresistible power,—the river could never mean to Judy what it meant to Auntie Sue.

"Hit sure is er fine night for to go 'possum huntin'," said the girl, at last, getting to her feet and standing in her twisted attitude, with her wry neck holding her head to one side. "Them there Jackson boys'll sure be out."

Auntie Sue laughed her low chuckling laugh.

From the edge of the timber that borders the fields of the bottom-lands across the river, came the baying of hounds. "There they be now," said Judy. "Hear 'em? The Billingses, 'cross from the clubhouse, 'll be out, too, I reckon. When hit's moonlight, they're allus a-huntin' 'possum an' 'coon. When hit's dark, they're out on the river a-giggin' for fish. Well, I reckon I'll be a-goin' in, now, ma'm," she concluded, with a yawn. "Ain't no use in a body stayin' up when there ain't nothin' ter do but ter sleep, as I kin see."

With an awkward return to Auntie Sue's "Good-night and sweet dreams, dear," the mountain girl went into the house.

For an hour longer, the old gentlewoman sat on the porch of her little log house by the river, looking out over the moonlit scene. Nor did she now, as when she had watched the sunset, crave human companionship. In spirit, she was far from all earthly needs or cares,—where no troubled thoughts could disturb her serene peace and her dearest dreams were real.

The missing letter was forgotten.

CHAPTER IV.

THE WILL OF THE RIVER.

AD Auntie Sue remained a few minutes longer on the porch, that evening, she might have seen an object drifting down the river, in the gentle current of The Bend.

Swinging easily around the curve above the club-house, it would not have been visible at first, because of the deep shadows of the reflected trees and mountains. But, presently, as it drifted on into the broader waters of The Bend, it emerged from the shadows into the open moonlit space, and then, to any one watching from the porch, the dark object, drawing nearer and nearer in the bright moonlight, would have soon shaped itself into a boat—an empty boat, the watcher would have said, that had broken from its moorings somewhere up the river;—and the watcher would have heard, through the still, night air, the dull, heavy roar of the mad waters at Elbow Rock.

Drifting thus, helpless in the grip of the main

current, the little craft apparently was doomed to certain destruction. Gently, it would float on the easy surface of the quiet, moonlit Bend. In front of the house, it would move faster and faster. Where the river narrows, it would be caught as if by mighty hands hidden beneath the rushing flood, and dragged onward still faster and faster. About it, the racing waters would leap and boil in their furious, headlong career, shaking and tossing the helpless victim of their might with a vicious strength from which there would be no escape, until, in the climax of the river's madness, the object of its angry sport would be dashed against the cliff, and torn, and crushed, and hammered by the terrific weight of the rushing flood against that rocky anvil, into a battered and shapeless wreck.

The drifting boat drew nearer and nearer. It reached the point where the curve of the opposite bank draws in to form the narrow raceway of the rapids. It began to feel the stronger pull of those hidden hands that had carried it so easily down The Bend. And then—and then—the unguided, helpless craft responded to the gentle pressure of some swirl or cross-current in the main flow of the stream, and swung a little to one side. A few feet farther, and the new impulse became stronger. Yielding easily to the current that drew it so gently across the invisible dividing-line between safety and destruction, the boat swung in toward the shore. A minute more, and it had drifted into that encircling curve of the bank where the current of the eddy carried it around and around.

The boat seemed undecided. Would it hold to the harbor of safety into which it had been drawn by the friendly current? Would it swing out, again, into the main stream, and so to its own destruction?

Three times the bow, pointing out from the eddy, crossed the danger-line, and, for a moment, hung on the very edge. Three times, the invisible hands which held it drew it gently back to safety. And so, finally, the little craft, so helpless, so alone, amid the many currents of the great river, came to rest against the narrow shelf of land at the foot of the bank below Auntie Sue's garden.

The light in the window of Auntie Sue's room went out. The soft moonlight flooded mountain and valley and stream. The mad waters at Elbow Rock roared in their wild fury. Always, always,—irresistibly, inevitably, unceasingly,—the river poured its strength toward the sea.

51

CHAPTER V.

EFORE the sun was high enough to look over Schoolhouse Hill, the next morning, Judy went into the garden to dig some potatoes.

Tom Warden's boys would come, some day before long, and dig them all, and put them away in the cellar for the winter. But there was no need to hurry the gathering of the full crop, so the boys would come when it was most convenient; and, in the meantime, Judy would continue to dig from day to day all that were needed for the kitchen in the little log house by the river. In spite of her poor crooked body, the mountain girl was strong and well used to hard work, so the light task was, for her, no hardship at all.

As one will when first coming out of doors in the morning, Judy paused a moment to look about. The sky, so clear and bright the evening before, was now a luminous gray. The mountains were lost in a ghostly world of fog, through which the river moved in stealthy silence,—a dull thing of mystery, with

52

only here and there a touch of silvery light upon its clouded surface. The cottonwoods and willows, on the opposite shore, were mere dreams of trees,—gray, formless, and weird. The air was filled with the dank earth-smell. The heavy thundering roar of the never-ending war of the waters at Elbow Rock came louder and more menacing, but strangely unreal, as if the mist itself were filled with threatening sound.

But to Judy, the morning was only the beginning of another day;—she looked, but did not see. To her, the many ever-changing moods of Nature were without meaning. With her basket in hand, she went down to the lower end of the garden, where she had dug potatoes the time before, and where she had left the fork sticking upright in the ground.

A few minutes served to fill the basket; but, before starting back to the house, the mountain girl paused again to look out over the river. Perhaps it was some vague memory of Auntie Sue's talk, the night before, that prompted her; perhaps it was some instinct, indefinite and obscure;—whatever it was that influenced her, Judy left her basket, and went to the brink of the high bank above the eddy for a closer view of the water.

The next instant, with the quick movement of an untamed creature of her native mountain forests, the girl sprang back, and crouched close to the ground to hide from something she had seen at the foot of the bank. Every movement of her twisted body expressed amazement and fear. Her eyes were wild and excited. She looked carefully about, as if for dangers that might be hidden in the fog. Once, she opened her mouth as if to call. Half-rising, she started as if to run to the house. But, presently, curiosity apparently overruled her fear, and, throwing herself flat on the ground she wormed her way back to the brink of the river-bank. Cautiously, without making a sound, she peered through the tall grass and weeds that fringed the rim above the eddy.

The boat, which some kindly impulse of the river had drawn so gently aside from the stronger current that would have carried it down the rapids to the certain destruction waiting at Elbow Rock, still rested with its bow grounded on the shore, against which the eddying water had pushed it. But the thing that had so startled Judy was a man who was lying, apparently unconscious, on the wet and muddy bottom-boards of the little craft.

Breathlessly, the girl, looking down from the top of the bank, watched for some movement; but the dirty huddled heap of wretched humanity was so still that she could not guess whether it was living or dead. Fearfully, she noted that there were no oars in the boat, nor gun, nor fishing-tackle of any sort. The man's hat was missing. His clothing was muddy and disarranged. His position was such that she could not see the face.

Drawing back, Judy looked cautiously about; then, picking up a heavy clod of dirt from the ploughed edge of the garden, and crouching again at the brink of the bank, ready for instant flight, she threw the clod into the water near the boat. The still form in the boat made no movement following the splash. Selecting a smaller clod, the girl threw the bit of dirt into the stern of the boat itself, where it broke in fragments. And, at this, the figure moved slightly.

"Hit's alive, all right," commented Judy to herself, with a grin of satisfaction, at the result of her investigation. "But hit's sure time he was a-gittin' up."

Carefully selecting a still smaller bit of dirt, she deliberately tossed it at the figure itself. Her aim was true, and the clod struck the man on the shoulder, with the result that he stirred uneasily, and, muttering something which Judy could not hear, half-turned on his back so that the girl saw the haggard, un-shaven face. She saw, too, that, in one hand, the man clutched an empty whisky bottle.

At sight of the bottle, the mountain girl rose to her feet with an understanding laugh. "Hell!" she said aloud; "drunk,—that's all—dead drunk. I'll sure fetch him out of hit." And then, grinning with malicious delight, she proceeded to pelt the man in the boat with clods of dirt until he scrambled to a sitting posture, and looked up in bewildered confusion.

"If you please," he said, in a hoarse voice, to the sallow, old-young face that grinned down at him from the top of the bank, "which one of the Devil's imps are you?"

As she looked into that upturned face, Judy's grin vanished. "I sure 'lowed as how you-all was dead," she explained.

"Well," returned the man in the boat, wearily, "I can assure you that it's not in the least my fault if I disappoint you. I feel as bad about it as you do.

However, I don't think I am so much alive that it makes any material difference." He lifted the whisky bottle, and studied it thoughtfully.

"You-all come dad burned near not bein' ary bit alive," returned the girl.

"Yes?" said the man, inquiringly.

"Yep; you sure did come mighty nigh hit. If your old John-boat had a-carried you-all on down ter Elbow Rock, 'stead of bein' ketched in the eddy here, you-all would sure 'nough been a-talkin' to the Devil by now."

The man, looking out over the river into the fog, muttered to himself, "I can't even make a success of dying, it seems."

Again, he regarded the empty bottle in his hand with studied interest. Then, tossing the bottle into the river, he looked up, once more, to the girl on the bank above.

"Listen, sister!" he said, nervously. "Is there any place around here where I can buy a drink? I need something rather badly. Where am I, anyway?"

"You-all are at Auntie Sue's place," said Judy; "an' there sure ain't no chance for you-all ter git ary licker here. Where'd you-all come from, anyhow?

How'd you-all git here 'thout no oars ner paddle ner nothin'? Where was you-all aimin' ter go?"

"Your questions, my good girl, are immaterial and irrelevant," returned the man in the boat. "The all-important matter before us for consideration is,— how can I get a drink? I *must* have a drink, I tell you!" He held up his hands, and they were shaking as if with palsy. "And I must have it damned quick!"

"You-all sure do talk some powerful big words," said Judy, with critical interest. "You-all sure must be some eddecated. Auntie Sue, now, she talks—"

The man interrupted her: "Who is 'Auntie Sue'?"

"I don't know," Judy returned; "she's just Auntie Sue—that's all I know. She sure is—"

Again the man interrupted: "I think it would be well for me to interview this worthy aunt of yours." And then, while he raised himself, unsteadily, to his feet, he continued, in a muttering undertone: "You don't seem to appreciate the situation. If I don't get some sort of liquor soon, things are bound to happen."

He attempted to step from the boat to the shore; but the instability of the light, flat-bottomed skiff,

together with his own unsteady weakness, combined
to land him half in the water and half on the muddy
bank where he struggled helplessly, and, in his weak-
ened condition, would have slipped wholly into the
river had not Judy rushed down the rude steps to his
assistance.

With a strength surprising in one of her apparent weakness, the mountain girl caught the stranger
under his shoulders and literally dragged him from
the water. When she had further helped him to his
feet, Judy surveyed the wretched object of her benefi-
cence with amused and curious interest.

The man, with his unkempt hair, unshaven, haggard face, bloodshot eyes, and slovenly dishevelled
dress, had appeared repulsive enough while in the
boat; but, now, as he stood dripping with water and
covered with mud, there was a touch of the ridiculous
in his appearance that brought a grin to the un-
lovely face of his rescuer, and caused her to exclaim
with unnecessary frankness: "I'll be dad burned if
you-all ain't a thing ter look at, mister!"

As the poor creature, who was shaking as if with
the ague, regarded the twisted form, the wry neck,
and the sallow, old-young face of the girl, who was

laughing at him, a gleam of sardonic humor flashed in his bloodshot eyes. "Thanks," he said, huskily; "you are something of a vision yourself, aren't you?"

The laughter went from Judy's face as she caught the meaning of the cruel words. "I ain't never laid no claim ter bein' a beauty," she retorted in her shrill, drawling monotone. "But, I kin tell you-all one thing, mister: Hit was God-A'mighty Hisself an' my drunken pap what made me ter look like I do. While you,—damn you!—you-all just naturally made yourself what you be."

At the mountain girl's illiterate words, so pregnant with meaning, a remarkable change came over the face and manner of the man. His voice, even, for the moment, lost its huskiness, and vibrated with sincere feeling as he steadied himself; and, bowing with courteous deference, said: "I beg your pardon, miss. That was unkind. You really should have left me to the river."

"You-all would a-drownded, sure, if I had," she retorted, somewhat mollified by the effect of her observation.

"Which," he returned, "would have been so beautifully right and fitting that it evidently could not be."

And with this cynical remark, his momentary bearing of self-respect was gone.

"Are you-all a-meanin' ter say that you-all was a-wantin' ter drown?"

"Something like that," he returned. And then, with a hint of ugliness in his voice and eyes, he rasped: "But, look here, girl! do you think I'm going to stand like this all day indulging in idle conversation with you? Where is this aunt of yours? Can't you see that I've got to have a drink?"

He started uncertainly toward the steps that led to the top of the bank, and Judy, holding him by his arm, helped him to climb the steep way. A part of the ascent he made on hands and knees. Several times he would have fallen except for the girl's support. But, at last, they gained the top, and stood in the garden.

"That there is the house," said Judy, pointing. "But I don't reckon as how you-all kin git ary licker there."

The wretched man made no reply; but, with Judy still supporting him, stumbled forward across the rows of vegetables.

The two had nearly reached the steps at the end of

61

the porch when Auntie Sue came from the house to see why Judy did not return with the potatoes. The dear old lady paused a moment, startled at the presence of the unprepossessing stranger in her garden. Then, with an exclamation of pity, she hurried to meet them.

The man, whose gaze as he shambled along was fixed on the ground, did not notice Auntie Sue until, feeling Judy stop, he also paused, and raising his head looked full at the beautiful old lady.

"Why, Judy!" cried Auntie Sue, her low, sweet voice filled with gentle concern. "What in the world has happened?"

With an expression of questioning bewilderment and rebuke on his haggard face, the man also turned to the mountain girl beside him.

"I found him in er John-boat what done come ashore last night, down there in the eddy," Judy explained to Auntie Sue. To the man, she said: "This here is Auntie Sue, mister; but, I don't reckon as how she's got ary licker for you."

"'Liquor'?" questioned Auntie Sue. "What in the world do you mean, child?" Then quickly to the stranger;—"My dear man, you are wringing wet.

You must have been in the river. Come, come right in, and let us do something for you." As she spoke, she went toward him with outstretched hands.

But the wretched creature shrank back from her, as if in fear;—his whole body shaking with emotion; his fluttering hands raised in a gesture of imploring protest;—while the eyes that looked up at the saintly countenance of the old gentlewoman were the eyes of a soul sunken in the deepest hell of shame and humiliation.

Shocked with pitying horror, Auntie Sue paused.

The man's haggard, unshaven face twitched and worked with the pain of his suffering. He bit his lips and fingered his quivering chin in a vain effort at self-control; and then, as he looked up at her, the sunken, bloodshot eyes filled with tears that the tormented spirit had no power to check.

And Auntie Sue turned her face away.

For a little, they stood so. Then, as Auntie Sue faced him again, the stranger, with a supreme effort of his will, gained a momentary control of his shattered nerves. Drawing himself erect and standing steady and tall before her, he raised a hand to his uncovered head as if to remove his hat. When his

63

hand found no hat to remove, he smiled as if at some jest at his own expense.

"I am so sorry, madam," he said,—and his voice was musically clear and cultured. "Please pardon me for disturbing you? I did not know. This young woman should have explained. You see, when she spoke of 'Auntie Sue,' I assumed, of course,—I mean, —I expected to find a native woman who would—" He paused, smiling again, as if to assure her that he fully appreciated the humor of his ridiculous predicament.

"But, my dear sir," cried Auntie Sue, eagerly, "there is nothing to pardon. Please do come into the house and let us help you."

But the stranger drew back, shaking his head sadly. "You do not understand, madam. It is not that my clothes are unpresentable,—it is I, myself, who am unfit to stand in your presence, much less to enter your house. I thank you, but I must go."

He was turning away, when Auntie Sue reached his side and placed her gentle old hand lightly on his arm.

"Please, won't you come in, sir? I shall never forgive myself if I let you go like this."

The man's voice was hoarse and shaking, now, as he answered: "For God's sake, madam, don't touch me! Let me go! You must! I—I—am not myself! You might not be safe with me! Ask her— she knows!" He turned to Judy.

"He's done said hit, ma'm," said Judy, in answer to Auntie Sue's questioning look. "My pap, he was that way when he done smashed me up agin the wall, when I was nothin' but a baby, an' hit made me grow up all crooked an' ugly like what I be now."

With one shamed glance at Auntie Sue, the wretched fellow looked down at the ground. His head drooped forward. His shoulders sagged. His whole body seemed to shrink. Turning sadly away, he again started back toward the river.

"Stop!" Auntie Sue's voice rang out imperiously. The man halted.

"Look at me," she commanded.

Slowly, he raised his eyes. The gentle old teacher spoke with fine spirit, now, but kindly still: "This is sheer nonsense, my boy. You wouldn't hurt me. Why, you couldn't! Of course, you are not yourself; but, do you think that I do not know a gentleman when I meet one? Come—" She held out her hand.

A moment he stood, gazing at her in wondering awe. Then his far-overtaxed strength failed;—his abused nerves refused to bear more,—and he sank,—a pitiful, cowering heap at her feet. Hiding his face in his shaking hands, he sobbed like a child.

CHAPTER VI.

IN THE LOG HOUSE BY THE RIVER.

THOSE two women managed, somehow, to get the almost helpless stranger into the house, where Auntie Sue, after providing him with nightclothes, left by one of her guests, by tactful entreaty and judicial commands, persuaded him to go to bed.

Then followed several days and nights of weary watching. There were times when the man lay with closed eyes, so weak and exhausted that he seemed to be drifting out from these earthly shores on the deep waters of that wide and unknown sea into which all the streams of life finally flow. But, always, Auntie Sue miraculously held him back. There were other times when, by all the rules of the game, he should have worn a strait-jacket;—when his delirium filled the room with all manner of horrid creatures from the pit; when leering devils and loathsome serpents and gibbering apes tormented him until his unnatural strength was the strength of a fiend, and his tortured nerves shrieked in agony. But Auntie Sue perversely ignored the rules of the game. And never did the man, even in his most terrible moments, fail to recognize in the midst of the hellish crew of his diseased imagination the silvery-haired old teacher as the angel of his salvation. Her gentle voice had always power to soothe and calm him. He obeyed her implicitly, and, like a frightened child, holding fast to her hand would beg piteously for her to protect and save him.

But no word of the man's low-muttered, broken sentences, nor of his wildest ravings, ever gave Auntie Sue a clue to his identity. She searched his clothes, but there was not a thing to give her even his name.

And, yet, that first day, when Judy would have gone to neighbor Tom's for help, Auntie Sue said "No." She even positively forbade the girl to mention the stranger's presence in the house, should she chance to talk with passing neighbors. "The river brought him to us, Judy, dear," she said. "We must save him. No one shall know his shame, to humiliate and wound his pride and drag him down after he is himself again. Until he has recovered and is once more the man I believe him to be, no one must see him or know that he is here; and no one must ever know how he came to us."

And late, one evening, when Judy was fast asleep, and the man was lying very still after a period of feverish tossing and muttering, the dear old gentlewoman crept quietly out of the house into the night. She was gone some time, and when she returned again to the stranger's bedside she was breathless and trembling as from some unusual exertion. And the following afternoon, when Judy came to her with the announcement that the boat which had brought the man to them was no longer in the eddy below the garden, Auntie Sue said, simply, that she was glad it was gone, and cautioned the girl, again, that the stranger's presence in the house must not be made known to any one.

When the mountain girl protested, saying, "You-all ain't got no call ter be a-wearin' yourself ter the bone a-takin' care of such as him," Auntie Sue answered, "Hush, Judy! How do you know what the poor boy really is?"

To which Judy retorted: "He's just triflin' an' ornery an' no 'count, that's what he is, or he sure wouldn't been a-floatin' 'round in that there old John-boat 'thout ary gun, or fishin' lines, or hat even, ter say nothin' of that there whisky bottle bein' plumb empty."

Auntie Sue made no reply to the mountain girl's harsh summing-up of the damning evidence against the stranger, but left her and went softly to the bed-side of their guest.

It was perhaps an hour later that Judy, quietly entering the room, happened upon a scene that caused her to stand as if rooted to the spot in open-mouthed amazement.

The man was sleeping, and the silvery-haired old maiden-lady, seated on the side of the bed, was bending over the unconscious stranger and gently stroking his tumbled, red-brown hair, even as a mother might lovingly caress her sleeping child. And then, as Judy watched, breathless with wonder, the proud old gentlewoman, bending closer over that still form on the bed, touched her lips—soft as a rose-petal—to the stranger's brow.

When she arose and saw Judy standing there, Auntie Sue's delicate old cheeks flushed with color, and her eyes were shining. With a gesture, she commanded the girl to silence, and the two tiptoed from the room. When they were outside, and Auntie Sue had cautiously closed the door, she faced the speechless Judy with a deliciously defiant air that could not wholly hide her lovely confusion.

"I—I—was thinking, Judy, how he—how he—might have been—my son."

"Your 'son'!" ejaculated the girl. "Why, ma'm, you-all ain't never even been married, as I've ever hearn tell, have you?"

Auntie Sue drew her thin shoulders proudly erect, and, lifting her fine old face, answered the challenging question with splendid spirit: "No, I have never been married; but I might have been; and if I had, I suppose I could have had a son, couldn't I?"

The vanquished Judy retreated to the kitchen, where, in safety, she sank into a chair, convulsed with laughter, which she instinctively muffled in her apron.

Then came the day when the man, weak and worn with his struggle, looked up at his gentle old nurse with the light of sanity in his deep blue eyes. Very tired eyes they were, and filled with painful memories,—filled, too, with worshipping gratitude and wonder.

She smiled down at him with delighted triumph, and drawing a chair close beside the bed, seated herself and placed her soft hand on his where it lay on the coverlid.

"You are much better, this morning," she said cheerily. "You will soon be all right, now." And as she looked into the eyes that regarded hers so questioningly, there was in her face and manner no hint of doubt, or pretense, or reproach;—only confidence and love.

He spoke slowly, as if feeling for words: "I have been in Hell; and you—you have brought me out. Why did you do it?"

"Because you are mine," she answered, with her low chuckling laugh. It was so good to have him able to talk to her rationally after those long hours of fighting.

"Because I am yours?" he repeated, puzzling over her words.

"Yes," she returned, with a hint of determined proprietorship in her voice; "because you belong to me. You see, that eddy where your boat landed is my property, and so anything that drifts down the river and lodges there belongs to me. Whatever the river brings to me, is mine. The river brought you, and so—" She finished with another laugh,—a laugh that was filled with tender mother-yearning.

The blue eyes smiled back at her for a moment; then she saw them darken with painful memories.

"Oh, yes; the river," he said. "I wanted the river to do something for me, and—and it did something quite different from what I wanted."

"Of course," she returned, eagerly, "the river is always like that. It always does the thing you don't expect it to do. Just like life itself. Don't you see? It begins somewhere away off at some little spring, and just keeps going and going and going; and thousands and thousands of other springs, scattered all over the country, start streams and creeks and branches that run into it, and make it bigger and bigger, as it winds and curves and twists along, until it finally reaches the great sea, where its waters are united with all the waters from all the rivers in all the world. And in all of its many, many miles, from that first tiny spring to the sea, there are not two feet of it exactly alike. In all the centuries of its being, there are never two hours alike. An infinite variety of days and nights—an infinite variety of skies and light and clouds and daybreaks and sunsets—an infinite number and variety of currents and shoals and deep places and quiet spots and dangerous rapids and eddies—and, along its banks, an endless change of hills and mountains and flats and forests and meadows and farms and cities—and—" She paused, breathless. And then, when he did not speak, but only watched her, she continued: "Don't you see? Of course, the river never could be what you expect, any more than life could be exactly what you want and dream it will be."

"Who in the world are you?" he asked, wonderingly. "And what in the world are you doing here in the backwoods?"

Smiling at his puzzled expression, she answered: "I am Auntie Sue. I am *living* here in the backwoods."

"But, your real name? Won't you tell me your name? I must know how to address you."

"Oh, my name is Susan E. Wakefield—*Miss* Wakefield, if you please. I shall be seventy-one years old the eighteenth day of next November. And you must call me 'Auntie Sue,'—just as every one else does."

"Wakefield—Wakefield—where have I seen that name?" He wrinkled his brow in an effort to remember. "Wakefield—I feel sure that I have heard it, somewhere."

"It is not unlikely," she returned, lightly. "It is not at all an uncommon name. And now that I am properly introduced, don't you think—?"

He hesitated a moment, then said, deliberately, "My name is Brian Kent."

"That is an Irish name," she said quickly; "and that is why your hair is so nearly red and your eyes so blue."

"Yes," he returned, "from my mother. And please don't ask me more now, for I can't lie to you, and I won't tell you the truth." And she saw, again, the dark shadows of painful memories come into the blue eyes.

Bending over the bed, she laid her soft hand on his brow, and pushed back his heavy hair; and her sweet old voice was very low and gentle as she said: "My dear boy, I shall never ask you more. The river brought you to me, and you are mine. You must not even think of anything else, just now.

When you are stronger, and are ready, we will talk of your future; but of your past, you—"

A loud knock sounded at the door of the living room.

"There is someone at the door," she said hastily. "I must go. Lie still, and go to sleep like a good boy; won't you?"

Swiftly, she leaned over, and, before he realized, he felt her lips touch his forehead. Then she was gone, and Brian Kent's Irish eyes were filled with tears. Turning to the wall, he hid his face in the pillow.

CHAPTER VII.

OFFICERS OF THE LAW.

AS Auntie Sue was closing the door of her guest's room carefully behind her, Judy came from the kitchen in great excitement, and the knocking at the front door of the house was repeated.

"Hit's the Sheriff, ma'm," whispered Judy. "I was just a-comin' ter tell you. I seed 'em from the kitchen-winder. He's got two other men with him. Their hosses is tied ter the fence in front. What in hell will we do, now? They are after him in there, sure 's death!"

Auntie Sue's face was white, and her lips trembled,—but only for a moment.

"Go back into the kitchen, Judy, and stay there," she commanded, in a whisper; and went to open the front door as calmly as if nothing unusual had happened.

Sheriff Knox was a big man, with a bluff, kindly manner, and a voice that made nothing of closed doors. He returned Auntie Sue's greeting heartily, and, with one of his companions,—a quiet, business-looking gentleman,—accepted her cordial invitation to come in. The third man of the party remained near the saddle-horses at the gate.

"Well, Auntie Sue," said the Sheriff, settling his ponderous bulk in one of the old lady's rocking-chairs, which certainly was not built to carry such a weight, "how are you? I haven't seen you in a coon's age. I'll swear, though, you ain't a minute older than you was when you first begun teachin' the little Elbow Rock school up there on the hill, are you?"

"I don't know, Sheriff," Auntie Sue returned, with a nervous little laugh. "I sometimes think that I am a few days older. I have watched a good many sunsets since then, you know."

The big officer's laughter almost shook the log walls of the house. To his quiet companion, who had taken a chair near the window, he said: "I'll have to tell you, Ross, that Auntie Sue owns every sunset in these Ozark Mountains. What was it you paid for them?" He turned again to their smiling hostess. "Oh, yes; fifty cents an acre for the land

78

and fourteen dollars and a half for the sunsets. You'll have to be blamed careful not to trespass on the sunsets in this neighborhood, Ross." Again, his hearty laugh roared out, while his chair threatened to collapse with the quaking of his massive body.

The gentleman seated at the window laughed quietly, in sympathy.

"You'll be all right, though, Ross," the Sheriff continued, "as long as you're with me. Auntie Sue and me have been friends for about twenty year, now. I always stop to see her whenever I'm passing through the Elbow Rock neighborhood, if I ain't in too big a hurry. Stayed with her a week, once, five years ago, when we was after that Lewis gang. She knows I'd jail any man on earth that would even touch one of her sunsets."

Then, as if the jesting allusion to his office reminded him of his professional duties, he added: "I plumb forgot, Auntie Sue, this gentleman is Mr. Ross. He is one of William J. Burns's crack detectives. Don't be scared, though, he ain't after you."

Auntie Sue, while joining in the laughter, and acknowledging the introduction, regarded the business-looking gentleman by the window with intense interest.

"I think," she said, slowly,—and the sweetness of her low, cultured voice was very marked in contrast to the Sheriff's thundering tones,—"I think, sir, that this is the first time in my life that I ever saw a real detective. I have read about them, of course."

Mr. Ross was captivated by the charm of this beautiful old gentlewoman, who regarded him with such child-like interest, and who spoke with such sweet frankness and dignity. Smilingly, he returned: "I fear, madam, that you would find me very disappointing. No one that I ever knew in my profession could hope to live up to the reputation given us by the story-books. No secret service man living can remotely approximate the deeds performed by the detectives of fiction. We are very, very human, I can assure you."

"I am sure that you, at least, must be very kind," returned Auntie Sue, gently. And the cheeks of the experienced officer flushed like the cheeks of a schoolboy.

"Mr. Ross, Auntie Sue," said the Sheriff, "is, as

I was telling you, one of William J. Burns's big men."

Auntie Sue gave her attention to her big friend: "Yes?"

The Sheriff continued: "Now, the Burns people, you see, protect the banks all over the country."

"Yes?" came, again, in a tone so low and gentle that the monosyllable was scarcely heard.

The officer's loud voice went on: "And Mr. Ross, here, works most of his time on these bank cases. Just now, he is trailing a fellow that got away with a lot of money from the Empire Consolidated Savings Bank, of Chicago, about a month ago;—that is, the man disappeared about a month ago. He had been stealing along from the bank for about a year,— worked for them, you see."

"The Empire Consolidated Savings Bank!" Auntie Sue spoke the words in a voice that was little more than a whisper. It was to the Empire Consolidated Savings Bank that she had sent the money which she had received from her brother in Buenos Aires; and Homer T. Ward, the president of that bank, was one of her old pupils. Why, her stranger guest, in the other room there, was that very moment wearing one of the bank president's nightshirts.

"And do you"—Auntie Sue addressed the detective—"do you know the man's name, Mr. Ross?"

"Oh, yes," returned the officer, "his name is Brian Kent."

Some source of strength, deep-hidden in her gentle nature, enabled Auntie Sue to control her emotions, though her voice broke a little as she slowly repeated the man's name, "Brian Kent. And do I understand, sir, that you have traced the man to this— neighborhood?"

The detective was too skilled not to notice Auntie Sue's manner and the break in her voice; but he never dreamed that this old gentlewoman's agitation was caused by a deeper interest than a quite natural fear that a dangerous criminal might be lurking in the immediate vicinity.

"Not exactly, Mrs.—ah—"

"Miss Wakefield,"—she supplied her name with a smile.

With a courteous bow, the detective continued: "We do not know for sure that the man is in this neighborhood, Miss Wakefield. There is really no cause for you to be alarmed. Even if he should call at your house, here, you need not be frightened, for I assure you the man is not at all a dangerous character."

"I am glad," said Auntie Sue; and she laughed a little with a relief more genuine than her callers knew.

Detective Ross continued as if anxious to finish his unpleasant duty: "It is too bad for us to be disturbing you with this business, Miss Wakefield, and I hope you will forgive us; but, the case is like this: We traced our man to the little town of Borden, some forty miles up the river from here. He disappeared from the hotel one night, leaving his suit-case and, apparently, everything he had with him, and not a soul that we can find has seen him since. Of course, everybody says 'suicide.' He had been drinking heavily and acting rather queer the two or three days he was at the hotel,—it seems. But I am not willing, yet, to accept the suicide idea as final, because it would be too easy for him to give things that appearance in order to throw us off; and I can't get away from the fact that a John-boat that was tied to the bank near the hotel managed to break loose and drift off down the river that same night. Working on my theory, we are following down the river, trying to get trace of either the boat or the man. So far, we haven't heard of either, which rather strengthens me in my belief that the boat and the man went away together. He is probably traveling nights, and lying up under the willows in daylight. But he will be compelled to show himself somewhere, soon, in order to get something to eat, for he couldn't have taken much with him, trying, as he was, to create the impression that he had committed suicide. You have a wonderful view of the river here, Miss Wakefield."

"Yes, sir; it is beautiful from the porch."

"You spend a good deal of time on the porch, do you?"

"Yes, sir."

"And you would be quite likely to notice any boat passing, wouldn't you?"

"Yes, sir."

"Could you see a boat at night,—in the moonlight, I mean?"

"I could if it were well out in the middle of the

stream, away from the shadow of the trees, along the bank."

"Have you seen any boats pass lately, Miss Wakefield?"

"No, sir; I haven't seen a boat on the river for a month, at least."

"Dead certain about it, are you, Auntie Sue?" asked the Sheriff.

"Yes, sir; I am very sure," she returned. "Judy and I were talking about it yesterday."

"Who is Judy?" asked the detective.

The Sheriff answered, "Just a girl that lives with Auntie Sue."

And Auntie Sue added: "I know Judy has seen no boats passing, because, as I say, we were talking about it."

"I see," said the detective. "And may I ask, Miss Wakefield, if any one—any stranger, I mean—has called at the house lately, or if you have seen any one in the vicinity?"

The gentle old lady hesitated.

The officers thought she was searching her memory to be sure before she answered.

Then Auntie Sue said, deliberately: "No, sir; we have not seen a stranger in this vicinity for several weeks. The last one was a mule-buyer, who stopped to ask if he was on the right road to Tom Warden's; and that must have been fully six weeks ago."

The detective looked at Sheriff Knox.

"Well," said the big officer, "I reckon we might as well push along."

The two men arose.

"Oh, but surely you will stay for dinner," said Auntie Sue, while her dear heart was faint with fear lest they accept, and thus bring about who could say what disastrous consequences through their meeting with Judy.

"Not this time, Auntie Sue," returned the Sheriff. "Mr. Ross is anxious to get on down the river as fast as he can. He's got men on watch at White's Crossing, and if our man ain't passed there, or if we don't strike his trail somewhere before we get there, we will jump back on the railroad, and get some boy to bring the horses through later."

"I see," returned Auntie Sue. And to the detective she added, smiling: "I am sure it must be very

86

difficult for any one to escape you, Mr. Ross. I have read such wonderful things about Mr. Burns and the work of his organization; and now that I have met you,—a real live detective,—I shall be very careful, indeed, about what I do in the future. I shouldn't want to have you on my track, I assure you."

The two men laughed heartily, and the detective, as he extended his hand in farewell, returned: "I count it a great privilege to have met you, Miss Wakefield; and if you will promise to do one thing for me, I'll agree to be very lenient with you if I am ever assigned to a case in which you are to be brought to justice."

"I promise," returned the old lady, quickly. "I really wouldn't dare to refuse under the circumstances, would I? What do you want me to do, Mr. Ross?"

"If this man Brian Kent should happen to appear in this vicinity, will you get a message as quickly as possible, at any cost, to Sheriff Knox?"

"Why, of course," agreed Auntie Sue. "But you have not yet told me what the man looks like, Mr. Ross."

"He is really a fine looking chap," the detective

answered. "Thirty years old—fully six feet tall—rather slender, but well built—weighs about one hundred fifty—a splendid head—smooth shaven—reddish hair—dark blue eyes—and a high, broad forehead. He is of Irish extraction—is cultured—very courteous in his manner and speech—dresses well—and knows a lot about books and authors and such things."

"I would surely know him from that description," said Auntie Sue, thinking of the wretched creature who had fallen, sobbing, at her feet so short a time before. "But, you do not make him seem like a criminal at all. It is strange that a man such as you describe should be a fugitive from the law, is it not?"

"We come in contact with many strange things in our business, Miss Wakefield," the Burns operative answered—a little sadly, Auntie Sue thought. "Life itself is so strange and complex, though you in your quiet retreat, here, can scarcely find it so."

"Indeed, I find life very wonderful, Mr. Ross, even here in my little house by the river," she answered, slowly.

Sheriff Knox held out a newspaper to Auntie Sue: "Just happened to remember that I had it in my pocket," he said. "It gives a pretty full account of this fellow Kent's case. You will notice there is a big reward offered for his capture. If you can catch him for us, you'll make enough money to keep you mighty nigh all the rest of your life." And the officer's great laugh boomed out at the thought of the old school-teacher as a thief-catcher.

"By the way, Sheriff," said Auntie Sue, as they were finally saying good-bye at the door, "you didn't happen to ask at Thompsonville for my mail, did you, as you came through?" Her voice was trembling, now, with eagerness and anxiety.

"I'm plumb sorry, Auntie Sue, but I didn't. You see, we were so busy on this job, I clean forgot about stopping here; and, besides, we might have caught our man before we got this far, you see."

"Of course," returned Auntie Sue, "I should have thought of that; but I have been rather anxious about an important letter that seems to have been delayed. Some of the neighbors will probably be going to the office to-day, though. Good-bye! You know you are always welcome, Sheriff; and you, too, Mr. Ross, if you should ever happen to be in this part of the country again."

"A wonderful old woman, Ross," commented Sheriff Knox as they were riding away. And the quiet, business-looking detective, whose life had been spent in combating crime and deception, answered, as he waved farewell to Auntie Sue, who watched them from the door of the little log house by the river, "A very wonderful woman, indeed,—the loveliest old lady I have ever met,—and the most remarkable."

CHAPTER VIII.

THAT WHICH IS GREATER THAN THE LAW.

WHEN she had watched Sheriff Knox and his two companions ride out of sight, Auntie Sue turned slowly back into the house to face Judy, who stood accusingly in the kitchen doorway.

For what seemed a long time, the old gentlewoman and the deformed mountain girl stood silently looking at each other. Then Auntie Sue nervously crossed the room to lay the newspaper, which the Sheriff had given her, on the table beside her basket of sewing.

Without speaking, Judy followed her, watching every movement intently.

Turning to face her companion again, Auntie Sue stood, still speechless, clasping and unclasping her thin old hands.

Judy spoke in her shrill, drawling monotone: "You-all have sure fixed hit this here time, hain't you? Can't you-all see what a hell of a hole you've done got us inter?"

When Auntie Sue apparently could not reply,

Judy continued: "Just as if hit wasn't more 'n enough for you-all ter go an' wear yourself plumb out a-takin' keer of that there ornery, no-'count feller, what I never ought ter dragged out of the river nohow. An', now, you-all got ter go an' just naturally lie like you did ter the Sheriff an' that there deteckertive man. I was plumb scared to death a-listenin' ter you through the crack in the kitchen door. I 'lowed every minute they'd ketch you, sure. My Lord-A'mighty! ma'm, can't you-all figger what'll happen ter weuns if they ever finds out that weuns done had him hid right here in this here house all the time? I never heard tell of such dad burned, fool doin's in all my born days! I sure wish ter God that there old John-boat had a-tuck him off down the river an' smashed him up agin Elbow Rock, like hit ort, an' not a-fetched him ter our door ter git weuns in jail for savin' his worthless, no-'count hide, —I sure do!"

"But, Judy, I never in all my life did such a thing before," said Auntie Sue in a tremulous whisper, too overwrought to speak aloud.

"You-all ain't a-needin' ter do hit but onct, neither. Onct is sure a heap plenty for that there big Sheriff

92

man. Just look what he did ter my pap! He's jailed pap seven times, that I kin rec'lect. God-A'mighty knows how many times he ketched him 'fore I was borned. An' pap, he didn't do so mighty much ary time, neither."

"I just had to do it, Judy, dear," protested Auntie Sue. "It seemed as if I simply could not tell the truth: something wouldn't let me."

Judy, unheeding her companion's agitation, continued reviewing the situation: "An' just look at all the money you-all done lost!"

"Money?" questioned Auntie Sue.

"Yep, 'money:'—that there reward what they'd a-paid you-all if you-all hadn't a-lied like you did. I reckon as how there'd a-been as much, maybe, as what was in that there letter you-all done sent ter the bank an' ain't never heard tell of since. Hit's most likely clean gone by now, an' here you done gone an' throw'd this other away,—plumb throw'd hit away!"

At this, Auntie Sue's spirit suddenly flashed into fiery indignation.

"Judith Taylor," she said sharply, "how can you suggest such a wicked thing? Why, I would—I would—*die* before I would accept a penny for doing such a thing!"

And it was Judy, now, who stood silent and abashed before the aroused Auntie Sue.

"Don't ever speak of such a thing again!" continued the old lady. "And remember, we must be more careful than ever, now, not to let any one— not a soul—know that Mr.—Mr.—Burns is in the house, or that we ever saw him!"

"That there deteckertive man said as how the feller's name was Brian Kent, didn't he?" muttered the sullen Judy.

"I don't care what the detective man said!" retorted Auntie Sue. "I am telling you that his name is Brian Burns, and you had better remember it! You had better remember, too, that if anybody ever finds out the truth about him, you and I will go right along to jail with him!"

"Yes, ma'm; I sure ain't aimin' ter forgit that," replied the humbled Judy; and she slouched away to the kitchen.

Auntie Sue went to the door of Brian Kent's room. But, with her hand outstretched toward the latch, she hesitated. Had he heard? The Sheriff's voice had been so loud. She feared to enter, yet she knew that she must. At last, she knocked timidly, and, when there was no answer, knocked again, louder. Cautiously, she opened the door.

The man lay with his face to the wall,—to all appearances fast asleep.

She tiptoed to the bed, and stood looking down upon the stranger for whom, without a shadow of reason,—one would have said,—she had violated one of the most deeply rooted principles of her seventy years.

To Auntie Sue, daughter of New England Puritanism. and religious to the deeps of her being, a lie was abhorrent,—and she had lied,—deliberately, carefully, and with painstaking skill she had lied. She had not merely evaded the truth; she had lied,—and that to save a man of whom she knew nothing except that he was a fugitive from the law. And the strangest thing about it was this, that she was glad. She could not feel one twinge of regret for her sin. She could not even feel that she had, indeed, sinned. She had even a feeling of pride and triumph that she had lied so successfully. She was troubled, though, about this new and wholly unexpected development in her life. It had been so easy for her. She had lied so naturally, so instinctively.

She remembered how she had spoken to Brian Kent of the river and of life. She saw, now, that the river symbolized not only life as a whole, with its many ever-changing conditions and currents, amid which the individual must live;—the river symbolized, as truly, the individual life, with its ever-changing moods and motives,—its ever-varying and often-conflicting currents of instinct and training,—its infinite variety of intellectual deeps and shallows,—its gentle places of spiritual calm,—and its wild and turbulent rapids of dangerous passion.

"What hitherto unsuspected currents in her life-river," she asked herself, "had carried her so easily into falsehood? What strange forces were these," she wondered, "that had set her so suddenly against honesty and truthfulness and law and justice? And this stranger,—this wretched, haggard-faced, drunken creature, who had been brought by the mysterious currents of life to her door,—what was there in him that so compelled her protecting interest? What was it within him, deeply hidden under the repellent exterior of his being, that had so awakened in her that strange feeling of possession,—of motherhood?"

It was not strange that, in her mental and spiritual

extremity, the dear old gentlewoman's life-long habit should lead her to kneel beside the stranger's bed and pray for understanding and guidance. It was significant that she did not ask her God to forgive the lie.

And, presently, as she prayed, she felt the man on the bed move. Then a hand lightly touched her hair. She remained very still for a little,—her head still bowed. The hand that touched so reverently the silvery gray hair trembled a little. Slowly, the old teacher raised her face to look at him; and the Irish blue eyes of Brian Kent were wide with wondering awe and glowing with a light that warmed her heart and strengthened her.

"Why did you do it?" he asked. "You wonderful, wonderful woman! Why did you do it?"

Slowly, she rose from her knees to sit beside him on the bed. "You heard?"

He nodded his head, not trusting himself to speak.

"I was afraid the Sheriff talked too loud," she said.

"But, why did you do it?" he persisted.

"I think it was because I couldn't do anything else," she answered, with her little chuckling laugh. Then she added, seriously: "How could I let them take you away? Are you not mine? Did not the river bring you to me?"

"I must tell you," he answered, sadly, "that what the detective told you about me is true."

"Yes?" she answered, smiling.

"I was a clerk in the Empire Consolidated Savings Bank," he continued, "and I stole money,—for nearly a year I stole,—not large sums, but a little at a time. Then, when I knew that it was going to be discovered, I took quite a lot, and ran away."

"Yes?" said Auntie Sue.

"Do you not care that I am a thief?" he questioned, wonderingly.

"Oh, yes; I care very much," she returned. "But, you see, after all, your stealing is a little thing that can be made all right. Your being a thief is so small in comparison with other things which you might have been, but which you are not, and of so little importance in comparison with what you really *are,* that I can't feel so very bad about it."

"But—but—my drinking,—my condition when—" He could not go on.

"Why, you see," she answered, "I can't think of *that* man as being *you* at all. *That* was something

that the accident of your being a thief did to you,—
like catching cold, and being sick, after accidentally
falling in the river."

After a little silence, the man spoke, slowly: "I
suppose every thief, when he is caught, says the same
thing; but I really never wanted to do it. Circumstances—" he paused, biting his lip, and turning
away.

"What was she like?" asked Auntie Sue, gently.

"She?" and his face reddened.

"Yes, I have observed that, to a man, 'circumstances' nearly always mean a woman. To a woman,
of course, it is a man."

"I cannot tell you about her, now," he said.
"Some day, perhaps, when I am further away from
it. But she is not at all like you."

And this answer, for some strange reason, brought
a flush of pleasure to the face of the old school-
teacher.

"I did not mean for you to tell me now," she
returned. "I only wanted you to know that, even
though I am an old maid, I can understand."

She left him then, and went to attend to her simple
household duties.

It was not until quite late in the evening that
Auntie Sue took up the newspaper which Sheriff
Knox had given her. Judy had retired to her room,
and Brian Burns—as they had agreed he should be
called—was fast asleep.

To-morrow, Brian was going to sit up. His clothing had been washed and ironed and pressed, and
Auntie Sue was making some little repairs in the
way of darning and buttons. She had finished, and
was putting her needle and scissors in the sewing-
basket on the table beside her, when she noticed the
paper, which she had forgotten.

The article headed "BANK CLERK DISAP-
PEARS" was not long. It told, in a matter-of-fact,
newspaper way, how Brian Kent had, at different
times, covering a period of several months, taken
various sums from the Empire Consolidated Savings
Bank, and gave, so far as was then known, the
accumulated amount which he had taken. The dis-
honest clerk had employed several methods in his
operations; but the particular incident—read Auntie
Sue—which had led to the exposure of Kent's steal-
ings was the theft of a small sum of money in bank-

notes, which had been sent to the bank in a letter by one of the bank's smaller depositors.

The newspaper fell from Auntie Sue's hand. Mechanically, she fingered the garment lying in her lap.

She, too, had sent a sum of money in a letter for deposit to her small account in this bank from which Brian Kent had stolen. She would not have sent the familiar paper currency of the United States that way; but this money was in Argentine notes. Her brother from far-away Buenos Aires had sent it to her, saying that it would help to keep her during the closing years of her life; and she had added it to her small savings with a feeling of deepest gratitude that her last days were now fully provided for. And she had received from the bank no acknowledgment of her letter with its enclosures.

Taking up the paper with hands that trembled so she scarce could distinguish the words, she read the paragraph again.

Suddenly, she recalled the man's puzzled expression when she had told him her name, and she seemed to hear him say, again, "Wakefield? Wakefield? Where have I seen that name?"

She looked at the date of the paper. Beyond all doubt, the man sleeping there in the other room;— the man whom she had saved from a suicide's end in the river;—whom she had nursed through the hell of delirium tremens;—whom she had yearned over as over her own son, and for whom, to save from the just penalty of his crime, she had lied—beyond all doubt that man had robbed her of the money that was to have insured to her peace and comfort in the closing years of her life.

Carefully, Auntie Sue laid the garment she had just mended with such loving care, with the rest of Brian Kent's clothing, on the near-by chair. Rising, she went with slow, troubled step to the porch.

There was no moon, that night, to turn the waters of The Bend into a stream of silvery light. But the stars were shining bright and clear, and she could see the river where it made its dark, mysterious way between the walls of shadowy hills; and borne to her ears on the gentle night wind came the deep, thundering roar of the angry waters at Elbow Rock.

For a long time she stood there on the porch looking into the night, with the light from the open door of her little house behind her; and she felt very

102

lonely, very tired, and very old. With her beautiful old face upturned to the infinite sky, where shining worlds are scattered in such lavish profusion, she listened, listened to the river that, with its countless and complex currents, swept so irresistibly onward along the way that was set for it by Him who swung those star-worlds in the limitless space of that mighty arch above. And something of the spirit that broods ever over the river must have entered into the soul of Auntie Sue. When she turned back into the house, there was a smile on her face, though her eyes were wet with tears.

Going to the chair that held Brian Kent's clothing, she took the garments in her arms and pressed them to her lips. Then she carried them to his room.

For some time she remained in that darkened chamber beside the sleeping man.

When she returned to the living-room, she again took up the newspaper. Very carefully, that her sleeping companions in the house might not hear her, she went to the kitchen, the paper in her hand. Very carefully, that no sound should betray her act, she burned the paper in the kitchen stove.

CHAPTER IX.

AUNTIE SUE'S PROPOSITION.

URING the next few days, Brian Kent rapidly regained his strength. No one seeing the tall, self-possessed gentleman who sat with Auntie Sue on the porch overlooking the river, or strolled about the place, could have imagined him the wretchedly repulsive creature that Judy had dragged from the eddy so short a time before. And no one,—excepting, perhaps, detective Ross,—would have identified this bearded guest of Auntie Sue's as the absconding bank clerk for whose arrest a substantial reward was offered.

But Mr. Ross had departed from the Ozarks, to report to the Empire Consolidated Savings Bank that, to the best of his knowledge and belief, Brian Kent had been drowned. Homer T. Ward, himself, wrote Auntie Sue about the case, for the detective had told the bank president about his visit to the little log house by the river, and the banker knew that his old teacher would wish to hear the conclusion of the affair.

The facts upon which the detective based his conclusion that Brian Kent was dead, were, first of all, the man's general character, temperament, habits, and ambitions,—aside from his thefts from the bank,— prior to the time of his exposure and flight, and his known mental and physical condition at the time he disappeared from the hotel in the little river town of Borden.

The detective reasoned (and there are thousands of cases that could be cited to support his contention) that by such a man as Brian Kent,—knowing, as he must have known, the comparative certainty of his ultimate arrest and conviction, and being in a mental and nervous condition bordering on insanity, as a result of his constant brooding over his crime and the excessive drinking to which he had resorted for relief, —by such a man, death would almost inevitably be chosen rather than a life of humiliation and disgrace and imprisonment.

Acting upon the supposition, however, that the man had gone down the river in that missing boat, and that the appearance of suicide was planned by the fugitive to trick his pursuers, the detectives ascertained that he had provided no supplies for a trip down the river. The man would be compelled to seek food. The mountain country through which he must pass was sparsely settled, and for a distance that would have taken a boat many days to cover, the officers visited every house and cabin and camp on either side of the river without finding a trace of the hunted man. The river had been watched night and day. The net set by the Burns operatives touched every settlement and village for many miles around. And, finally, the battered and broken wreck of the lost boat had been found some two miles below Elbow Rock.

". . . And so, my dear Auntie Sue," Banker Ward wrote, in conclusion, "you may rest in peace, secure in the certainty that my thieving bank clerk is not lurking anywhere in your beautiful Ozarks to pounce down upon you unawares in your little house beside the river. The man is safely dead. There is no doubt about it. I regret, more than I can express, that you have been in any way disturbed by the affair. Please think no more about it.

"By the way, you made a great impression upon detective Ross. He was more than enthusiastic over your graciousness and your beauty. I never heard him talk so much before in all the years I have known him. Needless to say, I indorsed everything he said about the dearest old lady in the world, and then we celebrated by dining together and drinking a toast to Auntie Sue. . . ."

Auntie Sue went with the letter to Brian, and acquainted him with that part of the banker's communication which related to the absconding clerk; but, about her relation to the president of the Empire Consolidated Savings Bank, she said nothing.

"Isn't it splendid!" she finished, her face glowing with delight.

"Splendid?" he echoed, looking at her with grave, questioning eyes.

"Why, yes, of course!" she returned. "Aren't you glad to be so dead, under the circumstances? Think what it means! You are free, now. No horrid old detectives dogging your steps, or waiting behind every bush and tree to pounce upon you. There is nothing, now, to prevent your being the kind of man that you always meant to be,—and really *are*, too,—except for your—your accidental tumble in the river," she finished with her low chuckling laugh. "And, some day," she went on, with conviction, "when you have established yourself,—when you have asserted your *real* self, I mean,—and have paid back every penny of the money, Homer T. Ward and Mr. Ross and everybody will be glad that they didn't catch you before you had a chance to save yourself."

"And you, Auntie Sue?" Brian's voice was deep with feeling: "And you?"

"Me? Oh, I am as glad, now, as I can ever be, because, you see, to me it is already done."

For a long minute he looked at her without speaking, then turned his face away to gaze out over the river and the hills; but his eyes were the eyes of one who looks without seeing.

Slowly, he said: "I wish I could be sure. There was a time when I was—when I believed in myself. It seems to me, now, that it was years and years ago. I thought, then, that nothing could shake me in my purpose; that nothing could check me in my ambition. I saw myself going straight on to the goal I had set for myself as certainly as—well, as your river over there goes on to the sea. But now——" He shook his head sadly.

Auntie Sue laughed. "You foolish boy. My river out there doesn't go straight at all. It meets all sorts of obstacles, and is beset by all sorts of conflicting influences, and so is forced to wind and twist and work its way along; but, the big, splendid thing about the river is that it keeps going on. It never stops to turn back. No matter what happens to it, it never stops. It goes on and on and on unto the very end, until it finally loses itself in the triumph of its own achievement,—the sea."

"And you think that I can go on?" he asked, doubtingly.

"I know you can go on," she answered with conviction.

"But, why are you so sure?"

"Perhaps," she returned, smiling, "seventy years makes one sure of some things."

He exclaimed passionately: "But you do not know—you cannot know—how my life, my dreams, my plans, my hopes, my—everything—has been broken into bits!"

She answered calmly, pointing to Elbow Rock: "Look there, Brian. See how the river is broken into bits. See how its smoothly flowing, onward sweep is suddenly changed to wild, chaotic turmoil; how it rages and fumes and frets and smashes itself against the rocks. But it goes on just the same. Life cannot be always calm and smoothly flowing like the peaceful Bend. But life can always go on. Life must always go on. And you will find, my dear boy, that a little way below Elbow Rock there is another quiet stretch."

When he spoke again there was a note of almost reverence in his voice.

"Auntie Sue, was there ever a break in your life? Were your dreams and plans ever smashed into bits?"

For a little, she did not answer; then she said, bravely: "Yes, Brian; several times. Once,— years and years ago,—I do not know how I managed to go on. I felt, then, as you feel now; but, somehow, I managed, and so found the calm places. The last hard spot came quite recently." She paused, wondering what he would do if she were to tell him how he himself had made the hard spot. "But,

110

now," she continued, "I am hoping that the rest of the way will be calm and untroubled."

"I wish I could help to make it so!" he cried impulsively.

"Why, you can," she returned quickly. "Of course you can. Perhaps that is why the current landed your boat at my garden, instead of carrying you on down the rapids to Elbow Rock. Who can say?"

A new light kindled in the man's eyes as his sensitive nature took fire at Auntie Sue's words. "I could do anything for a woman like you, Auntie Sue," he said quietly, but with a conviction that left no room for doubt. "But you must tell me what I am to do."

She answered: "You are simply to go on with your life—just as if no Elbow Rock had ever disturbed you; just as the river goes on—to the end."

She left him, then, to think out his problem alone; for the teacher of so many years' experience was too wise not to know when a lesson was finished.

But when the end of the day was come, they again sat together on the porch and watched the miracle of the sunset hour. And no word was spoken by them, now, of life and its problems and its meanings.

THE RE-CREATION OF BRIAN KENT

As one listens to the song of a bird without thought of musical notes or terms; as one senses the fragrance of a flower without thought of the chemistry of perfume; as one feels the presence of spring in the air without thought of the day of the week, so they were conscious of the beauty, the glory, and the peace of the evening.

Only when the soft darkness of the night lay over the land, and river and mountain and starry sky were veiled in dreamy mystery, did Auntie Sue speak: "Oh, it is so good to have some one to share it with, —some one who understands. I am very lonely, sometimes, Brian. I wonder if you know?"

"Yes, Auntie Sue, I know, for I have been lonely, too."

And so the old gentlewoman, whose lifework was so nearly finished, and the man in the flush of his manhood years, whose life had been so nearly wrecked, were drawn very close by a something that came to them out of the beauty and the mystery of that hour.

The next day, Brian told Auntie Sue that he would leave on the morrow.

112

"Leave?" she echoed in dismay. "Why, Brian, where are you going?"

"I don't exactly know," he returned; "but, of course, I must go somewhere, out into the world again."

"And why must you 'go somewhere, out into the world again'?" she demanded.

"To work," he answered, smiling. "If I am to go on, as you say, I must go where I can find something to do."

"If that isn't just like you—you child!" cried the old teacher. "You are all alike,—you boys and girls. You all must have something to do; always, it is 'something to do'."

"Well," he returned, "and must we not have something to do?"

"You will do something, certainly," she answered; "but, before you can *do* anything that is worth doing, you must *be* something. Life isn't *doing*;—it is *being*."

"I wonder if that was not the real reason for my wretched failures," said Brian, thoughtfully.

"It is the real reason for most of our failures,"

she returned. "And so you are not going to fail again. You are not going away somewhere, you don't know where, to do something you don't know what. You are going to stay right here, and just *be* something. Then, when the time comes, you will do whatever is yours to do as naturally and as inevitably as the birds sing, as the blossoms come in the spring, or as the river finds its way to the sea."

And more than ever Brian Kent felt in the presence of Auntie Sue as a little boy to whom the world had grown suddenly very big and very wonderful.

But, after a while, he shook his head, smiling wistfully. "No, no, Auntie Sue, that sounds all true and right enough, but it can't be. I must go just the same."

"Why can't it be, Brian?"

"For one thing," he returned, "I cannot risk the danger to you. After all, as long as I am living, there is a chance that my identity will be discovered, and you—no, no; I must not!"

"As for that," she answered quickly, "the chances of your being identified are a thousand times greater if you go into the world again too soon. Some day, of course, you must go; but you are safer now right

114

here. And"—she added quickly—"it would be no easier for me, dear boy, to—to—have it happen somewhere away from me. You are mine, you know, no matter where you go."

"But, Auntie Sue," he protested, "I am not a gentleman of means that I can do nothing indefinitely; neither am I capable of living upon your hospitality for an extended period. I must earn my bread and butter."

The final sentence came with such a lifting of his head, such a look of stern decision, and such an air of pride, that the gentle old school-teacher laughed until her eyes were filled with tears; and Judy, at the crack in the kitchen door, wondered if the mistress of the little log house by the river were losing her mind.

"Oh, Brian! Brian!" cried Auntie Sue, wiping her eyes. "I knew you would come to the 'bread and butter' at last. That is where all our philosophies and reasonings and arguments come at last, don't they? Just 'bread and butter,' that is all. And I love you for it. Of course you can't live upon my hospitality,—and I couldn't let you if you would. And if you *would,* I wouldn't let you if I could. I am no more a lady of means, my haughty sir, than you are a gentleman of independent fortune. The fact is, Brian, dear, I suspect that you and I are about the two poorest people in the world,—to be anything like as pretentiously respectable and properly proud as we are."

When the man could make no reply, but only looked at her with a much-puzzled and still-proud expression, she continued, half-laughingly, but well pleased with him: "Please, Brian, don't look so haughtily injured. I had no intention of insulting you by offering charity. Far from it."

Instantly, the man's face changed. He put out his hands protestingly, and his blue eyes filled, as he said, impulsively: "Auntie Sue, after what you have done for me, I—"

She answered quickly: "We are considering the future. What has been, is past. Our river is already far beyond that point in its journey. Don't let us try to turn the waters back. I promise you I am going to be very, very practical, and make you pay for *everything*."

Smiling, now, he waited for her to explain.

"I must tell you, first," she began, "that, except

for a very small amount in the—in a savings bank, I have nothing to provide for my last days except this little farm."

"What a shame," Brian Kent exclaimed, "that a woman like you can give her life to the public schools for barely enough salary to keep her alive during her active years, and then left in her old age with no means of support. It is a national disgrace."

Auntie Sue chuckled with appreciation of the rather grim humor of the situation. What would Brian Kent, indignant at the public neglect of the school-teacher, say of the man who had robbed her of the money that was to provide for her closing years? "After all, most public sins are only individual sins at the last," she said, musingly.

"I beg your pardon," said Brian, not in the least seeing the relevancy of her words.

Auntie Sue came quickly back to her subject: "Only thirty acres of my little farm is under cultivation. The remaining fifty acres is wild timberland. If I could have that fifty acres also in cultivation, with the money that the timber would bring, —which would not be a great deal,—I would be fairly safe for the—for the rest of my evening," she finished with a smile. "Do you see?"

"You mean that I—that you want me to stay here and work for you?"

"I mean," she answered, "that, if you choose to stay for awhile, you need not feel that you would be accepting my hospitality as charity," she returned gently. "I am not exactly offering you a job: I am only showing you how you could, without sacrificing your pride, remain in this quiet retreat for awhile before returning to the world."

"It would be heaven, Auntie Sue," he returned earnestly. "I want to stay so bad that I fear myself. Let me think it over until to-morrow. Let me be sure that I am doing the right thing, and not merely the thing I want to do."

She liked his answer, and did not mention the subject again until Brian himself was ready. And, strangely enough, it was poor, twisted Judy who helped him to set matters straight.

CHAPTER X.

BRIAN KENT DECIDES.

BRIAN had walked along the river-bank below the house to a spot just above the point where the high bluff jutting out into the river-channel forms Elbow Rock.

The bank here is not so high above the roaring waters of the rapids, for the spur of the mountain which forms the cliff lies at a right angle to the river, and the greater part of the cliff is thus on the shore, with its height growing less and less as it merges into the main slope of the mountain-side. From the turn in the road, in front of the house, a footpath leads down the bank of the river to the cliff, and, climbing stairlike up the face of the steep bluff, zigzags down the easier slope of the down-river side, to come again into the road below. The road itself, below Elbow Rock, is forced by the steep side of the mountain-spur and the precipitous bluff to turn inland from the river, and so, climbing by an easier grade up past Tom Warden's place, crosses the ridge above the schoolhouse, and comes back down the mountain again in front of Auntie Sue's place, to its general course along the stream. The little path forms thus a convenient short cut for any one following the river road on foot.

Brian, seated on the river-bank a little way from the path where it starts up the bluff, was trying to decide whether it would be better for him to follow his desire and stay with Auntie Sue for a few weeks or months, or whether he should not, in spite of the land he might clear for her, return to the world where he could more quickly earn the money to pay back that which he had stolen.

And as he sat there, the man was conscious that he had reached one of those turning-points that are found in every life where results, momentous and far-reaching, are dependent upon comparatively un-important and temporary issues. He could not have told why, and yet he felt a certainty that, for him, two widely separated futures were dependent upon his choice. Nor could he, by thinking, discover what those futures held for him, nor which he should choose. Even as his boat that night had hung on the edge of the eddy,—hesitating on the dividing-line between the two currents,—so the man himself now felt the pull of his life-currents, and hesitated,—undecided.

Looking toward the house, he thought how like the life offered by Auntie Sue was to the quiet waters of The Bend, and—his mind finished the simile— how like the life to which he would go was to the rapids at Elbow Rock; and, yet, he reflected, the waters could never reach the sea without enduring the turmoil of the rapids. And, again, the thought came, "The Bend is just as much the river as the troubled passage around the rock."

When he had given up life, and, to all intent and purpose, had left life behind him, the river, without his will or knowledge, had mysteriously elected to save him from the death he had chosen as his only refuge from the utter ruin that had seemed so inevitable. As the currents of the river had carried his boat to the eddy at the foot of Auntie Sue's garden, the currents of life had mysteriously brought him to the saving influence of Auntie Sue herself. Should he push out again into the stream to face the danger he knew beset such a course? or should he wait for a season in the secure calm of the harbor she offered until he were stronger? Brian Kent knew, instinctively, that there was in the wisdom and love of Auntie Sue's philosophy and faith a strength that would, if he could make it his, insure his safe passage through every danger of life, and yet—

The man's meditations were interrupted by a chance look toward the bluff which towered above him.

Judy was climbing the steep trail.

Curiously, Brian watched the deformed mountain girl as she made her way up the narrow, stairlike path, and her cutting words came back to him: "God-A'mighty and my drunken pap made me like I am. But you,—damn you!—you made yourself what you be." And Auntie Sue had said that the all-important thing in life was not to *do* something, but to *be* something.

The girl, who had gained a point halfway to the top of the bluff, paused to look searchingly about, and Brian, who was half-hidden by the bushes, started to call to her, thinking she might be looking for him; but some impulse checked him and he remained silently watching her. Climbing hurriedly a little higher up the path Judy again stopped to look carefully around, as if searching the vicinity for some one. Then, once more, she went on until she stood on top of the cliff; and now, as she looked about over the surrounding country, she called: "Mr. Burns! Oh, Mr. Burns! Who-o-e-e! Mr. Burns!"

Brian's lips were parted to answer the call when something happened on top of the bluff which held him for the moment speechless.

From beyond where Judy stood on the brink of the cliff, a man's head and shoulders appeared. Brian saw the girl start and turn to face the newcomer as if in sudden fear. Then she whirled about to run. Before she could gain the point where the path starts down from the top, the man caught her and dragged her roughly back, so that the two disappeared from Brian's sight. Brian was halfway up the bluff when he heard the girl's shrill scream.

There was no sign of weakness, now, in the man that Judy had dragged from the river. He covered the remaining distance to the top in a breath. From among the bushes, a little way down the mountainside, came the sound of an angry voice mingled with Judy's pleading cries.

An instant more, and Brian reached the spot where

123

poor Judy was crouching on the ground, begging the brute, who stood over her with menacing fists, not to hit her again.

The man was a vicious-looking creature, dressed in the rough garb of the mountaineer; dirty and unkempt, with evil, close-set eyes, and a scraggly beard that could not hide the wicked, snarling mouth.

He stood for a second looking at Brian, as if too surprised by the latter's sudden appearance to move; then he went down, felled by as clean a knockout as was ever delivered by an Irish fist.

"Are you hurt, Judy?" demanded Brian, as he lifted the girl to her feet. "Did he strike you?"

"He was sure a-fixin' ter lick me somethin' awful when you-all put in," returned the poor girl, trembling with fear. "I know, 'cause he's done hit to me heaps er times before. He's my pap."

"Your father!" exclaimed Brian.

Judy nodded;—then screamed: "Look out! He'll git you, sure!"

Judy's rescuer whirled, to see the man on the ground drawing a gun. A vigorous, well-directed kick, delivered in the nick of time, sent the gun whirling away into the bushes and rendered the native's right arm useless.

"Get up!" commanded Brian.

The man rose to his feet, and stood nursing his damaged wrist and scowling at Judy's companion.

"Are you this girl's father?"

"I reckon I am," came the sullen reply. "I'm Jap Taylor, an' you-all are sure goin' to find that you can't come between a man an' his lawful child in these here mountains, mister,—if you-all be from the city."

"And you will find that you can't strike a crippled girl in my presence, even if she is your daughter,—in these mountains or anywhere else," retorted Brian. "What are you trying to do with her, anyway?"

"I aim ter take her back home with me, where she belongs."

"Well, why didn't you go to the house for her like a man, instead of jumping on her out here in the woods!"

"Hit ain't none of your dad burned business as I can see," came the sullen reply.

"I am making it my business, just the same," returned Brian.

He turned to the girl, who had drawn back a little behind him. "Judy," he said, kindly, "I think perhaps you better tell me about this."

"Pap, he was a-layin' for me in the bresh 'cause he dassn't come to the house ter git me," said the girl, fearfully.

"But, why does he fear to come to the house?" persisted Brian.

" 'Cause he done give me ter Auntie Sue."

"Gave you to Auntie Sue?" repeated the puzzled Brian.

Jap Taylor interrupted with, "I didn't sign ary paper, an'—"

"Shut up, you!" snapped Brian. "Go on, Judy."

"Hit was a year last corn-plantin'," explained the girl. "My maw, she died. He used ter whip her, too. An' Auntie Sue was there helpin' weuns; an' Tom Warden an' some other folks they was there, too; an' they done fixed hit so that I was ter go an' live with Auntie Sue; an' pap, he give me ter her. He sure did, Mr. Burns, an' I ain't a-wantin' ter go with him, no more."

126

The poor girl's shrill monotone broke, and her twisted body shook with her sobs.

"I didn't sign ary paper," repeated Judy's father, with sullen stubbornness. "An' what's more, I sure ain't a-goin' ter. I 'lows as how she'll just go home an' work for me, like she ort, 'stead of livin' with that there old-maid schoolma'am. I'm her paw, I am, an' I reckon I got rights."

He started toward the girl, who drew closer to Brian, and begged piteously: "Don't let him tech me! 'Fore God, Mr. Burns, he'll kill me, sure!"

Brian drew the girl behind him as he faced the father with a brief, "Get out!"

The mountaineer hesitated.

Brian went one step toward him: "Do you hear? Get out! And if you ever show your dirty face in this vicinity again, I'll not leave a whole bone in your worthless carcass!"

And Jap Taylor saw something in those Irish blue eyes that caused him to start off down the mountain toward the river below Elbow Rock.

When he had placed a safe distance between himself and the man who appeared so willing and able to make good his threat, Judy's father turned, and, shaking his uninjured fist at Brian, delivered a volley of curses, with: "I'll sure git you-all for this! Jap Taylor ain't a-lettin' no man come between him an' his'n. I'll fix you, an' I'll fix that there schoolma'am, too! She's nothin' but a damned old—"

But Brian started toward him, and Jap Taylor beat a hasty retreat.

"Never mind, Judy," said Brian, when the native had disappeared in the brush and timber that covered the steep mountain-side. "I'll not let him touch you. Come, let us sit down and talk a little until you are yourself again. Auntie Sue must not see you like this. We don't want to let her know anything about it. You won't tell her, will you?"

"I ain't aimin' ter tell nobody," said Judy, between sobs. "I sure ain't a-wantin' ter make no trouble,—not for Auntie Sue, nohow. She's been powerful good ter me."

When they were seated on convenient rocks at the brink of the cliff overlooking the river, Judy gradually ceased crying, and presently said, in her normal, querulous monotone: "Did you-all mind what pap 'lowed he'd do ter Auntie Sue, Mr. Burns?"

"Yes, Judy; but don't worry, child. He is not going to harm any one while I am around."

"You-all are aimin' ter stay then, be you? I'm sure powerful glad," said Judy, simply.

Brian started. A new factor had suddenly been injected into his problem.

"I was powerful scared you-all was aimin' ter go away," continued Judy. "Hit was that I was a-huntin' you-all to tell you 'bout, when pap he ketched me."

"What were you going to tell me, Judy?"

"I 'lowed ter tell you-all 'bout Auntie Sue. She'd sure be powerful mad if she know'd I'd said anythin' ter you, but she's a-needin' somebody like you ter help her, mighty bad. She—she's done lost a heap of money, lately: hit was some she sent—"

Brian interrupted: "Wait a minute, Judy. You must not tell me anything about Auntie Sue's private affairs; you must not tell any one. Anything she wants me to know, she will tell me. Do you understand?" he finished with a reassuring smile.

"Yes, sir; I reckon you-all are 'bout right, an' I won't tell nobody nothin'. But 'tain't a-goin' ter hurt none ter say as how you-all ort ter stay, I reckon."

"And why do you think I ought to stay, Judy?"

" 'Cause of what Auntie Sue's done for you-all,—a-nursin' you when you was plumb crazy an' plumb dangerous from licker, an' a-lyin' like she did ter the Sheriff an' that there deteckertive man," returned Judy stoutly; "an' 'cause she's so old an' is a-needin' you-all ter help her; an' 'cause she is a-lovin' you like she does, an' is a-wantin' you-all ter stay so bad hit's mighty nigh a-makin' her plumb sick."

Brian Kent did not answer. The mountain girl's words had revealed to him the selfishness of his own consideration of his problem so clearly that he was stunned. Why had he not, in his thinking, remembered the dear old gentlewoman who had saved him from a shameful death?

Judy went on: "Hit looks ter me like somebody just naturally's got ter take care of Auntie Sue, Mr. Burns. All her whole life she's a-been takin' care of everybody just like she tuck me, an' just like she tuck you-all, besides a heap of other ways; an' now she's so old and mighty nigh plumb wore out, hit

130

sure looks like hit was time somebody was a-fixin'
ter do somethin' for her. That was what I was a-
huntin' you-all ter tell you when pap ketched me,
Mr. Burns."

"I am glad you told me, Judy;—very glad. You
see, I was not thinking of things in just that way."

"I 'lowed maybe you mightn't. Seems like folks
mostly don't."

"But it's all right, now!" Brian cried heartily.
"You have settled it. I'll stay. We'll take care of
Auntie Sue,—you and I, Judy. Come on, now;
let's go to the house, and tell her. But we won't say
anything about your father, Judy;—that would only
make her unhappy; and we must never make Auntie
Sue unhappy—never." He was as eager and enthusiastic, now, as a schoolboy.

" 'Course," said Judy, solemnly; " 'course you just
naturally got ter stay an' take care of her now, after
what pap's done said he'd do."

"Yes, Judy; I've just naturally got to stay," returned Brian.

Together they went down the steep cliff trail and
to the little log house by the river to announce Brian's
decision to Auntie Sue. They found the dear old

lady in her favorite spot on the porch overlooking the river.

"Why, of course you will stay," she returned, when Brian had told her. "The river brought you to me, and you know, my dear boy, the river is never wrong. Oh, yes, I know there are cross-currents and crooked spots and sand-bars and rocks and lots of places where it *seems* to us to be wrong. But, just the same, it all goes on, all the time, toward the sea for which it starts when it first begins at some little spring away over there somewhere in the mountains. Of course you will stay with me, Brian,—until the river carries you on again."

CHAPTER XI.

RE-CREATION.

ROM the very day of his decision, to which he had been so unexpectedly helped by Judy, Brian Kent was another man. The gloomy, despondent, undecided spirit that was the successor of the wretched creature that Judy had helped to Auntie Sue's that morning was now succeeded by a cheerful, hopeful, contented man, who went to his daily task with a song, did his work with a smile and a merry jest, and returned, when the day was done, with peace in his heart and laughter on his lips.

As the days of the glorious Ozark autumn passed, Brian's healthful, outdoor work on the timbered mountain-side brought to the man of the cities a physical grace and beauty he had lacked,—the grace of physical strength and the beauty of clean and rugged health. The bright autumn sun and the winds that swept over the many miles of tree-clad hills browned his skin; while his work with the ax

133

developed his muscles and enforced deep breathing of the bracing mountain air, thus bringing a more generous supply of richer blood, which touched his now firmly rounded cheeks with color.

The gift of humor and the faculty of quaint and witty conversational twists, with the genius of story-telling that was his from his Irish mother, made quick friends for him of the mountain neighbors who welcomed this new pupil of their old school-teacher with whole-hearted pleasure, and quoted his jests and sayings throughout the country with never-failing delight. And Judy,—it is not too much to say that Judy became his most ardent admirer and devoted slave.

But the dear old mistress of the little log house by the river alone recognized that these outward changes in the human wreck that the river had brought to her were but manifestations of a more potent transformation that was taking place in the man's inner life; and it was this inner change that filled the teacher's loving heart with joy, and which she watched with keen and delighted interest.

It was not, after all, a new life that was coming

to this man, Auntie Sue told herself; it was his own old and more real life that was reasserting itself. It was the real Brian Kent that had been sojourning in a far country that was now coming home to his own. It was the wealth of his heart and mind and soul which had been deep-buried under an accumulation of circumstances and environment that was now being brought to the surface.

Might it not be that Auntie Sue's genius for absorbing beauty and making truth her own had, in her many years of searching for truth and beauty in whatever humanity she encountered, developed in her a peculiar sensitiveness? And was it not this that had made her feel instinctively the real nature of the man in whom a less discerning observer would have recognized nothing worthy of admiration or regard? Without question, it was the true,—the essential,—the underlying,—elements in the character of the absconding bank clerk that had aroused in this remarkable old gentlewoman the peculiar sense of kinship—of possession—that had determined her attitude toward the stranger. The law that like calls to like is not less applicable to things spiritual than to things material. The birds of a feather that always flock together are not of necessity material birds of material feathers.

Nor was Brian Kent himself unconscious of his Re-Creation. The man knew what he was, as every man knows deep within himself the real self that is. And that was the horror of the situation which had set him adrift on the river that night when, in his last drunken despairing frenzy, he had left the world with a curse in his heart and had faced the black unknown with reckless laughter and a profane toast. It is to be doubted if there can be a hell of greater torment than that experienced by one who, endowed by nature with a capacity for great living, is betrayed by the very strength of his genius into a situation that is intolerable of his real self, and is forced, thus, to a continuous self-crucifixion and death.

In his new environment the man felt the awakening of this self which he had mourned as dead. Thoughts, emotions, dreams, aspirations, which had, as he believed, been killed, he found were not dead, but only sleeping; and in the quickening of their vitality and strength he knew a joy as great as had been his despair.

The beauty of nature, that had lost its power of appeal to his sodden soul, now stirred him to the very depth of his being. The crisp, sun-sweet air of the autumn mornings, when he went forth with his ax to the day's clean labor, was a draught of potent magic that set every nerve of him tingling with delight. The woodland hillside, where he worked, was a wonderland of beautiful creations that inspired a thousand glowing fancies. Sometimes, at his heavy task, he would pause for a moment's rest, and so would look out and away over the vast expanse of country that from his feet stretched in all its charm of winding river and wooded slopes, and tree-fringed ridges to the far, blue sky-line; and the very soul of him would answer to the call as he had thought he never could answer again. The very clouds that drifted past on their courses to unseen ports beyond the hills were freighted with meaning for him now. The winds that came laden with the subtly blended perfume of ten thousand varieties of trees and grasses and shrubs and flowers whispered words of life which he now could hear. The loveliness of the glowing morning skies, as he saw them when he rose for the day's work, and the glories of the sunsets, as he watched them with Auntie Sue from the porch when the day's task was accomplished, filled him with an exquisite gladness which he had never hoped to know again.

Most of all, did the river speak to him; not, indeed, as it had spoken that dreadful night, when, from the window of his darkened room, he had listened to its call: the river spoke, now, in the full day as his eye followed its winding length through the hills in all its varied beauty of sunshine and shadow;—of gleaming silver and living green and russet-brown. It talked to him in the evening when the waters gave back the glories of the sky and the deepening twilight wrapped the world in its dusky veil of mystery. It spoke to him in the soft darkness of the night, as it swept on its way under the stars, or in the light of the golden moon. And, in time, some of these things which the river said to him, he, in turn, told to Auntie Sue.

And Auntie Sue, delighted with the man's awakening self, and charmed with his power of thought and his gift of expression, led him on. With artful suggestion and skilful question and subtle argument, she stimulated his mind and fancy to lay hold of the truths and beauties that life and nature offered. But ever the rare old gentlewoman was his teacher, revealing himself to himself; guiding him to a fuller discovery and knowledge of his own life and its meaning, which, indeed, is the true aim and end of all right teaching.

So the days of the autumn passed. The hills changed their robes of varied green for costumes of brown and gold, with touches here and there of flaming scarlet and brilliant yellow. And then winter was at hand, and that momentous evening came when 'Auntie Sue said to her pupil, after an hour of most interesting talk, "Brian, why in the world don't you write a book?"

" 'A book'!" exclaimed Brian, in a startled tone.

Judy laughed. "He sure ought ter. Lord knows he talks like one."

"I am in earnest, Brian," said Auntie Sue, her lovely old eyes shining with enthusiasm and her gentle voice trembling with excitement. "I have been thinking about it for a long time, now, and, to-night,

I just can't keep it to myself any longer. Why don't you give to the world some of the thoughts you have been wasting on Judy and me?"

"Hit's sure been a-wastin' of 'em on me," agreed Judy. " 'Fore God, I don't sense what he's a-talkin' 'bout, more'n half the time."

Brian laughed. "Judy is prophetic, Auntie Sue. She voices perfectly the sentiment of the world toward any book I might write."

Auntie Sue detected a note of bitterness underlying the laughing comment, and wondered.

Judy spoke again as she arose to retire to her room for the night: "I reckon as how there's a right smart of things youuns talk that'd be mighty fine if a body only had the learnin' ter sense 'em. An' there must be heaps of folks where youuns come from what would know Mr. Burns's meaning if he was to write hit all out plain. Everybody ain't like me. Hit's sure a God's-blessin' they ain't, too."

"And there, Brian, dear, is your answer," said Auntie Sue, as Judy left the room. "Any book has meaning only for those who have the peculiar sympathy and understanding needed to interpret it. A book that means nothing to one may be rich in meaning for another. Every writer writes for his own peculiar readers, just as every individual has his own peculiar friends."

"Or enemies," said Brian.

"Or enemies," agreed Auntie Sue.

Brian went to the window, and stood for some time, looking out into the night. Then turning, with a nervous gesture, he paced uneasily up and down the room; while Auntie Sue watched him in silence with an expression of loving concern on her dear old face.

At last, she spoke: "Why, Brian, what is the matter? What have I said? I did not mean to upset you like this. Come, sit down here, and tell me about it. What is it troubles you so?"

With a short laugh, Brian came and stood before her. "I suppose it had to come sooner or later, Auntie Sue. I have been trying for days to muster up courage enough to tell you about it. You have touched the one biggest thing in my life."

"Why, what do you mean, Brian?"

"I mean just what we have been talking about,— writing," answered Brian.

"Oh!" she cried, with quick and delighted

141

triumph. "Then I *am* right. You have been thinking about it, too."

"Thinking about it!" he echoed, and in his voice she felt the nervous intensity of his mood. "I have thought of nothing else. All day long when I am at work, I am writing, writing, writing. It is the last thing on my mind when I go to sleep. I dream about it all night. And it is the first thing I think about in the morning."

Auntie Sue clasped her hands to her heart with an exclamation of joyous interest.

Brian, with a quiet smile at her enthusiasm, went on: "I know exactly what I want to say, and why i want to say it. There is a world of people, Auntie Sue, whose lives have been broken and spoiled by one thing or another, and who have more or less cut themselves loose from everything, and are just drifting, they don't care a hang where, because they think they have failed so completely that there is nothing more in life for them. People like me,—I don't mean thieves and criminals necessarily,—who have had that which they know to be the best and biggest and truest part of themselves tortured and warped and twisted and denied and smashed and beaten and betrayed and killed; and who, because they feel that their real selves are dead within them, don't care what happens to that part which is left."

He was walking the floor again now, and speaking with a depth of feeling which he had never before revealed to his gentle companion.

"It is not so much the love of wrong-doing that makes people turn bad,"—he continued,—"it is having their real selves misunderstood and doubted and smothered and their realest loves and dreams and aspirations never recognized, or else distorted and twisted and made to appear as something they hate. I want to make the people—and there are many thousands of them—who are suffering in the living hell that tormented me, feel that I know and understand. And then, Auntie Sue, then I want to tell them about you and your river.

"I would teach them the things you have taught me. I would say to every one that I could persuade to listen: 'It doesn't in the least matter what your experience is, the old river is still going on to the sea. No matter if every woman you ever knew has proved untrue, virtuous womanhood still *is*. No matter if every man you ever knew has proved false, true manhood still *is*. If every friend you ever had has betrayed your friendship, loyal friendship still *is*. If you have found nothing in your experience but dishonesty and falsehood and infidelity and hypocrisy, it is only because you have been unfortunate in your experience; because honesty and fidelity and sincerity are existing *facts*. They are the very foundation facts of life, and can no more fail life than the river can fail to reach the sea.

" 'Your little individual experience, my little individual experience,—what are they? They are nothing more than the tiny bubbles, swirls, ripples, and breaks on the surface of the great volume of water that flows so inevitably onward. The bit of foam, the tiny wave caused by twig or branch or blade of water-grass, or the great rocks and cliffs that make the roaring whirlpools and rapids,—do they stay the waters, or turn the river back on its course, or in any way prevent its onward flow? No more can the twigs of circumstances, or the boughs of environment, or the grasses of accident that make the tiny waves of our individual experiences,—or even the great rocks and cliffs of national or racial import,—

such as wars, and pestilence, and famine,—finally check or stay the river of life in its onward flow toward the sea of its final and infinite meaning.' "

He went again to the window, and stood looking out into the night as though listening to the voices.

"Why, Auntie Sue," he said, turning back to the old gentlewoman,—and his face was radiant with the earnestness of this thought,—"Auntie Sue, there are as many currents in our river out there as there are human lives. A comparatively few great main or dominant currents in the river flow—a comparatively few great dominant currents in the river flow of life. But if you look closer, you will see that in each one of those established principal currents there are countless thousands—millions—of tiny currents all turning and twisting across, and back, and up, and down in every direction,—weaving themselves together,—pulling themselves apart,—criss-crossing,— clashing,—interlacing,—tangled and confused,—and these are the individual lives. And no matter what the conflict or confusion; no matter what direction they take for the moment, they all, *all*, go to make up the river;—they, all together, *are* the river,—and they all together move onward,—ceaselessly, inevitably, irresistibly."

He paused to stand smiling down at her, as she sat there in her low chair beside the table with the lamplight on her silvery hair,—there in the little log house by the river.

"That is what you have made your river mean to me, Auntie Sue; and that is what I would give to the world."

With trembling hands, the gentle old teacher reached for her handkerchief, which lay in the sewing-basket on the table beside her. Smilingly, she wiped away the tears that filled her eyes. Lovingly, she looked up at him,—standing so tall and strong before her, with his reddish hair tumbled and tossed, and his Irish blue eyes lighted with the fire of his inspiration.

"Well," she said, at last, "why don't you do it, Brian?"

As a breath of air puts out the light of a candle, so the light went from Brian Kent's face. Dropping into his chair, he answered hopelessly, "Because I am afraid."

"Afraid?" echoed Auntie Sue, troubled and

amazed. "What in the world are you afraid of, Brian?"

And the bitter, bitter answer came, "I am afraid of another failure."

Auntie Sue's quick mind caught the significance of his words. *"Another* failure, Brian? Then you, —then you have written before?"

"Yes," he returned. And not since his decision to remain with her had she seen him so despondent. "To write was the dream and the passion of my life. I tried and tried. God, how I worked and slaved at it! The only result from my efforts was the hell from which you dragged me."

After a little silence, Auntie Sue said gently: "I don't think I understand, Brian. You have never told me about your trouble, you know."

"It is an old, old story," he returned. "I am only one of thousands. My wretched experience is not at all uncommon."

"I know," she answered. "But don't you think that perhaps you had better tell me? Perhaps, in the mere telling of it to me, now that it is all over, you may find the real reason for—for what happened to you."

Wise Auntie Sue!—wise in that rarest of all wisdom,—the sympathetic understanding of human hearts and souls.

"You know about my earlier life," he began; "how, in my boyhood, after mother's death, I worked at anything I could do to keep myself alive, and how I managed to gain a little schooling. I was always dreaming of writing, even then. I took the business course in a night-school, not because I liked it, but because I thought it would help me to earn a living in a way that would give me more time for what I really wanted to do. And after I finished school, and had finally worked up to a good position in that bank, I did have more time for my writing. But," —he hesitated—"I—well,—other interests had come into my life,—and—"

Auntie Sue said, softly, "She did not understand, Brian."

"No, she did not understand," he continued, accepting Auntie Sue's interpretation without comment. "And when my writing brought no money, because no publisher would accept my stuff, and the conditions under which I wrote became intolerable because of misunderstanding and opposition and dis-

148

belief in my ability and charges of neglect, I—I— stole money from my employers to gain temporary relief until my writing should amount to something. You see, I could not help believing that I would succeed, in time. I suppose all dreamers have more or less confidence in their dreams: they must, you know, or their dreams would never be realized. I always expected to pay back the money I took with the money I would earn by my pen. But I failed to earn anything, you see; and then—then the inevitable happened, and the river brought me to you."

"But, my dear boy!" cried Auntie Sue, "all this that you have told me is no reason why you should fear to write now. Indeed, it is a very good reason why you should not fear."

He looked at her questioningly, and she continued: "You have given every reason in the world why you failed. Your whole life was out of tune. How could you expect to produce anything worthy from such a jangling discord? You should have been afraid, indeed, to write *then*. But, *now*,—now, Brian, you are ready. You are a long, long way down the river from the place of your failures. The disturbing, distracting things are past,—just as in the quiet reach of the river below Elbow Rock the turmoil of the rapids is past. You say that you know exactly what you want to write, and why you want to write it—and you do know—and because you know,—because you have suffered,—because you have learned,—because you can do this thing for others,—it is yours to do, and so you must do it. What you really mean when you say you are 'afraid to write' is, that you are *afraid not to,*" she finished with a little laugh of satisfaction.

And Brian Kent, as he watched her glowing face and felt the sincerity and confidence that vibrated in her voice, was thrilled with a new courage. The fires of his inspiration shone again in his eyes, as he answered, with deep conviction, "Auntie Sue, I believe you are right. What a woman you are!"

CHAPTER XII.

SO Brian wrote his book that winter.

When the days were fair, he worked with his ax on the mountain-side. But his note-book was ever at hand, and many a thought that went down on the pages of his manuscript was born while he wrought with his hands in the wholesome labor which gave strength to his body and clearness to his brain. In the evenings, he wrote in the little log house by the river, with Auntie Sue sitting in her chair beside the table,—the lamp-light on her silvery hair, and her sewing-basket within reach of her hand, —engaged with some bit of needlework, a book, or perhaps with one of her famous letters to some other pupil, far away. The stormy days gave him many hours with his pen, and so the book grew.

And always as the man endeavored to shape his thoughts for the printed pages that would carry his message to the doubting, disconsolate, and fearful world that he knew so well, he heard in his heart the voices of the river. From the hillside where he worked in the timber he could see the stream winding through the snowy hills like a dark line carelessly drawn with many a crook and curve and break on the sheet of white. From the porch he saw the quiet Bend a belt of shining ice and snow, save for a narrow line in the centre, which marked the course of the strongest currents; while the waters of the rapids crashed black and dreadful against the Elbow Rock cliff, which stood gaunt and grim amid the surrounding whiteness; and in the deathlike hush of the winter twilight, the roar of the turmoil sounded with persistent menace. And all that the river said to him he put down,—so far as it was given him to do.

And that which Brian Kent wrote was good. He knew it—in his deepest, truest self he knew. And Auntie Sue knew it; for, of course, he read to her from his manuscript as the book grew under his hand. Even Judy caught much of his story's meaning, and marvelled at herself because she, too, could understand.

So the spring came, and the first writing of the book was nearly finished.

And now the question arose: What would they

do about the final preparation of the manuscript for the printers? Brian explained that he should have a typewritten copy of his script, which he would work over, correct, and revise, and from which perfected copy the final manuscript would be typewritten. But neither Auntie Sue nor Brian would consider his finishing the book anywhere but in the little log house by the river; even if there had been no other reason why Brian should not go to the city, if it could be avoided.

"There is only one thing to do,"—said Auntie Sue, at last, when the matter had been discussed several times,—"we must send for Betty Jo. She has been studying stenography in a business college in Cincinnati, and, in her latest letter to me, she wrote that she would finish in April. I'll just write her to come right here, and bring her typewriter along. She will need a vacation, and she can have it and do your work at the same time. Besides, I need to see Betty Jo. She hasn't been to visit me since before Judy came."

Brian thought that Auntie Sue seemed a little nervous and excited as she spoke, but he attributed it to her combined interest in the book and in the pro-

THE RE-CREATION OF BRIAN KENT

posed typist. The man could not know the real cause
of his gentle old companion's agitation, nor with
what anxiety she had considered the matter for many
days before she announced her plan. The fact was
that Auntie Sue was taking a big chance, and she
realized it fully. But she could find no other way
to secure the services of a competent stenographer
for Brian, and, as Brian must have a competent stenographer in order to finish his book properly, she
had decided to accept the risk.

"That sounds all right, Auntie Sue," returned
Brian. "But who, pray tell, is Betty Jo?"

"Betty Jo is,"—Auntie Sue paused and laughed
with a suggestion of embarrassed confusion,—"Betty
Jo is—just Betty Jo, Brian," she finished.

Brian laughed now. "Fine, Auntie Sue! That describes her exactly,—tells me her life's history and
gives me a detailed account of her family,—ancestors and all."

"It describes her with more accuracy than you
think," retorted Auntie Sue, smiling in return at
his teasing manner.

"I reckon as how she's got more of er name than
that, ain't she?" said Judy, who was a silent, but

intensely interested, listener. "I've allus took notice that folks with funny names'll stand a right
smart of watchin'."

Brian and Auntie Sue laughed together at this,
but the old lady said, with a show of spirit: "Judy!
You know nothing about it! You never even saw
Betty Jo! You shouldn't say such things, child."

"Might as well say 'em as ter think 'em, I reckon,"
Judy returned, her beady-black eyes stealthily watching Brian.

"What is your Betty Jo's real name, Auntie Sue?"
asked Brian, curiously.

Again Auntie Sue seemed to hesitate; then—"Her
name is Miss Betty Jo Williams," and as she spoke
the old teacher looked straight at Brian.

"A perfectly good name," Brian returned; "but
I never heard of her before."

Judy's black eyes, with their stealthy, oblique look,
were now watchfully fixed on Auntie Sue.

"She is the orphan-niece of one of my old pupils,"
Auntie Sue continued. "I have known her since
she was a baby. When she finished her education
in the seminary, and had travelled abroad for a few
months, she decided all at once that she wanted a

course in a business college, which was just what any one knowing her would expect her to do."

"Sounds steady and reliable," commented Brian. "But will she come?"

"Yes, indeed, she will, and be tickled to death over the job," returned Auntie Sue. "I'll write her at once."

While Auntie Sue was preparing to write her letter, Judy muttered, in a tone which only Brian heard: "Just the same, 'tain't no name for a common gal ter have; hit sure ain't. There's somethin' dad burned queer 'bout hit somewhere."

"Nonsense! Judy," said Brian in a low voice; "don't worry Auntie Sue."

"I ain't aimin' ter worry her none," returned the mountain girl; "but I'll bet you-all a pretty that this here gal'll worry both of youuns 'fore you are through with her;—me, too, I reckon."

For some reason, Auntie Sue's letter to Betty Jo seemed to be rather long. In fact, she spent the entire evening at it; which led Judy to remark that "hit sure looked like Auntie Sue was aimin' ter write a book herself."

A neighbor who went to Thompsonville the following day with a load of hogs for shipment, posted the letter. And, in due time, another neighbor brought the answer. Betty Jo would come.

It was the day following the evening when Brian wrote the last page of his book that another letter came to Auntie Sue,—a letter which, for the second time, very nearly wrecked Brian Kent's world.

CHAPTER XIII.

JUDY TO THE RESCUE.

BRIAN was working in the garden. It was early in the afternoon, and the man, as he worked in the freshly ploughed ground, was rejoicing at the completion of his book.

Straightening up from his labor, he drew a deep breath of the fragrant air. About him on every side, and far away into the blue distance, the world was dressed in the gala dress of the season. The river, which at the breaking of the winter had been a yellow flood that washed the top of the bank in front of the house and covered the bottom-lands on the opposite side, was again its normal self, and its voice to him, now, was a singing voice of triumphal gladness.

For Brian, too, the world was new, and fresh, and beautiful. The world of his winter was gone. He had found himself in his work, and in the glorious consciousness of the fact he felt like shouting with sheer joy of living.

"And Auntie Sue, dear Auntie Sue," he thought, looking with love in his eyes toward the house, how wonderful she had been in her helpful understanding and never-failing faith in him. After all, it was Auntie Sue's triumph more than it was his.

His happy musing was interrupted by a neighbor who, on his way home from Thompsonville, stopped at the garden fence with the letter for Auntie Sue.

Brian took the letter with a jest which brought a roar of laughter from the mountaineer, and, when the latter had gone on his way up the hill, started toward the house to find Auntie Sue.

Glancing at the envelope in his hand, Brian noticed the postmark "Buenos Aires." He stopped suddenly, staring dumbly at the words in the circular mark and at the name written on the envelope. Over and over, he read "Buenos Aires,—Miss Susan Wakefield; Buenos Aires,—Miss Susan Wakefield." Something— His brain seemed to be numb. His hands trembled. He looked about at the familiar surroundings, and everything seemed suddenly strange and unreal to him. He looked again at the letter in his hand, turning it curiously. A strange feeling of oppression and ominous foreboding possessed him as though the bright spring sky were all at once overcast with heavy and menacing storm-clouds. What was it? "Buenos Aires,—Susan Wakefield?" Where had he seen that combination before? What was it that made the name of the Argentine city in connection with Auntie Sue's name seem so familiar? Slowly, he went on to the house, and, finding Auntie Sue, gave her the letter.

"Oh!" cried the old lady, as she saw the postmark on the envelope. "It must be from brother John. It is not John's writing, though," she added, as she opened the envelope.

And at her words the feeling of impending disaster so oppressed Brian Kent that only by an effort could he control himself. He was possessed of the strange sensation of having at some time in the past lived the identical experience through which he was at that moment passing. "Susan Wakefield;—a brother John in Buenos Aires, Argentine;—the letter!" It was all so familiar that the allusion was startling in its force. But that ominous cloud,— that sense of some great trouble near that filled him with such unaccountable dread—what could it mean?

An exclamation from Auntie Sue drew his attention. She looked at him with tear-filled eyes, and her sweet voice broke as she said: "Brian! Brian! John is dead! This—this letter is from the doctor who attended him."

Tenderly, as he would have helped his own mother, Brian assisted Auntie Sue to her room. For a little while he sat with her, trying to comfort her with such poor words as he could find.

Briefly, she told him of the brother who had lived in Argentine for many years. He had married a South-American woman whom Auntie Sue had never seen, and while not wealthy had been moderately prosperous. But he had never forgotten his sister who was so alone in the world. "Several times, when he could, he sent me money for my savings-bank account," she finished simply, her sweet old voice low and tender with the memories of the years that were gone. "John and I were always very fond of each other. He was a good man, Brian."

Brian Kent sat like a man stricken dumb. Auntie Sue's words, "he sent me money for my savings-bank account," had made the connection between the names "Buenos Aires, Argentine; John Wakefield; Susan Wakefield," and the thing for which his mind had been groping with such a sense of impending disaster.

In her grief over the death of her brother, and in her memories of their home years so long past, dear old Auntie Sue had forgotten the peculiar meaning her words might have for the former clerk of the Empire Consolidated Savings Bank who sat beside her, and to whom she turned in her sorrow as a mother to a dearly beloved son.

"But it is all right, Brian, dear," she said with brave cheerfulness. "When one has watched the sunsets for seventy years, one ceases to fear the coming of the night, for always there is the morning. Just let me rest here alone for a little while, and I will be myself again."

She looked up at him with a smile, and Brian Kent, kneeling beside the bed, bowed his head and caught the dear old hands to his lips. Without trusting himself to speak again, the man left the room,— closing the door.

He moved about the apartment as one in a dream. With a vividness that was torture, he lived again that hour in the bank when, opening the afternoon mail, he had found the letter from Susan Wakefield

162

with the Argentine notes, which her letter said she had received from her brother John in Buenos Aires, and which she was sending to the bank for deposit to her little account. It had been a very unbusiness-like letter and a very unbusinesslike way to transmit money. It was, indeed, this nature of the transaction that had tempted the hard-pressed clerk.

Mechanically, Brian stopped at his writing-table to finger the manuscript which he had finished the evening before. Was it only the evening before? Taking up the volume of closely written sheets which were bound together by a shoestring that Auntie Sue had laughingly found for him, when he had so joyously announced the completion of the last page of his book, he turned the leaves idly,—reading here and there a sentence with curious interest. The terrific mental strain of his situation completely divorced him, as it were, from the life which he had lived during those happy months just past, and which was so fully represented by his work.

Again the river, swinging around a sudden turn in its course, had come upon a passage where its peaceful flow was broken by the wild turmoil of the troubled waters.

"And Auntie Sue,"—something within the man's self was saying,—"dear Auntie Sue, who had saved him, not only from death, but from the hell of the life that he had formerly lived, as well; and whose loving companionship and sympathetic understanding had so inspired and strengthened him in the work which had been the passionate desire of his heart;— the gentle old teacher whose life had been so completely given to others, and who, in the helplessness of her last years, was so alone,—Auntie Sue was depending upon that money which her brother had sent her as the only support of the closing days of her life. Auntie Sue believed that her money was safe in the bank. That belief was to her a daily comfort. Auntie Sue did not know that she was almost penniless;—that the man whom she had saved with such a wondrous salvation had robbed her, and left her so shamefully without means for the necessities of life. Auntie Sue did not know. But she would know,"—that inner voice went on. "The time would come when she would learn the truth. It was certain to come. It might come any day. Then— then—"

As one moving without conscious purpose, Brian

Kent went from the house,—the manuscript in his hand.

Judy was sitting idly on the porch steps. At sight of the mountain girl the man knew all at once that there was one thing he must do. He must make sure that there was no mistake. He was already sure, of course; but still, as a condemned man at the scaffold hopes against hope for a stay of sentence, so he caught at the shadowy suggestion of a possibility.

"Come with me, Judy," he said, forcing himself to speak coolly; "I want to talk with you."

Judy arose, and, looking at him in her stealthy, oblique way, said, in her drawling monotone: "What's happened ter Auntie Sue? Was there somethin' in that there letter Bud Jackson give you-all for her what's upset her?"

"Auntie Sue's brother is dead, Judy," Brian answered. "She wishes to be alone, and we must not disturb her. She will be all right in a little while. Come, let us walk down toward the bluff."

When they had reached a spot on the river-bank a short distance above the Elbow Rock cliff, Brian said to his companion: "Judy, I want you to tell me something. Did Auntie Sue ever send money in a letter to the Empire Consolidated Savings Bank, in Chicago?"

The black, beady eyes shifted evasively, and the mountain girl turned her sallow, old-young face away from Brian's direct gaze.

"Look at me, Judy."

She sent a stealthy, oblique glance in his direction.

"You must tell me."

"I done started ter tell you-all onct,—that time pap ketched me,—an' you-all 'lowed as how I oughten ter tell nothin' 'bout Auntie Sue to nobody."

"But it is different now, Judy," returned Brian. "Something has happened that makes it necessary for me to know."

"Meanin' that there letter 'bout her brother bein' dead?" asked Judy, shrewdly.

"Yes."

"What you-all got ter know for?"

"Because—" Brian could not finish.

Judy's beady eyes were watching him intently, now. "Hit looks like you-all ain't a-needin' me ter tell you-all anythin'," she observed dryly.

"Then Auntie Sue did send money?"

"She sure did. I seed her fix hit in the letter, myself," came the answer.

"What kind of money?"

"I dunno,—some funny kind hit was,—what her brother done sent her from some funny place, I dunno just where."

"When did she send it?"

" 'Bout a month 'fore you come."

"And—and did any letter ever come from the bank to tell her that the money was received by them all right?"

The mountain girl did not answer, but again turned her face away.

"Tell me," Brian insisted. "I—I—must know, Judy," and his voice was harsh and broken with emotion.

The answer came reluctantly: "I reckon you-all knows where that there money went ter."

The girl's answer sent a new thought like a hot iron into Brian Kent's tortured brain. He caught Judy's arm in quick and fearful excitement. "Judy!" he gasped, imploringly, "Judy, do you—? does Auntie Sue know—? does she know that I—?"

"How could she help knowin'? She ain't no fool. An' I done heard that there Sheriff an' the detecker-tive man tellin' her 'bout you an' the bank. An' the Sheriff, he done give her a paper what he said told all 'bout what you-all done, an' she must er burned the paper, er done somethin' with hit, 'cause I couldn't never find hit after that night. An' what would she do that for? And what for did she make me promise not ter ever say nothin' ter you-all 'bout that there money letter? An' why ain't she said nothin' to you 'bout the letter from the bank not comin', if she didn't know hit was you 'stead of them what done got the money?"

The girl paused for a moment, and then went on in a tone of reverent wonder: "An' to think that all the time she could a-turned you-all over to that there Sheriff an' got the money-reward to pay her back what you-all done tuck."

Brian Kent was as one who had received a mortal hurt. His features were distorted with suffering. With eyes that could not see, he looked down at the manuscript to which he still unconsciously clung; and, again, he fingered the pages of his work as though some blind instinct were sending his tormented soul to seek relief in the message which, during the happy months just past, he had written for others.

And the deformed mountain girl, who stood before him with twisted body and old-young face, grew fearful as she watched the suffering of this man whom she had come to look upon as a superior being from some world which she, in her ignorance, could never know.

"Mr. Burns," she said at last, putting out her hand and plucking at his sleeve, "Mr. Burns, you-all ain't got no call ter be like this. You-all ain't plumb bad. I knows you ain't, 'count of the way you-all have been ter me an' 'cause you kept pap from hurtin' me, an' 'cause you are takin' care of Auntie Sue like you're doin'. Hit ain't no matter 'bout the money, now, 'cause you-all kin take care of her allus."

Brian looked up from the manuscript in his hand, and stared dumbly at the girl, as if he failed to hear her clearly.

"An' just think 'bout your book," Judy continued pleadingly. "Think 'bout all them fine things you-all have done wrote down for everybody ter read,—'bout the river allus a-goin' on just the same, no matter what happens, an' 'bout Auntie Sue an'—"

She stopped, and drew away from him, frightened at the look that came into the man's face.

"Don't, Mr. Burns! Don't!" she half-screamed. "'Fore God, you-all oughten ter look like that!"

The man threw up his head, and laughed,— laughed as the wild, reckless and lost Brian Kent had laughed that black night when, in the drifting boat, he had cursed the life he was leaving and had drunk his profane toast to the darkness into which he was being carried.

Raising the manuscript, which represented all that the past months of his re-created life had meant to him, and grasping it in both hands, he shook it contemptuously, as he said, with indescribable bitterness and the reckless surrendering of every hope: "'All them fine things that I have wrote down for everybody ter read.'" He mimicked her voice with a sneer, and laughed again. Then: "It's all a lie, Judy, dear;—a damned lie. Auntie Sue is a saint, and believes it. She made me believe it for a little while,—her beautiful, impossible dream-philosophy

170

of the river. The river,—hell!—the river is as treacherous and cruel and false and tricky and crooked as life itself! And I am as warped and twisted in mind and soul as you are in body, Judy, dear. Neither of us can help it. We were made that way by the river. To hell with the whole impossible mess of things!" With a gesture of violent rage, he turned toward the river, and, taking a step forward, lifted the manuscript high above his head.

Judy screamed, "Mr. Burns, don't!"

He paused an instant, and, turning his head, looked at her with another laugh.

"'Fore God, you dassn't do that!" she implored.

And then, as the man turned his face from her, and his arms went back above his head for the swing that would send the manuscript far out into the tumbling waters of the rapids, she leaped toward him, and, catching his arm, hampered his movement so that the book fell a few feet from the shore, where the water, checked a little in its onward rush to the cliff by the irregular bank, boiled and eddied among the rocky ledges and huge boulders that retarded its force. Another leap carried the mountain girl to the edge of the bank, where she crouched like a runner ready for the report of the starter's pistol, her black, beady eyes searching the stream for the volume of manuscript, which had disappeared from sight, drawn down by the troubled swirling currents.

The man, watching her, laughed in derision; but, while his mocking laughter was still on his lips, the boiling currents brought the book, again, to the surface, and Brian saw the girl leave the bank as if thrown by a powerful spring. Straight and true she dived for the book, and even as she disappeared beneath the surface her hands clutched the manuscript.

For a second, Brian Kent held his place as if paralyzed with horror. Then, as Judy's head appeared farther down the stream, he ran with all his strength along the bank to gain a point a little ahead of the swimming girl before he should leap to her rescue.

But Judy, trained from her birth on that mountain river, knew better than Brian what to do. A short distance below the point where she had plunged into the stream, a huge boulder, some two or three feet from the shore, caused a split in the current, one fork of which set in toward the bank. Swimming desperately, the girl gained the advantage of this current, and, just as Brian reached the spot, she was swept against the bank, where, with her free hand, she caught and held fast to a projecting root. Had she been carried past that point, nothing could have saved her from being swept on into the wild turmoil of the waters at Elbow Rock.

It was the work of a moment for Brian to throw himself flat on the ground at the edge of the bank and, reaching down, to grasp the girl's wrist. Another moment, and she was safe beside him, his manuscript still tightly held under one arm.

Not realizing, in his excitement, what he was doing, Brian shook the girl, saying angrily: "What in the world do you mean, taking such a crazy-fool chance as that!"

She broke away from him with: "Well, what'd you-all go an' do such a dad burned fool thing for? Hit's you-all what's crazy yourself—plumb crazy!"

Brian held out his hand: "Give me that manuscript!"

Judy clutched the book tighter, and drew back defiantly. "I won't. You-all done throwed hit away onct. 'Tain't your'n no more, nohow."

"Well, what do you purpose to do with it?" said the puzzled man, in a gentler tone.

"I aims ter give hit ter Auntie Sue," came the startling reply. "I reckon she'll know what ter do. Hit allus was more her'n than your'n, anyhow. You done said so yourself. I heard you only last night when you-all was so dad burned tickled at gittin' hit done. You-all ain't got no right ter sling hit inter the river, an', anyway, I ain't a-goin' ter let you."

"Which sounds very sensible to me," came a clear voice from a few feet distant.

Judy and Brian turned quickly, to face a young woman who stood regarding them thoughtfully, with a suggestion of a smile on her very attractive face.

CHAPTER XIV.

BETTY JO CONSIDERS.

THE most careless eye would have seen instantly that the newcomer was not a native of that backwoods district. She was not a large woman, but there was, nevertheless, a full, rounded strength, which saved her trim and rather slender body from appearing small. Neither would a discriminating observer describe her by that too-common term "pretty." She was more than that. In her large, gray eyes, there was a look of frank, straightforward interest that suggested an almost boyish good-fellowship, while at the same time there was about her a general air of good breeding; with a calm, self-possessed and businesslike alertness which, combined with a wholesome dignity, commanded a feeling of respect and confidence. Her voice was clear and musical, with an undertone of sympathetic humor. One felt when she spoke that while she lacked nothing of intelligent understanding and sympathetic interest, she was quite ready to laugh at you just the same.

When the two stood speechless, she said, looking straight at Brian: "It seems to me, sir, that the young lady has all the best of the argument. But I really think she should have some dry clothes as well."

She turned to the dripping and dishevelled Judy: "You poor child. Aren't you cold? It is rather early in the season for a dip in the river, I should think. Let me take whatever you have there, and you make for the house as fast as you can go,—the run will warm you."

As she spoke, she went to the mountain girl, holding out her hand to take the manuscript, and smiling encouragingly.

But Judy backed away, her stealthy, oblique gaze fixed with watchful surprise on the fair stranger.

"This here ain't none of your put-in," and her shrill drawling monotone contrasted strangely with the other's pleasing voice. "Where'd you-all happen from, anyhow? How'd you-all git here?"

"I came over the bluff by the path," answered the other. "You see, I left the train from the south at

White's Crossing because I knew I could drive up from there by the river road quicker than I could go by rail away around through the hills to Thompsonville, and then make the drive down the river from there. When I reached Elbow Rock, I was in such a hurry, I took the short cut, while the man with my trunk and things went by the road over Schoolhouse Hill, you know. I arrived here just as this gentleman was pulling you from the water."

Before Brian could speak, Judy returned with excitement: "I know who you-all be now. I ought ter knowed the minute I set eyes on you. You-all are the gal with that there no-'count name, an' you've come ter work for him, there,"—she pointed to Brian,—"a-helpin' him ter write his book, what ain't his'n no more, nohow, 'cause he done throwed hit away,—plumb inter the river."

"I am Miss Williams," returned the other. "My 'no-'count name,' I suppose, is Betty Jo." She laughed kindly. "Perhaps it won't seem so 'no-'count' when we are better acquainted, Judy. Won't you run along to the house, and change to some dry clothes? You will catch your death of cold if you stand here like this."

"How'd you-all know I was Judy?"

"Why, Auntie Sue wrote me about you, of course."

"An' you knowed me 'cause I'm so all crooked an' ugly, I reckon," came the uncompromising return.

Betty Jo turned to Brian: "You are Mr. Burns, are you not, for whom I am to work?"

Brian made no reply,—he really could not speak.

"And this,"—Betty Jo included Judy, the manuscript, and the river in a graceful gesture,—"this, I suppose, is the result of what is called 'the artistic temperament'?"

Still the man could find no words. The young woman's presence and her reference to his work brought to him, with overwhelming vividness, the memory of all to which he had so short a time before looked forward, and which was now so hopelessly lost to him. He felt, too, a sense of rebellion that she should have come at such a moment,—that she could stand there with such calm self-possession and with such an air of competency. Her confidence and poise in such contrast to the chaotic turmoil of his own thoughts, and his utter helplessness in the situation which had so suddenly burst upon him, filled him with unreasoning resentment.

178

Betty Jo must have read in Brian Kent's face something of the suffering that held him there dumb and motionless before her, and so sensed a deeper tragedy than appeared on the surface of the incident; and her own face and voice revealed her understanding as she said, with quiet, but decisive, force: "Mr. Burns, Judy must go to the house. Won't you persuade her?"

Brian started as one aroused from deep abstraction, and went to Judy; while Betty Jo drew a little way apart, and stood looking out over the river.

"Give me the manuscript, Judy," said Brian gently, "and go on to the house."

"You-all ain't a-goin' ter sling hit inter the river again?" The words were half-question and half-assertion.

"No," said Brian. "I promise not to throw it into the river again."

As Judy gave him the manuscript, she turned her beady eyes in a stealthy, oblique look toward Betty Jo, and whispered: "You-all best tell her 'bout hit. I sure hate her poison-bad; but hit's easy ter see she'd sure know what ter do."

"Be careful that Auntie Sue doesn't see you like this,

179

Judy," was Brian's only answer; and Judy started off for her much-needed change to dry clothing.

When the mountain girl was gone, Brian stood looking at the water-stained volume of manuscript in his hand. He had no feeling, now, of more than a curious idle interest in this work to which, during the months just past, he had given so without reserve the best of himself. It was, he thought, strange how he could regard with such indifference a thing for which a few hours before he would have given his life. Dumbly, he was conscious of the truth of Judy's words,—that the book was no longer his. Judy was right—this book which he had called his had always been, in reality, Auntie Sue's. So the matter of his work, at least so far as he had to do with it, was settled—definitely and finally settled.

But what of himself? What was to become of him? Of one thing only he was certain about himself;—he never could face Auntie Sue again. Knowing, now, what he had done, and knowing that she knew;—that all the time she was nursing him back to health, all the time she had been giving him the inspiration and strength and peace of her gentle, loving companionship, in the safe and quiet harbor of her little house by the river, she had known that it was he who had—

A clear, matter-of-fact, but gentle, voice interrupted his bitter thoughts: "Is it so very badly damaged, Mr. Burns?"

He had forgotten Betty Jo, who now stood close beside him.

"Let me see?" She held out her hand as he turned slowly to face her.

Without a word, he gave her the manuscript.

Very businesslike and practical, but with an underlying feeling of tenderness that was her most compelling charm, Betty Jo examined the water-stained volume.

"Why, no," she announced cheerfully; "it isn't really hurt much. You see, the sheets being tied together so tightly, the water didn't get all the way through. The covers and the first and last pages are pretty wet, and the edges of the rest are rather damp. It'll be smudged somewhat, but I don't believe there is a single word that can't be made out. It is lucky it didn't prolong its bath, though, isn't it? All we need to do, now, is to put it in the sun to dry for a few minutes."

Selecting a sunny spot near by, she arranged the volume against a stone and deftly separated the pages so that the air could circulate more freely between them; and one would have said, from her manner of ready assurance, that she had learned from long experience exactly how to dry a manuscript that had been thrown in the river and rescued just in the nick of time. That was Betty Jo's way. She always did everything without hesitation,—just as though she had spent the twenty-three years of her life doing exactly that particular thing.

Kneeling over the manuscript, and gently moving the wet sheets, she said, without looking up: "Do you always bath your manuscripts like this before you turn them over to your stenographer to type, Mr. Burns?"

In spite of his troubled state of mind, Brian smiled.

The clear, matter-of-fact voice went on, while the competent hands moved the drying pages. "You see, I never worked for an author before. I suspect I have a lot to learn."

She looked up at him with a Betty Jo smile that

went straight to his heart, as Betty Jo's smiles had a curious way of doing.

"I hope you will be very patient with me, Mr. Burns. You will, won't you? There is no real danger of your throwing *me* in the river when the 'artistic temperament' possesses you, is there?"

It was no use. When Betty Jo set out to make a man talk, that man talked. Brian yielded not ungracefully: "I owe you an apology, Miss Williams," he said.

"Indeed, no," Betty Jo returned, giving her attention to the manuscript again. "It is easy to see that you are terribly upset about something; and everybody is so accustomed to being upset in one way or another that apologies for upsetments are quite an unnecessary bother, aren't they?"

That was another interestingly curious thing about Betty Jo,—the way she could finish off a characteristic, matter-of-fact statement with a question which had the effect of making one agree instantly whether one agreed or not.

Brian felt himself quite unexpectedly feeling that "upsetments" were quite common, ordinary, and to-be-expected events in one's life. "But I am really in very serious trouble, Miss Williams," he said in a way that sounded oddly to Brian himself, as though he were trying to convince himself that his trouble really was serious.

Betty Jo rose to her feet, and looked straight at him, and there was no mistaking the genuineness of the interest expressed in those big gray eyes.

"Oh, are you? Is it really so serious? I am so sorry. But don't you think you better tell me about it, Mr. Burns? If I am to work for you, I may just as well begin right here, don't you think?"

There it was again,—that trick-question. Brian felt himself agreeing in spite of himself, though how he was to explain his painful situation to this young woman whom, until a few minutes before, he had never even seen, he did not know. He answered cautiously, speaking half to himself: "That is what Judy said."

Betty Jo did not understand, and made no pretense,—she never made a pretense of anything. "What did Judy say?" she asked.

"That I had better tell you about it," he answered.

184

And the matter-of-fact Betty Jo returned: "Judy seems to be a very particular and common-sensing sort of Judy, doesn't she?"

And Brian realized all at once that Judy was exactly what Betty Jo said.

"But,—I—I—don't see how I *can* tell you, Miss Williams."

"Why?" laughed Betty Jo. "It is perfectly simple, Mr. Burns. Here, now, I'll show you: You are to sit down there on that nice comfortable rock,—that is your big office-chair, you know,—and I'll sit right here on this rock,—which is my little stenography-chair,—and you will just explain the serious business proposition to me with careful attention to details. I must tell you that 'detailing' is one of my strong points, so don't spare me. I really should have my notebook, shouldn't I?"

Again, in spite of himself, Brian smiled; also, before he was aware, they were both seated as Betty Jo had directed.

"But this is not a business matter, Miss Williams," he managed to protest half-heartedly.

Betty Jo was looking at her watch in a most

matter-of-fact manner, and she answered in a most matter-of-fact voice: "Everything is more or less a business matter, isn't it, Mr. Burns?"

And Brian, if he had answered, would have agreed.

Betty Jo slipped her watch back into her pocket, and continued: "You will have plenty of time before that man with my trunk and things can get away 'round over Schoolhouse Hill and down again to Auntie Sue's. He will be obliged to stop at neighbor Tom's, and tell them all about me, of course. We mustn't let him beat us to the house, though; so, perhaps, you better begin, don't you think?"

That "don't-you-think?" so characteristic of Betty Jo, did its work, as usual; and so, almost before Brian Kent realized what he was doing, it had been decided for him that to follow Judy's advice was the best possible thing he could do, and he was relating his whole wretched experience to this young woman, about whom he knew nothing except that she was a niece of an old pupil of Auntie Sue's, and that she had just finished a course in a business college in Cincinnati.

At several points in his story Betty Jo asked straightforward questions, or made short, matter-of-fact comments; but, always with her businesslike air of competent interest. Indeed, she managed to treat the situation as being wholly impersonal; while at the same time the man was never for a moment made to feel that she was lacking in sincere and genuine sympathy. Only when he told her that his name was Brian Kent, and mentioned the Empire Consolidated Savings Bank, did she for the moment betray excited surprise. When she saw that he had noticed, she said quickly: "I read of the affair in the papers, of course."

Auntie Sue had indeed taken a big chance when she decided for Betty Jo to come to help Brian with his book. But Auntie Sue had taken no chance on Betty Jo herself. Perhaps it was, in fact, the dear old teacher's certainty about Betty Jo herself that had led her to accept the risk of sending for the niece of her friend and pupil under such a peculiar combination of circumstances.

When Brian had finished his story with the account of his discovery of the distressing fact that he had robbed Auntie Sue and that she knew he had robbed her, Betty Jo said: "It is really a sad story, isn't it, Mr. Burns? But, oh, isn't Auntie Sue wonderful! Was there ever such another woman in the world! Don't you love her? And couldn't you do anything—anything that would make her happy? After all, when you think of Auntie Sue, and how wonderful she has been, this whole thing isn't so bad, is it?"

"Why, I—I—don't think I see what you mean," Brian replied, puzzled by the unexpected turn she had given to the situation, yet convinced by that little question with which she finished that she was somehow right.

"Well, I mean wouldn't *you* love to do for some one what Auntie Sue has done for you? I should if I were only big enough and good enough. It seems to me it would make one the happiest and contentedest and peacefulest person in the world, wouldn't it?"

Brian did not answer. While he felt himself agreeing with Betty Jo's view, he was wondering at himself that he could discuss the matter so calmly. It was not that he no longer felt deeply the shame of this terrible thing that he had done; it was not that he had ceased to suffer the torment that had caused his emotional madness, which had found expression in his attempt to destroy his manuscript; it was only that this young woman somehow made it possible for him to retain his self-control, and instead of venting his emotions in violent and wholly useless expressions of regret, and self-condemnation, and in irrational, temperamental action, to consider coolly and sanely what he must do. He was strangely possessed, too, of an instinctive certainty that Betty Jo knew exactly how he felt and exactly what she was doing.

While he was thinking these things, or, rather, feeling them, Betty Jo went to see how the manuscript was drying. She returned to her seat on the rock presently, saying: "It is doing very nicely,—almost dry. I think it will be done pretty soon. In the meantime, what are we going to do about everything? You have thought of something for you to do, of course?"

"I fear I have felt rather more than I have thought," returned Brian.

She nodded. "Yes, I know; but feeling alone never arrives anywhere. An excess of thoughtless feeling is sheer emotional extravagance. I sound like a book, don't I?" she laughed. "It is so just the

same, Mr. Burns. And now that you have—ah—
been properly—not to say gloriously—extravagant at
poor Judy's expense, we had better do a little thinking, don't you think?"

The man's cheeks reddened at her words; but the
straightforward, downright sincerity of those gray
eyes, that looked so frankly into his, held him steady;
while the interrogation at the end of her remark
carried its usual conviction.

"There is only one possible thing left for me to do,
Miss Williams," he said earnestly.

"And what is that?" A smile that sent a glow of
courage to Brian Kent's troubled heart accompanied
the flat question.

"I can't face Auntie Sue again, knowing what I
know now." He spoke with passion.

"Of course you would expect to feel that way,
wouldn't you?" came the matter-of-fact answer.

"The only thing I can do," he continued, "is to
give myself up, and go to the penitentiary; arranging, somehow, to do it in such a way that the reward
will go to Auntie Sue. God knows she deserves it!
Sheriff Knox would help me fix that part, I am sure."

For a moment there was a suspicious moisture in

Betty Jo's gray eyes. Then she said, "And you would really go to prison for Auntie Sue?"

"It is the least I can do for her now," he returned.

And Betty Jo must have felt the sincerity of his purpose, for she said, softly: "I am sure that it would make Auntie Sue very happy to know that you would do that; and"—she added—"I know that you could not possibly make her more unhappy and miserable than by doing it, could you?"

Again she had given an unexpected turn to the subject with the usual convincing question-mark.

"But what can I do?" he demanded, letting himself go a little.

Betty Jo steadied him with: "Well, suppose you listen while I consider? Did I tell you that 'considering' was another of my strong points, Mr. Burns? Well, it is. You may consider me while I consider, if you please.

"The first thing is, that you must make Auntie Sue happy,—as happy as you possibly can do at any cost. The second thing is, that you must pay her back that money, every penny of it. Now, it wouldn't make her happy for you to go to prison, and the reward wouldn't pay back all the money; and if you were in prison, you never could pay the rest; besides, if you were wasting your time in prison, she would just die of miserableness, and she wouldn't touch a penny of that reward-money—not if she was to die for want of it. So that settles that, doesn't it?"

And Brian was forced to admit that, as Betty Jo put it, it did.

"Very well, let us consider some more: Dear Auntie Sue has been wonderfully, gloriously happy in doing what she has for you this past winter,— meaning your book and all. I can see that she must have been. No one could help being happy doing such a thing as that. So you just simply can't spoil it all, now, by letting her know that you know what you know."

Brian started to speak, but she checked him with: "Please, Mr. Burns, I must not be interrupted when I am considering. Next to the prison,—which we have agreed won't do at all,—you could do nothing that would make Auntie Sue more unhappy than to spoil the happiness she has in your not knowing what you have done to her. That is very clear, isn't it? And think of her miserableness if, after all these weeks of happy anticipation, your book should never be published. No, no, no; you can't rob Auntie Sue of her happiness in you just because you stole her money, can you?"

And Brian knew in his heart that she was right.

"So, you see," Betty Jo continued, "the only possible way to do is to go right along just as if nothing had happened. And there is this final consideration,—which must be a dark secret between you and me,—when the book is finished, you must see to it that every penny that comes from it goes to Auntie Sue until she is paid back all that she lost through you. Now, isn't that pretty fine 'considering,' Mr. Burns?"

And Brian was convinced that it was. "But," he suggested, "the book may not earn anything. Nothing that I ever wrote before did."

"You never wrote one before just like this, did you?" came the very matter-of-fact answer. "And, besides, if your book never earns a cent, it will do Auntie Sue a world more good than your going to prison for her. That would be rather silly, now that you think of it, wouldn't it? And now that we have our conspiracy all nicely conspired, we must hurry to the house before that man arrives with my things."

She went for the manuscript as she spoke. "See," she cried, "it is quite dry, and not a bit the worse for its temperamental experience!" She laughed gleefully.

"But, Miss Williams," exclaimed Brian, "I—I—can't understand you! You don't seem to mind. What I have told you about myself doesn't seem to—to—make any difference to you—I mean in your attitude toward me."

"Oh, yes, it does," she returned. "It makes me very interested in you, Mr. Burns."

"But, how can you have any confidence— How can you help me with my book now that you know what I am?" he persisted, for he was sincerely puzzled by her apparent indifference to the revelation he had made of his character.

"Auntie Sue,"—she answered,—"just Auntie Sue. Come,—we must go."

"How in the world can I ever face her!" groaned Brian.

"You won't get the chance at her, for awhile, with me around;—she will be so busy with me that she won't notice anything wrong with you. So you will get accustomed to the conspiracy feeling before you are even suspected of conspiring. You know, when one has once arrived at the state of not feeling like a liar, one can lie with astonishing success. Haven't you found it so?"

They laughed together over this as they went toward the house.

As they reached the porch, Betty Jo whispered a last word of instruction: "You better find Judy, and fix her the first thing;—fix her good and hard. Here is Auntie Sue now. Don't worry about her noticing anything strange about you. I'll attend to her."

And the next minute, Betty Jo had the dear old lady in her arms.

CHAPTER XV.

A MATTER OF BUSINESS.

HE weeks that followed the coming of Betty Jo to the little log house by the river passed quickly for Brian Kent. Perhaps it was the peculiar circumstances of their first meeting that made the man feel so strongly that he had known her for many years, instead of for only those few short weeks. That could easily have been the reason, because the young woman had stepped so suddenly into his life at a very critical time;—when his mental faculties were so confused by the turmoil and suffering of his emotional self that the past was to him, at the moment, far more real than the present.

And Betty Jo had not merely come into his life casually, as a disinterested spectator; but, by the peculiar appeal of herself, she had led Brian to take her so into his confidence that she had become immediately a very real part of the experience through which he was then passing, and thus was identified with his past experience out of which the crisis of the moment had come.

Again Betty Jo, in the naturalness of her manner toward him, and by her matter-of-fact, impersonal consideration of his perplexing situation, had brought to his unsettled and chaotic mind a sense of stability and order; and by subtly insinuating her own practical decisions as to the course he should follow, had made herself a very literal part of his inner life. In fact, Betty Jo knew Brian Kent more intimately at the close of their first meeting than she could have known him after years of acquaintanceship under the ordinary course of development.

Brian's consciousness of this would naturally cause him to feel toward the young woman as though she had long been a part of his life. Still other causes might have contributed to the intimate companionship that so quickly became to them both an established and taken-for-granted fact; but, the circumstances of their first meeting, given, of course, their peculiar individualities, were, really, quite enough. The fact that it was springtime might also have had something to do with it.

The morning after her arrival, Betty Jo set to work typing the manuscript. Brian went to his work on the timbered hillside. In the evenings, Brian worked over the typewitten pages,—revising, correcting, perfecting,—and then, as Betty Jo made the final copy for the printers, they went critically over the work together.

So the hours flew past on busy wings, and the days of the springtime drew toward summer. The tender green of the new-born leaves and grasses changed to a stronger, deeper tone. The air, which had been so filled with the freshness and newness of bursting buds and rain-blessed soil, and all the quickening life of tree and bush and plant, now carried the perfume of strongly growing things,—the feel of maturing life.

To Brian, the voices of the river brought a fuller, deeper message, with a subtle undertone of steady and enduring purpose.

From the beginning, Betty Jo established for herself the habit of leaving her work at the typewriter in the afternoons, and going for a walk over the hills. Quite incidentally, at first, her walks occasionally led her by way of the clearing where Brian was at work with his ax, and it followed, naturally, that as the end of the day drew near, the two would go together down the mountain-side to the evening meal. But long before the book was finished, the little afternoon visit and the walk together at the day's close had become so established as a custom that they both accepted it as a part of their day's life; and to Brian, at least, it was an hour to which he looked forward as the most delightful hour of the twenty-four. As for Betty Jo,—well, it was really Betty Jo who established the custom and developed it to that point where it was of such importance.

Auntie Sue was too experienced from her life-long study of boys and girls not to observe the deepening of the friendship between the man and the woman whom she had brought together. But if the dear old lady felt any twinges of an apprehensive conscience, when she saw the pair day after day coming down the mountain-side through the long shadows of the late afternoon, she very promptly banished them, and, quite consistently, with what Brian called her "River philosophy," made no attempt to separate these two life currents, which, for the time at least, seemed to be merging into one.

And often, as the three sat together on the porch

199

after supper to watch the sunsets, or later in the evening as Auntie Sue sat with her sewing while they were busy with their work and unobserving, the dear old lady would look at them with a little smile of tender meaning, and into the gentle eyes would come that far-away look that was born of the memories that had so sweetened the long years of her life, and of the hope and dream of a joy unspeakable that awaited her beyond the sunset of her day.

In her long letter to Betty Jo, asking the girl to come, Auntie Sue had told the young woman the main facts of Brian's history as she knew them, omitting only the man's true name and the name of the bank. She had even mentioned her conviction that there had been a woman in his trouble. But Auntie Sue had not mentioned in her letter the money she had lost; nor did she now know that Brian had himself told Betty Jo at the time of their first meeting.

On the day that Betty Jo typed the last page, and the book was ready for the printers, the young woman went earlier than usual to the clearing where Brian was at work. The sound of his ax reached her while she was yet some distance away, and guided her to the spot where he was chopping a big white oak.

Brian, with his eyes fixed on the widening cut at the base of the tree, did not notice the girl, who stood watching him. She was smiling to herself at his ignorance of her presence and in anticipation of the moment when he should discover her, and there was in her eyes a look of wholesome womanly admiration for the man who swung his ax with such easy strength. In truth, Brian Kent at his woodman's labor made a picture not at all unattractive.

Swiftly, the cut in the tree-trunk widened as the ax bit deeply at every skilful stroke, and the chips flew about the chopper's feet. The acrid odor of the freshly cut oak mingled with the woodland perfume. The sun warmly flooded the clearing with its golden light, and, splashing through the openings in the forest foliage, formed pools of yellow beauty amid the dark, rich green of the shadowy undergrowth. The air was filled with the sense of life, vital and real, and strong and beautiful.

And the young woman, as she stood smiling there, was keenly conscious of it all. Most of all, perhaps

Betty Jo was conscious of the man, who worked with such vigor at his manly task.

Slowly, accurately, the bright ax sank deeper and deeper into the heart of the tree. The chips increased in scattered profusion. And then, as Betty Jo watched, the swinging ax cut through the last fibre of the tree's strength, and the leafy top swayed gently toward its fall. Almost imperceptibly, at first, it moved while Betty Jo watched breathlessly. Brian swung his ax with increasing vigor, now, while the wood, still remaining, cracked and snapped as the weight of the tree completed the work of the chopper. Faster and faster the towering mass of foliage swung in a wide graceful arc toward the ground. The man with the ax stepped back, his eyes fixed on the falling tree as, with swiftly increasing momentum, its great weight swept swiftly downward to its crashing end.

Betty Jo clapped her hands in triumph; and Brian, turning, saw her standing there. His face was flushed and glistening with perspiration; his broad chest heaved with the deep breathing gained by his exertion, and his eyes shone with the gladness of her presence.

"You are early, to-day!" he cried. "Have you finished? Is it actually completed?"

"All finished," she returned; and, going to the fallen tree, she put her hands curiously on the trunk, which lay a little higher than her waist. "Help me up," she commanded.

Brian set his ax against the stump, and, laughingly, lifted her to the seat she desired. Then he stood watching her face as she surveyed the tangled mass of branches.

"It looks so strange from here, doesn't it?" she said.

"Yes; and I confess I don't like to see it that way;" he returned. "I wish they didn't have to be cut. I feel like a murderer,—every one I fall."

She looked down into his eyes, as she returned: "I know you must. *You* would, of course. But, after all, it has to be, and I don't suppose the tree minds so much, do you?"

"No; I don't suppose it feels it much." He laughed, and, throwing aside his hat, he ran his fingers through his tumbled hair for all the world like a schoolboy confused by being caught in some sentimental situation which he finds not only embarrassing, but puzzling as well.

"I like you for feeling that way about it, though," Betty Jo confessed with characteristic frankness. "And I am sure it must be a very good thing for the world that every one is not so intensely practical that they can chop down trees without a pang. And that reminds me: Speaking of the practical, now that the book is finished, what are we going to do with it?"

"Send it to some publisher, I suppose," answered Brian, soberly; "and then, when they have returned it, send it to some other publisher."

"Have you any particular publisher to whom you will send it first?" she asked.

"They are all alike, so far as my experience goes," he returned.

"I suppose it would be best if you could take your book East, and interview the publishers personally, don't you think?"

Brian shook his head: "I am not sure that it would make any difference, and, in any case, I couldn't do it."

"I know," said Betty Jo, "and that is what I wanted to get at. Why don't you appoint me your agent, and let me take your book East, and make the publishing arrangements for you?"

Brian looked at her with such delighted surprise that Betty Jo smiled back at him well pleased.

"Would you really do it?" he demanded, as though he feared she was jesting.

"You are sure that you don't mean 'could I do it'?"—she returned,—"sure you could trust me?"

To which Brian answered enthusiastically: "You could do anything! If you undertake the job of landing a publisher for my stuff, it is as good as done."

"Thank you," she said, jumping down from the tree-trunk. "Now that we have settled it, let us go to the house and tell Auntie Sue, and I will start in the morning."

As they went down the hill, they discussed the matter further, and, later, at the house, Brian took a moment, when Auntie Sue was in her room, to hand an envelope to his assistant. "Your salary," he said, hurriedly, "and expense money for the trip."

"Oh!" Betty Jo's exclamation was one of surprise. Then she said, in her most matter-of-fact, businesslike tone: "Thank you. I will render a statement of my account, but—" For once, Betty Jo seemed at a loss for words. "You don't mind if I ask—is—is this money—?"

Brian's face was a study. "Yes," he said, "it is really Auntie Sue's money; but it is all I have, and I can't return it to her—without her knowing—so I—"

Betty Jo interrupted: "I understand. It is all we can do,—forgive me?"

Brian Kent did not know that Betty Jo, a few minutes later, buried the envelope he had given her deep in the bottom of her trunk without even opening it.

The next day, Brian drove to Thompsonville with Betty Jo, who took the noon train for the East.

The two were rather quiet as "Old Prince" jogged soberly along the beautiful river road. Only now and then did they exchange a few words of the most commonplace observation.

They were within sight of the little Ozark settlement when Brian said, earnestly: "I wish I could tell you, Miss Williams, just what your coming to help me with this work has meant to me."

"It has meant a great deal to me, too, Mr. Burns"

206

she returned. Then she added quickly: "I suppose the first real work one does after finishing school always means more than any position following could possibly mean, don't you think? Just like your book. No matter how many you may write in the future, this will always mean more to you than any one of them."

"Yes," he said slowly. "This book will always mean more to me than all the others I may write."

For a moment their eyes met with unwavering frankness. Then Betty Jo turned her face away, and Brian stiffened his shoulders, and sat a little straighter in the seat beside her. That was all.

Very brave they were at the depot purchasing Betty Jo's ticket and checking her trunk. With brave commonplaces they said good-bye when the train pulled in. Bravely she waved at him from the open window of the coach. And bravely Brian stood there watching until the train rounded the curve and disappeared from sight between the hills.

The world through which Brian Kent drove that afternoon on his way back to Auntie Sue and Judy in the little log house by the river was a very dull and uninteresting world indeed. All its brightness and its beauty seemed suddenly to have vanished. And as "Old Prince" jogged patiently on his way, sleepily content with thoughts of his evening meal of hay and grain, the man's mind was disturbed with thoughts which he dared not own even to his innermost self.

"Circumstances to a man," Auntie Sue had said, "always meant a woman." And Brian Kent, while he never under any pressure would have admitted it, knew within his deepest self that it was a woman who had set him adrift on the dark river that dreadful night when he had cursed the world which he thought he was leaving forever.

"Circumstances" in the person of Auntie Sue had saved him from destruction, and, in the little log house by the river, had brought about his Re-Creation.

And then, when that revelation of his crime toward Auntie Sue had come, and the labor of months, with all that it implied of the enduring salvation of himself and the happiness of Auntie Sue, hung wavering in the balance, it was the "Circumstances" of Betty Jo's coming that had set him in the right current of action again.

What waited for him around the next bend in the

208

river, Brian wondered,—calm and peaceful waters, with gently flowing currents, or the wild tumult of dangerous rapids wherein he would be forced to fight for his very existence? Would Betty Jo succeed as his agent to the publishers? If she did succeed in finding a publisher to accept his book, would the reading public receive his message? And if that followed, what then? When Betty Jo's mission in the East was accomplished, she was to return to Auntie Sue for the summer. Then—?

"Old Prince," of his own accord, was turning in at the gate, and Brian awoke from his abstraction to to see Auntie Sue and Judy waiting for him.

All during the evening meal and while he sat with Auntie Sue on the porch overlooking the river, as their custom was, Brian was preoccupied and silent; while his companion, with the wisdom of her seventy years, did not force the conversation.

It was the time of the full moon, and when Auntie Sue at last bade him good-night, Brian, saying that the evening was too lovely to waste in sleep, remained on the porch. For an hour, perhaps, he sat there alone; but his thoughts were not on the beauties of the scene that lay before him in all its dreamy charm of shadowy hills and moonlit river. He had no ear for the soft voices of the night. The gentle breeze carried to him the low, deep-toned roar of the crashing waters at Elbow Rock; but he did not hear. Moved at last by a feeling of restless longing, and the certainty that only a sleepless bed awaited him in the house, he left the porch to stroll along the bank of the river.

CHAPTER XVI.

THE SECRET OF AUNTIE SUE'S LIFE.

BRIAN KENT, strolling along the bank of the river in the moonlight, and preoccupied with thoughts that were, at the last, more dreams than thoughts, was not far from the house when a sound from behind some near-by bushes broke in upon his reveries. A moment, he listened. Then telling himself that it was some prowling animal, or perhaps, a bird that his presence had disturbed, he went on. But he had gone only a few feet farther when he was conscious of something stealthily following him. Stepping behind the trunk of a tree, he waited, watching. Then he saw a form moving toward him through the shadows of the bushes. Another moment, and the form left the concealing shadow, and, in the bright moonlight, he recognized Judy.

At first, the man's feeling was that of annoyance. He did not wish to be disturbed at such a time by the presence of the mountain girl. But his habitual gentleness toward poor Judy, together with a very natural curiosity as to why she was following him at that time of the night, when he had supposed her in bed and asleep, led him to greet her kindly as he came from behind the tree: "Well, Judy, are you, too, out enjoying the moonlight?"

The girl stopped suddenly and half-turned as if to run; but, at his words, stood still.

"What is it, Judy?" he asked, going to her. "What is the matter?"

"There's a heap the matter!" she answered, regarding him with that sly oblique look; while Brian noticed a feeling of intense excitement in her voice. "I don't know what you-all are a-goin' ter think of me, but I'm bound ter tell you just the same,—seems like I got ter,—even if you-all was ter lick me for hit like pap used ter."

"Why, Judy, dear," the puzzled man returned, soothingly, "you know I would never strike you, no matter what you did. Come, sit down here on this log, and tell me about whatever it is that troubles you; then you can go back to sleep again."

"I ain't a-wantin' ter set down. I ain't been asleep. Hit seems like I can't never sleep no more." She wrung her hands and turned her poor twisted

212

body about nervously; then demanded with startling abruptness: "When do you-all 'low she'll git back?"

The wondering Brian did not at first catch her meaning, and she continued, with an impatient jerk of her head: "Hit's that there gal with the no-'count name, Betty Jo, I'm a-talkin' 'bout."

"Oh, you mean Miss Williams," Brian returned. "Why, I suppose she will be back in two or three weeks, or a month, perhaps; I don't know exactly, Judy. Why?"

" 'Cause I'm a-tellin' you-all not ter let her come back here ever," came the startling answer, in a voice that was filled with menacing anger. Then, before Brian could find a word to reply, the mountain girl continued, with increasing excitement: "You-all dassn't let her come back here, nohow, 'cause, if you do, I'll hurt her, sure. You-all have been a-thinkin' as how I was plumb blind, I reckon; but I seen you, —every evenin', when she'd pretend ter just go for a walk an' then'd make straight for the clearin' where you was a-choppin', an' then you'd quit, an' set with her up there on the hill. Youuns never knowed I was a-watchin' from the bresh all the time, did you? Well, I was; an' when youuns'd walk down ter the house, so slow like an' close together, I'd sneak ahead, an' beat you home; but all the time I was a-seein' you, an' youuns never knowed, 'cause youuns just naturally couldn't see nor hear nothin' but each other. Don't you-all 'low as how I'd know by the way you looked at her, while youuns was a-fixin' that there book, every night, what you-all was a-thinkin' 'bout her? My God-A'mighty! hit was just as plain ter me as if you was a-sayin' hit right out loud all the time,—a heap plainer hit was than if you'd done writ' hit down in your book. I can't make out ter read print much, nohow, like youuns kin; but I sure kin see what I see. I—"

"Judy! Judy!" Brian broke the stream of the excited girl's talk. "What in the world are you saying? What do you mean, child?"

"You-all knows dad burned well what I'm a-meanin'!" she retorted, with increasing anger. "I'm a-meanin' that you-all are plumb lovin' that there Betty Jo gal,—that's what I'm a-meanin'!—an' you-all sure ain't got ary right for ter go an' do sich a thing, nohow!"

Brian tried to check her, but she silenced him with: "I won't neither hush! I can't! I tell you

214

I'm a-goin' ter say my say if you-all kills me! I've just naturally got ter! Seems like I was all afire inside an' would burn plumb up if I didn't! I've got rights, I reckon, if I be all crooked an' twisted out er shape, an' ugly-faced an' no learnin', ner nothin'."

A dry sob choked the torrent of words for an instant; but, with a savage effort she went on: "I know I ain't nothin' alongside of her, but you-all ain't a-goin' ter have her just the same,—not if I have ter kill her first! You ain't got no right ter have her, nohow, 'cause hit's like's not you-all done got a woman already somewheres, wherever 'twas you-all come from; an' even if you ain't got no woman already, I sure ain't a-goin' ter let you have her! What'd she ever do for you? Hit was me what dragged you-all from the river when you was mighty nigh dead from licker an' too plumb sick ter save yourself! Hit's me that's kept from tellin' the Sheriff who you be an' a-takin' that there reward-money! Hit was me what jumped inter the river above Elbow Rock just ter git your dad burned old book, when you'd done throwed hit plumb away!

"I knowed first time I heard Auntie Sue name her

215

what she'd do ter you! Any fool would a-knowed
what a woman with a half-gal, half-boy name like
her'n would do, an' she's done hit,—she sure has!
But she ain't a-goin' ter do no more! You-all belongs
ter me a heap more'n you do ter her,—if hit comes
ter that,—though, I ain't a-foolin' myself none
a-thinkin' that sich as you could ever take up with sich
as me,—me bein' what I am. No, sir; I ain't never
fooled myself ary bit like that, Mr. Burns. But hit
ain't a-makin' no difference how ugly an' crooked an'
no 'count I be outside; the inside of me is a-lovin'
you like she never could, ner nobody else, I reckon.
An' I'll just go on a-lovin' you, no matter what happens; an' I ain't a-carin' whether you got a woman
already er not, er whether you-all have robbed er
killed, er what you done. An'—an'—so I'm a-tellin'
you, you'd best not let her come back here no more,
'cause—'cause I just naturally can't stand hit ter see
youuns tergether! 'Fore God, I'm a-tellin' you true,
—I'll sure hurt her!"

The girl's voice raised to a pitch of frenzied excitement, and, whirling, she pointed to the river, as
she cried: "Look out there! What do you-all reckon
your fine Betty Jo lady would do if I was ter git her

216

ketched in them there rapids? What do you-all reckon the Elbow Rock water would do ter her? I'll tell you what hit'd do: Hit would smash an' grind an' tear an' hammer that there fine, straight body of hers 'til hit was all broken an' twisted an' crooked a heap worse'n what I be,—that's what hit would do; an' hit would scratch an' cut an' beat up that pretty face an' mess up her pretty hair an' choke her an' smother her 'til she was all blue-black an' muddy, an' her eyes was red an' starin', an' she was nothin' but just an ugly lump of dirt; an' hit wouldn't even leave her her fine clothes neither,—the Elbow Rock water wouldn't,—hit'd just naturally tear 'em off her, an' leave her 'thout ary thing what's makin' you love her like you're a-doin'! An' where would all her fine schoolin' an' smart talk an' pretty ways be then? Eh? She wouldn't be no better, ner half as good as me, I'm a-tellin' you, onct Elbow Rock got done with her!"

The poor creature finished in wild triumph; then suddenly, as though spent with the very fury of her passion, she turned from the river, and said dully: "You'd sure best not let her come back, sir! 'Fore God, I ain't a-wantin' ter do hit, but hit seems like

I can't help myself; I can't sleep for wantin' ter fix hit so,—so's you just couldn't want ter have her no more'n you're a-wantin' me. I—I—sure ain't a-foolin' myself none, not ary bit, a-thinkin' you-all could ever git ter likin' sich as me; but, I can't help sort of dreamin' 'bout hit an' a-pretendin', an'—an' all the while I'm a-knowin', inside er me like, that there ain't nobody,—not Auntie Sue, nor this here Betty Jo, nor that there other woman, nor anybody,— what kin care for you like I'm a-carin',—they just naturally couldn't care like me; 'cause—'cause, you see, sir, I ain't got nobody else,—ain't no man but you ever even been decent ter me. I sure ain't got nobody else—"

The distraught creature's sobs prevented further speech, and she dropped down on the ground, weak and exhausted; her poor twisted body shaking and writhing with the emotion she could not voice.

For a little while, Brian Kent himself was as helpless as Judy. He could only stand dumbly, staring at her as she crouched at his feet. Then, very gently, he lifted her from the ground, and tried as best he could to comfort her. But he felt his words to be very shallow and inadequate, even though his own voice was trembling with emotion.

"Come, Judy, dear," he said, at last, when she seemed to have in a measure regained her self-control. "Come. You must go back to the house, child."

Drawing away from his supporting arm, she answered, quietly: "I ain't no child, no more, Mr. Burns: I'm sure a woman, now. I'm just as much a woman as—as—she is, if I be like what I am. I'm plumb sorry I had ter do this; but I just naturally couldn't help hit. You ain't got no call ter be scared I'll do hit again."

When they were nearing the house, Judy stopped again, and, for a long minute, looked silently out over the moonlit river, while Brian stood watching her.

"Hit is pretty, ain't hit, Mr. Burns?" she said at last. "With the hills all so soft an'—an' dreamy-like, an' them clouds a-floatin' 'way up there over the top of Table Mountain; with the moon makin' 'em all silvery an' shiny 'round the edges, an' them trees on yon side the river lookin' like they was made er smoke er fog er somethin' like that; an' the old river hitself a-layin' there in The Bend like—like a long strip of shinin' gold,—hit sure is pretty! Funny, I couldn't never see hit that a-way before,—ain't hit?"

"Yes, Judy; it is beautiful to-night," he said.

But Judy, apparently without hearing him, continued: " 'Seems like I can sense a little ter-night what Auntie Sue an' youuns are allus a-talkin' 'bout the river,—'bout hit's bein' like life an' sich as that. An' hit 'pears like I kin kind of git a little er what you done wrote 'bout hit in your book,—'bout the currents an' the still places an' the rough water an' all. I reckon as how I'm a part of your river, too, ain't I, Mr. Burns?"

"Yes, Judy," he answered, wonderingly; "we are all parts of the river."

"I reckon you're right," she continued. "Hit sure 'pears ter be that a-way. But I kin tell you-all somethin' else 'bout the river what you didn't put down in your book, Mr. Burns: There's heaps an' heaps er snags an' quicksands an' sunk rocks an' shaller places where hit looks deep an' deep holes where hit looks shaller, an' currents what's hid 'way down

under that'll ketch an' drag you in when you ain't
a-thinkin', an' drown you sure. 'Tain't all of the
river what Auntie Sue an' youuns kin see from the
porch. You see, I knows 'bout hit,—'bout them other
things I mean,—'cause I was borned and growed up
a-knowin' 'bout 'em; an'—an'—the next time you-all
writes er book, Mr. Burns, I 'low you-all ought ter
put in 'bout them there snags an' things, 'cause folks
sure got ter know 'bout 'em, if they ain't a-wantin'
ter git drowned."

When Judy had gone into the house, Brian again
sat alone on the porch.

An hour, perhaps, had passed when a voice behind
him said: "Why, Brian, are you still up? I supposed you were in bed long ago."

He turned to see Auntie Sue, standing in the doorway.

"And what in the world are you prowling about
for, this time of the night?" Brian retorted, bringing
a chair for her.

"I am prowling because I couldn't sleep,—thinking about you, Brian," she answered.

"I fear that is the thing that is keeping me up,
too," he returned grimly.

"I know," she said gently. "Sometimes, one's self does keep one awake. Is it—is it anything you care to tell me? Would it help for me to know?"

For some time, he did not answer; while the old teacher waited silently. At last, he spoke, slowly: "Auntie Sue, what is the greatest wrong that a woman can do?"

"The greatest wrong a woman can do, Brian, is the greatest wrong that a man can do."

"But, what is it, Auntie Sue?" he persisted.

"I think," she answered,—"indeed I am quite sure,—that the greatest wrong is for a woman to kill a man's faith in woman; and for a man to kill a woman's faith in man."

Brian Kent buried his face in his hands.

"Am I right, dear?" asked the old gentlewoman, after a little.

And Brian Kent answered: "Yes, Auntie Sue, you are right—that is the greatest wrong."

Again they were silent. It was as though few words were needed between the woman of seventy years and this man who, out of some great trouble, had been so strangely brought to her by the river.

Then the silvery-haired old teacher spoke again:

"Brian, have you ever wondered that I am so alone in the world? Have you ever asked yourself why I never married?"

"Yes, Auntie Sue," he answered. "I have wondered."

"Many people have," she said, with simple frankness. Then—"I am going to tell you something, dear boy, that only two people in the world beside myself ever knew, and they are both dead, many years now. I am going to tell you, because I feel—because I think—that, perhaps, it may help you a little. I, too, Brian, had my dreams when I was a girl,—my dreams of happiness,—such as every true woman hopes for;—of a home with all that home means;—of a lover-husband;—of little ones who would call me 'mother';—and my dreams ended, Brian, on a battlefield of the Civil War. He went from me the very day we were promised. He never returned. I have always felt that we were as truly one as though the church had solemnized and the law had legalized our union. I promised that I would wait for him."

"And you—you have kept that promise? You have been true to that memory?" Brian Kent asked, wonderingly.

"I have been true to him, Brian;—all the years of my life I have been true to him."

Brian Kent bowed his head, reverently.

Rising, the old gentlwoman went close to him, and put her hands on his shoulders. "Brian, dear, I have told you my secret because I thought it might help you to know. Oh, my boy—my boy,—don't—don't let anything—don't let anyone—kill your faith in womanhood! No matter how bitter your experience, you can believe, now, that there are women who can be faithful and true. Surely, you can believe it now, Brian,—you must!"

And as he caught her hands in his, and raised his face to whisper, "I do believe, Auntie Sue," she stooped and kissed him.

Then, again, Brian Kent was alone in the night with his thoughts.

And the river swept steadily on its shining way through the moonlit world to the distant sea.

CHAPTER XVII.

AN AWKWARD SITUATION.

REQUENT letters from Betty Jo informed Brian and Auntie Sue of that practical and businesslike young woman's negotiations with various Eastern publishers, until, at last, the matter was finally settled to Betty Jo's satisfaction.

She had contracted with a well-known firm for the publication of the book. The details were all arranged. The work was to begin immediately. Betty Jo was returning to the little log house by the river.

Brian drove to Thompsonville the morning she was to arrive, and it seemed to him that "Old Prince" had never jogged so leisurely along the winding river road, yet he was at the little mountain station nearly an hour before the train was due.

Those weeks had been very anxious weeks to Brian, in spite of Auntie Sue's oft-repeated assurances that no publisher could fail to recognize the value of his work. And, to be entirely truthful, Brian himself, deep down in his heart, felt a certainty that his work would receive recognition. But, still, he would argue with himself, his feeling of confidence might very well be due to the dear old gentlewoman's enthusiastic faith in him rather than in any merit in the book itself; and it was a well-established fact—to all unpublished writers at least—that publishers are a heartless folk, and exceedingly loth to extend a helpful hand to unrecognized genius, however great the worth of its offering. He could scarcely believe the letters which announced the good news. It did not seem possible that this all-important first step toward the success which Auntie Sue so confidently predicted for his book was now an accomplished fact.

And now that Betty Jo's mission was completed, it seemed months ago that he had said good-bye to her and had watched the train disappear between the hills. But when at last the long whistle echoing and reechoing from the timbered mountain-sides announced the coming of the train that was bringing her back, and the train itself a moment later burst into view and, with a rushing roar of steam and wheels and brakes, came to a stop at the depot platform, and there was Betty Jo herself, it seemed that it was only yesterday that she had gone away.

Very calm and self-possessed and well poised was Betty Jo when she stepped from the train to meet him. She was very capable and businesslike as she claimed her baggage and saw it safely in the spring wagon. But still there was a something in her manner —a light in the gray eyes, perhaps, or a quality in the clear voice—that meant worlds more to the man than her simple statement, that she was glad to see him again. Laughingly, she refused to tell him about her trip as they rode home, saying that Auntie Sue must hear it all with him. And so conscious was the man of her presence there beside him that, somehow, the prospective success or failure of his book did not so much matter, after all.

In the excitement of the joyous meeting between Auntie Sue and Betty Jo, Judy's stoical self-repression was unnoticed. The mountain girl went about her part of the household work silently with apparent indifference to the young woman's presence. But when, after the late dinner was over, Auntie Sue and Brian listened to Betty Jo's story, Judy, unobserved, was nearby, so that no word of the conversation escaped her.

Three times that night, when all was still in the

little log house by the river, the door of Judy's room opened cautiously, and the twisted form of the mountain girl appeared. Each time, for a few minutes, she stood there in the moonlight that shone through the open window into the quiet room, listening, listening; then went stealthily to the door of the room where Betty Jo was sleeping, and each time she paused before that closed door to look fearfully about the dimly lighted living room. Once she crept to Brian's door, and then to Auntie Sue's, and once she silently put her hand on the latch of that door between her and Betty Jo; but, each time, she went stealthily back to her own room.

Betty Jo awoke early that morning. Outside her open window the birds were singing, and the sun, which was just above the higher mountain-tops, was flooding the world with its wealth of morning beauty. The music of the feathery chorus and the golden beauty of the light that streamed through the window into her room, with the fresh enticing perfume of the balmy air, were very alluring to the young woman just returned from the cities' stale and dingy atmosphere.

Betty Jo decided instantly that she must go for a

before-breakfast walk. From the window, as she dressed, she saw Brian going to the barn with the milk-pail, and heard him greet the waiting "Bess" and exchange a cheery good-morning with "Old Prince," who hailed his coming with a low whinny.

Quietly, so as not to disturb Auntie Sue, Betty Jo slipped from the house and went down the gentle slope to the river-bank, and strolled along the margin of the stream toward Elbow Rock,—pausing sometimes to look out over the water as her attention was drawn to some movement of the river life, or turning aside to pluck a wild flower that caught her eye. She had made her way thus leisurely two-thirds of the distance perhaps from the house to Elbow Rock bluff when Judy suddenly confronted her. The mountain girl came so unexpectedly from among the bushes that Betty Jo, who was stooping over a flower, was startled.

"Judy!" she exclaimed. "Goodness! child, how you frightened me!" she finished with a good-natured laugh. But as she noticed the mountain girl's appearance, the laugh died on her lips, and her face was grave with puzzled concern.

Poor Judy's black hair was uncombed and dishevelled. The sallow, old-young face was distorted with passion, and the beady eyes glittered with the light of an insane purpose.

"What is it, Judy?" asked Betty Jo. "What in the world is the matter?"

"What'd you-all come back for?" demanded Judy with sullen menace in every word. "I done told him not ter let you. Hit 'pears ter me youuns ought ter have more sense."

Alarmed at the girl's manner, Betty Jo thought to calm her by saying, gently: "Why, Judy, dear, you are all excited and not a bit like yourself. Tell me what troubles you. I came back because I love to be here with Auntie Sue, of course. Why shouldn't I come if Auntie Sue likes to have me?"

"You-all are a-lyin'," returned Judy viciously. "But you-all sure can't fool me. You-all come back 'cause he's here."

A warm blush colored Betty Jo's face.

Judy's voice raised shrilly as she saw the effect of her words.

"You-all knows dad burned well that's what you come back for. But hit ain't a-goin' ter do you no good; hit sure ain't. I done told him. I sure warned him what'd happen if he let you come back. I heard you-all a-talkin' yesterday evenin' all 'bout his book an' what a great man that there publisher-feller back East 'lows he's goin' ter be. An' I kin see, now, that you-all has knowed hit from the start, an' that's why you-all been a-fixin' ter git him away from me. I done studied hit all out last night; but I sure ain't a-goin' ter let you do hit."

As she finished, the mountain girl, who had worked herself into a frenzy of rage, moved stealthily toward Betty Jo, and her face, with those blazing black eyes, and its frame of black unkempt hair, and its expression of insane fury, was the face of a fiend.

Betty Jo drew back, frightened at the poor creature's wild and threatening appearance.

"Judy!" she said sharply. "Judy! What do you mean!"

With a snarling grin of malicious triumph, Judy cried: "Scared, ain't you! You sure got reason ter be, 'cause there ain't nothin' kin stop me now. Know what I'm a-goin' ter do? I'm a-goin' ter put you-all in the river, just like I told him, an' old Elbow Rock is a-goin' ter make you-all broken an' twisted an' ugly like what my pap made me. Oh, hit'll sure fix that there fine slim body of your'n, an' that there pretty face what he likes ter look at so, an' them fine clothes'll be all wet an' mussed an' torn off you. You-all sure will be a-lookin' worse'n what I ever looked the next time he sees you,—you with your no-'count, half-gal and half-boy name!"

As the mountain girl, with the quickness of a wild thing, leaped upon her, Betty Jo screamed—one piercing cry, that ended in a choking gasp as Judy's hands found her throat.

Brian, who was still at the barn, busy with the morning chores, heard. With all his might, he ran toward the spot from which the call came.

Betty Jo fought desperately; but, strong as she was, she could never have endured against the vicious strength of the frenzied mountain-bred Judy, who was slowly and surely forcing her toward the brink of the river-bank, against which the swift waters of the rapids swept with terrific force.

A moment more and Brian would have been too late. Throwing Judy aside, he caught the exhausted Betty Jo in his arms, and, carrying her a little back from the edge of the stream, placed her gently on the ground.

Betty Jo did not faint; but she was too spent with her exertions to speak, though she managed to smile at him reassuringly, and shook her head when he asked if she was hurt.

When Brian was assured that the girl was really unharmed, he turned angrily to face Judy. But Judy had disappeared in the brush.

Presently, as Betty Jo's breathing became normal, she arranged her disordered hair and dress, and told Brian what the mountain girl had said; and this, of course, forced the man to relate his experience with Judy that night when she had told him that Betty Jo must not come back.

"I suppose I should have warned you, Miss Williams," he finished; "but the whole thing seemed to me so impossible, I could not believe there was any danger of the crazy creature actually attempting to carry out her wild threat; and, besides,—well, you can see that it was rather difficult for me to speak of it to you. I am sorry," he ended, with embarrassment.

For a long moment, the two looked at each other silently; then Betty Jo's practical common sense came to the rescue: "It would have been awkward for you to try to tell me, wouldn't it, Mr. Burns? And now that it is all over, and no harm done, we must just forget it as quickly as we can. We won't ever mention it again, will we?"

"Certainly not," he agreed heartily. "But I shall keep an eye on Miss Judy, in the future, I can promise you."

"I doubt if we ever see her again," returned Betty Jo, thoughtfully. "I don't see how she would dare go back to the house after this. I expect she will return to her father. Poor thing! But we must be careful not to let Auntie Sue know." Then smiling up at him, she added: "It seems like Auntie Sue is getting us into all sorts of conspiracies, doesn't it? What *do* you suppose we will be called upon to hide from her next?"

At Brian's suggestion, they went first to the barn, where he quickly finished his work. Then, carrying the full milk-pail between them, they proceeded, laughing and chatting, to the house, where Auntie Sue stood in the doorway.

The dear old lady smiled when she saw them coming so, and, returning their cheery greeting happily, added: "Have you children seen Judy anywhere? The child is not in her room, and the fire is not even made in the kitchen-stove yet."

CHAPTER XVIII.

BETTY JO FACES HERSELF.

ALL that day Auntie Sue wondered about Judy, while Brian and Betty Jo exhausted their inventive faculties in efforts to satisfy the dear old lady with plausible reasons for the mountain girl's disappearance.

During the forenoon, Brian canvassed the immediate neighborhood, and returned with the true information that Judy had stopped at the first house below Elbow Rock for breakfast, where she had told the people that she was going back to her father, because she was "doggone tired of working for them there city folks what was a-livin' at Auntie Sue's."

This was, in a way, satisfactory to Auntie Sue, because it assured her that the girl had met with no serious accident and because she knew very well the mountain-bred girl's ability to take care of herself in the hills. But, still, the gentle mistress of the log house by the river was troubled to think that Judy would leave her so without a word.

Betty Jo was so occupied during the day by her efforts to relieve Auntie Sue that she had but little time left for thought of herself or for reflecting on the situation revealed in her encounter with Judy. But many times during the day the mountain girl's passionate accusation came back to her, "You-all are a-lyin'! You-all come back 'cause *he* is here." Nor could she banish from her memory the look that was on Brian Kent's face that morning when he was carrying her in his arms back from the brink of the river-bank, over which the frenzied Judy had so nearly sent her to her death. And so, when the day at last was over, and she was alone in her room, it was not strange that Betty Jo should face herself squarely with several definite and pointed and exceedingly personal questions.

It was like Betty Jo to be honest with herself and to demand of herself that her problems be met squarely.

"First of all, Betty Jo," she demanded, in her downright, straightforward way of going most directly to the heart of a matter, "are you in love with Brian Kent?"

Without hesitation, the answer came, "I have not permitted myself to love him."

237

"You have not permitted yourself to love him? That means that you would be in love with him if you dared, doesn't it?"

And Betty Jo, in the safe seclusion of her room, felt her cheeks burn as she acknowledged the truth of the deduction.

The next question was inevitable: "Is Brian Kent in love with you, Betty Jo?"

And Betty Jo, recalling many, many things, was compelled to answer, from the triumphant gladness of her heart: "He is trying not to be, but he can't help himself. And"—the downright and straightforward young woman continued—"because I know that Brian Kent is trying so hard not to love me is the real reason why I have not permitted myself to love him."

But the clear-thinking, practical Betty Jo protested quickly: "You must remember that you are wholly ignorant of Brian Kent's history, except for the things he has chosen to tell you. And those things in his life which he has confessed to you are certainly not the things that could win the love of a girl like you, even though they might arouse your

interest in the man. Interest is not love, Betty Jo.
Are you quite sure that you are not making the mistake that is most commonly made by young women?"

Betty Jo was compelled to answer that she was
not mistaking interest for love, because had such
been the case, she would not be able to so analyze
the situation. Betty Jo's quite womanly prejudice
is admitted, because the prejudice was so womanly,
and because Betty Jo herself was so womanly.

"Very well, Miss Betty Jo," the young woman
continued inexorably, "you are not permitting yourself to love Brian Kent because Brian Kent is trying not to love you. But, why is the man trying so
hard not to love you?"

Betty Jo thought very hard over this question,
and felt her way carefully to the answer. "It might
be, of course, that it is because he is a fugitive from
the law. A man under such circumstances could
easily convince himself that no good woman would
permit herself to love him, and he would therefore,
in reasonable self-defense, prevent himself from loving her if he could."

But surely Brian Kent had every reason to know

that Betty Jo did not at all regard him as a criminal. Betty Jo, as Auntie Sue, recognized only the re-created Brian Kent. If that were all, they need only wait for the restitution which was so sure to come through his book. And Brian Kent himself, through Auntie Sue's teaching and through his work, had come to recognize only his real self, and not the creature of circumstances which the river had brought to the little log house. Betty Jo felt sure that there was more than this that was forcing the man to defend himself against his love for her. Thus she was driven to the conclusion that there was something in Brian Kent's history that he had not made known to her,—a something that denied him the right to love her, and that,—reasoned poor Betty Jo in the darkness of her room,—could only be a woman,—a woman to whom he was bound, not by love indeed,— Betty Jo could not believe that,—but by ties of honor and of the law.

And very clearly Betty Jo reasoned, too, that Brian's attitude toward her evidenced unmistakably his high sense of honor. The very fact that he had so persistently—in all their companionship, in their most intimate moments together even—held this invisible and, to her, unknown barrier between them, convinced her beyond a doubt of the essential integrity of his character, and compelled her admiration and confidence.

"That is exactly it, Betty Jo," she told herself sadly; "you love him because he tries so hard to keep himself from loving you."

And thus Betty Jo proved the correctness of Auntie Sue's loving estimate of her character and justified the dear old teacher's faith in the sterling quality of her womanhood.

Face to face with herself, fairly and squarely, the girl accepted the truth of the situation for Brian and for herself, and determined her course. She must go away,—she must go at once.

She wished that she had not returned to the log house by the river. She had never fully admitted to herself the truth of her feeling toward Brian until Judy had so unexpectedly precipitated the crisis; but, she knew, now, that Judy was right, and that the real reason for her return was her love for him. She knew, as well, that her very love,—which, once fully admitted and recognized by her, demanded with all the strength of her young womanhood the nearness

241

and companionship of the mate her heart had chosen, —demanded, also, that she help him to keep that fine sense of honor and true nobility of character which had won her.

She understood instinctively that,—now that she had confessed her love to herself,—she would, in spite of herself, tempt him in a thousand ways to throw aside that barrier which he had so honorably maintained between them. Her heart would plead with him to disregard his better self, and come to her. Her very craving for the open assurance of his love would tempt him, perhaps beyond his strength. And, yet, she knew as truly that, if he should yield; if he should cast aside the barrier of his honor; if he should deny his best self, and answer her call, it would be disastrous beyond measure to them both.

To save the fineness of their love, Betty Jo must go. If it should be that they never met again, still she must go.

But there were other currents moving in the river that night. In the steady onward flow of the whole, Betty Jo's life-currents seemed to be setting away from the man she loved. But other currents, unknown to the girl, who faced herself so honestly, and who so bravely accepted the truth she found, were moving in ways beyond her knowledge. Directed and influenced by innumerable and unseen forces and obstacles, the currents which, combined, made the stream of life in its entirety, were weaving themselves together,—interlacing and separating,—drawing close and pulling apart,—only to mingle as one again.

Betty Jo saw only Brian Kent and herself, and their love which she now acknowledged, and she had, as it were, only a momentary glimpse of those small parts of the stream.

Betty Jo could not know of those other currents that were moving so mysteriously about her as the river poured itself onward so unceasingly to the sea.

CHAPTER XIX.

JUDY'S CONFESSION.

IN spite of all their care, Brian and Betty Jo did not wholly convince Auntie Sue that there was no more in Judy's disappearance than the report from the neighbors indicated. The dear old lady felt that there was something known to the young people that they were keeping from her; and, while she did not question their motives, and certainly did not worry,—for Auntie Sue never worried,—she was not satisfied with the situation. When she retired to her room for the night, she told herself, with some spirit, that she would surely go to the bottom of the affair the next morning.

It happened that Auntie Sue went to the bottom of the affair much sooner than she expected.

It must have been about that same hour of the night when Betty Jo, after reaching her decision to go away, retired to her bed, that Auntie Sue was aroused by a low knocking at the open window of her room.

The old teacher listened without moving, her first thought being that her fancy was tricking her. The sound came again, and, this time, there could be no mistake. Sitting up in her bed, Auntie Sue looked toward the window, and, at the sound of her movement, a low whisper came from without.

"Don't be scared, Auntie Sue. Hit ain't nobody but just me."

As she recognized Judy's voice, she saw the mountain girl's head and twisted shoulders outlined above the window-sill. A moment more, and Auntie Sue was at the window.

"Sh-h-h!" cautioned Judy. "Don't wake 'em up. I just naturally got ter tell you-all somethin', Auntie Sue; but, I ain't a-wantin' Mr. Burns an' that there Betty Jo woman ter hear. I reckon I best come through the winder."

Acting upon the word, she climbed carefully into the room.

"Judy, child! What—?"

The mountain girl interrupted Auntie Sue's tremulous whisper with: "I'll tell hit ter you, ma'm, in a little bit, if you'll just wait. I got ter see if they are sure 'nough a-sleepin' first, though."

She stole silently from the room, to return a few minutes later. "They are plumb asleep, both of 'em," she said in a low tone, when she had cautiously closed the door. "I done opened the doors ter their rooms, an' listened, an' shet 'em again 'thout ary one of 'em a-movin' even. I'll fix the winder, now, an' then we kin make a light."

Carefully, she closed the window and drew down the shade. Then she lit the lamp.

Auntie Sue, who was sitting on the bed, looked at the girl in bewildered amazement.

With a nervous laugh, Judy fingered her torn dress and dishevelled hair. "I sure am a sight, ain't I, ma'm? I done hit a-comin' through the bresh in the dark. But, don't—don't—look so kinder lost like; you-all ain't got no call ter be scared of me."

"Why, Judy, dear, I'm not afraid of you. Come, child; tell me what is the trouble."

At the kindly manner and voice of the old gentle-woman, those black eyes filled with tears, which, for the moment, the mountain girl stoically permitted to roll down her thin sallow cheeks unheeded. Then, with a quick resolute jerk of her twisted body, she drew her dress sleeve across her face, and said: "I—I—reckon I couldn't hate myself no worse'n I'm a-doin'. Hit seems like I been mighty nigh plumb crazy; but, I just naturally had ter come back an' tell you-all, 'cause you-all been so good ter me."

She placed a chair for Auntie Sue, and added: "You-all best make yourself comfortable, though, ma'm. I'm mighty nigh tuckered out myself. Hit's a right smart way from where pap's a-livin' ter here, an' I done come in a hurry."

She dropped down on the floor, her back against the bed, and clasped her knees in her hands, as Auntie Sue seated herself.

"Begin at the beginning, Judy, and tell me exactly what has happened," said Auntie Sue.

"Yes, ma'm, I will,—that's what I was aimin' ter do when I made up ter come back."

And she did. Starting with her observation of Brian and Betty Jo, and her conviction of their love, she told of her interview with Brian the night she warned him not to let Betty Jo return, and finished with the account of her attack on Betty Jo that morning.

Auntie Sue listened with amazement and pity. Here, indeed, was a wayward and troubled life-current.

"But, Judy, Judy!" exclaimed the gentle old teacher, "you would not really have pushed Betty Jo into the river. She would have been drowned, child. Surely, you did not mean to kill her, Judy."

The girl wrung her hands, and her deformed body swayed to and fro in the nervous intensity of her emotions. But she answered, stubbornly: "That there was just what I was aimin' ter do. I'd a-killed her, sure, if Mr. Burns hadn't a-come just when he did. I can't rightly tell how hit was, but hit seemed like there was somethin' inside of me what was a-makin' me do hit, an' I couldn't, somehow, help myself. An'—an'—that ain't all, ma'm; I done worse'n that," she continued in a low, moaning wail. "Oh, my God-A'mighty! Why didn't Mr. Burns sling me inter the river an' let me be smashed an' drowned at Elbow Rock while he had me, 'stead of lettin' me git away ter do what I've gone an' done!"

Auntie Sue's wonderful native strength enabled her to speak calmly: "What is it you have done, Judy? You must tell me, child."

The older woman's voice and manner steadied the girl, and she answered more in her usual colorless monotone, but still guarded so as not to awaken the other members of the household: "Hit seemed like Mr. Burns ketchin' me, like he did, an' me a-seein' him with her in his arms, made me plumb crazy-mad, an' I 'lowed I'd fix hit so's he couldn't never have her nohow, so I—I—done told pap 'bout him bein' Brian Kent what had robbed that there bank, an' how there was er lot of reward-money a-waitin' for anybody that'd tell on him."

Auntie Sue was too shocked to speak. Was it possible that, now, when the real Brian Kent was so far removed from the wretched bank clerk; when his fine natural character and genius had become so established, and his book was— No, no! It could not be! God could not let men be so cruel as to send Auntie Sue's Brian Kent to prison because that other Brian Kent, tormented by wrong environment, and driven by an evil combination of circumstances, had taken a few dollars of the bank's money! And Betty Jo— No, no! Auntie Sue's heart cried out in protest. There must be some way. She would find some way. The banker—Homer Ward! Auntie Sue's

mind, alert and vigorous as the mind of a woman of
half her years, caught at the thought of her old friend
and pupil. She leaned forward in her chair over
the girl who sat on the floor at her feet, and her voice
was strong and clear with the strength of the spirit
which dominated her frail body.

"Judy, did you tell any one else besides your
father?"

"There wasn't nobody else ter tell," came the
answer. "An' pap, he 'lowed he'd kill me if I said
anythin' ter anybody 'fore he'd got the money. He
aims ter git hit all for hisself."

"What will he do? Will he go to Sheriff Knox?"

"No, ma'm; pap, he 'lowed if he done that a-way,
the Sheriff he'd take most of the money. Pap's
a-goin' right ter that there bank feller hisself."

"Yes, yes! Go on, Judy!"

"You see, ma'm, I done remembered the name
of the bank an' where hit was an' Mr. Ward's name
an' all, on 'count of that there money letter what you
done sent 'em an' us bein' so worried 'bout hit never
gittin' there an' all that. An' pap, he knows er man
over in Gardner what's on the railroad, you see,
what'll let him have money enough for the trip,—a

licker-man, he is,—an' pap's aimin' ter make hit over ter Gardner ter git the money in time ter ketch that there early mornin' train. Hit's a right smart way over the mountains, but I reckon's how pap'll make hit. Soon's pap left, I got ter thinkin' what I'd done, an' the more I studied 'bout hit,—'bout Mr. Burns a-havin' ter go ter prison, an' 'bout you-all a-carin' for him the way you does, an' 'bout how happy you was over his book, an'—an'—how good you'd been ter me,—the sorrier I got, 'til I just couldn't stand a-thinkin' 'bout hit no longer; an'— an'—so I come fast as I could ter tell you. I 'lowed you'd make out ter fix hit some way so—Mr. Burns won't have ter go ter prison. Couldn't you-all send— send a telegraph ter the bank man, er somethin'? I'd git it inter Thompsonville for you, ma'm; an' Mr. Burns, he needn't never know nothin' 'bout hit."

Auntie Sue was dressing when Judy finished speaking. With a physical strength that had its source in her indomitable spirit, she moved about the room making the preparations necessary to her plan, and as she worked she talked to the girl.

"No, Judy, a telegram won't do. I must go to Homer Ward myself. That morning train leaves

Thompsonville at six o'clock. You must slip out of the house, and harness 'Old Prince' to the buggy as fast as you can. You will drive with me to Thompsonville, and bring 'Prince' back. You can turn him loose when you get near home, and he will come the rest of the way alone. You must not let Mr. Burns nor Betty Jo see you, because they mustn't know anything about what you have done. Do you understand, child?"

"Yes, ma'm," said Judy, eagerly. She was on her feet now.

"You can go to the neighbors and find some place to stay until I return," continued Auntie Sue.

"You don't need ter worry none 'bout me," said Judy. "I kin take care of myself, I reckon. But ain't you plumb scared ter go 'way on the cars alone an' you so old?"

"Old!" retorted Auntie Sue. "I have not felt so strong for twenty years. There is nothing for me to fear. I will be in St. Louis to-morrow night, and in Chicago the next forenoon. I guess I am not so helpless that I can't make a little journey like this. Homer Ward shall never send my boy to prison,—never,—bank or no bank! Go on, now, and get

'Prince' and the buggy ready. We must not miss that train." She pushed Judy from the room, and again cautioned her not to awaken Brian or Betty Jo.

When she had completed her preparations for the trip, Auntie Sue wrote a short note to Betty Jo, telling her that she had been called away suddenly, and that she would return in a few days, and that she was obliged to borrow Betty Jo's pocket-book. Grave as she felt the situation to be, Auntie Sue laughed to herself as she pictured the consternation of Betty Jo and Brian in the morning.

Silently, the old lady stole into the girl's room to secure the money she needed and to leave her letter. Then, as silently, she left the house, and found Judy, who was waiting with "Old Prince" and the buggy, ready to start.

The station agent at Thompsonville was not a little astonished when Auntie Sue and Judy appeared, and, with the easy familiarity of an old acquaintance greeted her with, "Howdy, Auntie Sue! What in thunder are you doin' out this time of the day? No bad news, I hope?"

"Oh, no, Mr. Jackson," Auntie Sue answered

easily. "I'm just going to Chicago for a little visit with an old friend."

"Sort of a vacation, eh?" returned the man behind the window, as he made out her ticket. "Well, you sure have earned one, Auntie Sue. It's gittin' to be vacation time now, too. Bunch of folks come in yesterday to stay at the clubhouse for a spell. Pretty wild lot, I'd say,—wimmen as well as the men. I reckon them clubhouse parties don't disturb you much, though, if you be their nearest neighbor, —do they?"

"They never have yet, Mr. Jackson," she returned. "Their place is on the other side of the river, and a mile above my house, you know. I see them in their boats on The Bend, though, and once in a while they call on me. But the Elbow Rock rapids begin in front of my place, and the clubhouse people don't usually come that far down the river."

She turned to Judy, and, with the girl, went out of the waiting room to the platform, where she whispered: "You must start back right away, Judy. If your father is on the train, he might see you."

"What if pap ketches sight of you-all?" Judy returned nervously.

"He will not be so apt to notice me as he would you," she returned, "even if he does catch a glimpse of me. And it can't be helped if he does. I'll be in Chicago as quick as he will, and I know I will see Mr. Ward first. Go on now, dear, and don't let Mr. Burns or Betty Jo see you, and be a good girl. I feel sure that everything will be all right."

With a sudden awkward movement, poor Judy caught the old gentlewoman's hand and pressed it to her lips; then, turning, ran toward the buggy.

When the train arrived, the station agent came to help Auntie Sue with her handbag aboard, and she managed to keep her friend between herself and the coaches, in case Jap Taylor should be looking from a window. As the conductor and the agent assisted her up the steps, the agent said: "Mind you take good care of her, Bill. Finest old lady God-Almighty ever made! If you was to let anything happen to her, you best never show yourself in this neighborhood again; we'd lynch you, sure!"

The conductor found a good seat for his lovely old passenger, and made her as comfortable as possible. As he punched her ticket, he said, with a genial smile, which was the voluntary tribute paid to Auntie

Sue by all men: "You are not much like the passengers I usually carry in this part of the country, ma'm. They are mostly a rather rough-lookin' lot."

She smiled back at him, understanding perfectly his intended compliment. "They are good people, though, sir,—most of them. Of course, there are some who are a little wild, sometimes, I expect."

The railroad man laughed again, shaking his head. "I should say so. You ought to see the specimen I've got in the smoker. I picked him up back there at Gardner. Perhaps you have heard of him—Jap Taylor. He is about the worst in the whole country, I reckon."

"I have heard of him," she returned. "I do hope he won't come into this coach."

"Oh, he won't start anything on my train," laughed the man in blue reassuringly. "He would never come in here, anyhow. Them kind always stay in the smoker. Seems like they know where they belong. He is half-scared to death himself, anyway; he is going to Chicago, too, and I'll bet it's the first time in his life he has ever been farther from these hills than Springfield."

CHAPTER XX.

BRIAN AND BETTY JO KEEP HOUSE.

WHEN Brian went to the barn the next morning he found "Old Prince" standing at the gate. While he was still trying to find some plausible explanation of the strange incident, after unharnessing the horse and giving him his morning feed, an excited call from Betty Jo drew his attention. With an answering shout, he started for the house. The excited girl met him halfway, and gave him Auntie Sue's note.

When Brian had read the brief and wholly inadequate message, they stood looking at each other, too mystified for speech. Brian read the note, again, aloud, speaking every word with slow distinctness. "Well, I'll be hanged!" he ejaculated, at the close of the remarkable communication, staring at Betty Jo.

"It wouldn't in the least surprise me if we were both hanged before night," returned Betty Jo. "After this from Auntie Sue, I am prepared for anything. What on earth *do* you suppose has happened?"

Brian shook his head: "It is too much for me!"

Together they went to the house, and the place seemed strangely deserted. Every possible explanation that suggested itself, they discussed and rejected.

"One thing we can depend upon," said Brian, at last, when they had exhausted the resources of their combined imaginations: "Auntie Sue knows exactly what she is doing, and she is doing exactly the right thing. I suppose we will know all about it when she returns."

Betty Jo looked again at the note: " 'I will be back in a few days,' " she read slowly. " 'Be good children, and take care of things.' "

Again, they regarded each other wonderingly.

Then Betty Jo broke the silence with an odd little laugh: "I feel like we were cast away on some desert island, don't you?"

"Something like that," Brian returned. Then, to relieve the strain of the situation, he added: "I suppose 'Bess' will have to be milked and the chores finished just the same."

"And I'll get breakfast for us," agreed Betty Jo, as he started back to the barn.

In the safe seclusion of the stable, with no one but "Old Prince" and "Bess" to witness his agitation, Brian endeavored to bring his confused and unruly thoughts under some sort of control.

"Several days; several days." The words repeated themselves with annoying persistency. And they—Betty Jo and he, Brian Kent—were to "take care of things";—they were to keep house together; —they were to live together, alone,—in the log house by the river,—alone. She was even then preparing their breakfast. They would sit down at the table alone. And there would be dinner and supper; and the evening,—just for them. He would work about the place. She would attend to her household duties. He would go to his meals, and she would be there expecting him,—waiting for him. And when the tasks of the day were finished, they would sit on the porch to watch the coming of the night,—Betty Jo and he, Brian Kent— "What in God's name," the man demanded of the indifferent "Bess," did Auntie Sue mean by placing him in such a situation? Did she think him more than human?

It had not been easy for Brian to maintain that barrier between himself and Betty Jo, even with the constant help of Auntie Sue's presence. Many, many times he had barely saved himself from declaring his love; and, now, he was asked to live with her in the most intimate companionship possible.

For the only time in his life Brian Kent was almost angry at Auntie Sue. "By all that was consistent, and reasonable, and merciful, and safe," he told himself, "if it was absolutely necessary for the dear old lady to disappear so mysteriously, why had she not taken Betty Jo along?"

In the meantime, while Brian was confiding his grievances to his four-footed companions in the barn, Betty Jo was expressing herself in the kitchen.

"Betty Jo," she began, as she raked the ashes from the stove preparatory to building the fire, "it appears to me that you have some serious considering to do, and"—with a glance toward the barn, as she went out to empty the ash-pan—"you must do it quickly before that man comes for his breakfast. You were very right, last night, in your decision, to go away. It is exactly what you should have done. I am more than ever convinced of that, this morning. But you can't go now. Even if Auntie Sue had not taken your pocket-book and every penny in it, you couldn't run away with Auntie Sue herself gone. If she hadn't wanted you to stay right here for some very serious reason, Betty Jo, she would have taken you with her last night. Auntie Sue very pointedly and definitely expects you to be here when she returns. And she will be away several days,—several days, Betty Jo." She repeated the words in a whisper. "And during those several days, you are to keep house for the man you love;—the man who loves you;—the man whom you must keep from telling you his love,—no matter how your heart pleads for him to tell you, you must not permit him to speak. He will be coming in to breakfast in a few minutes, and you will sit down at the table with him,—across the table from him,—facing him,—Betty Jo,—just like—"

She looked in the little mirror that hung beside the kitchen window, and, with dismay, saw her face flushed with color that was not caused by the heat of the stove. "And you will be forced to look at him across the table, and he will look at you,—and—and you must not,—" she stamped her foot,—"you dare not look like *that*, Betty Jo.

"And then there will be the dinner that you will

cook for him, and the supper; and the evenings on the porch. O Lord! Betty Jo, what ever will you do? How will you ever save the fineness of your love? If you were afraid to trust yourself with the help of Auntie Sue's presence, what in the world can you do without her—and you actually keeping house with him? Oh, Auntie Sue! Auntie Sue!" she groaned, "you are the dearest woman in the world and the best and wisest, but you have blundered terribly this time! Why *did* you do such a thing! It is not fair to him! It is not fair to me! It is not fair to our love!

"All of which,"—the practical Betty Jo declared a moment later, wiping her eyes on the corner of her apron, and going into the other room to set the table for breakfast,—"all of which, Betty Jo, does not in the least help matters, and only makes you more nervous and upset than you are.

"One thing is certain sure," she continued, while her hands were busy with the dishes and the table preparations: "If we can endure this test, we need never, never, never fear that anything nor anybody can ever, ever make us doubt the genuineness of our love. Auntie Sue has certainly arranged it most beautifully for Brian Kent and Betty Jo Williams to become thoroughly acquainted."

Betty Jo suddenly paused in her work, and stood very still: "I wonder," she said slowly,—"can it be,—is it possible,—what if Auntie Sue has brought about this situation for that very reason?"

"Breakfast ready?" cried Brian at the kitchen-door, and his voice was so hearty and natural that the girl answered as naturally: "It will be as soon as you are ready for it. I forget, do you like your eggs three minutes or four?"

They really managed that breakfast very well, even if they did sit opposite each other so that each was forced to look straight across the table into the face of the other. Or, perhaps, it was because they looked at each other so straight and square and frankly honest that the breakfast went so well.

And because the breakfast went so well, they managed the dinner and the supper also.

"I have been thinking," said Brian at the close of their evening meal, looking straight into the gray eyes over the table, "perhaps it might be better for you to stay at neighbor Tom's until Auntie Sue returns. I'll hitch up 'Old Prince' and drive you over, if you say. Or, we might find some neighbor woman to come here to live with us, if you prefer."

"You don't like my housekeeping, then?" asked Betty Jo.

"Like it!" exclaimed Brian; and the tone of his voice approached the danger-point.

Betty Jo said quickly: "I'll tell you exactly what I think, Mr. Burns: Auntie Sue said we were to be good children, and take care of things until she returned. She did not say for me to shirk my part by going to neighbor Tom's or by having any one come here. Don't you think we can do exactly what Auntie Sue said?"

"Yes," returned Brian, heartily; "I am sure we can. And do you know,—come to think about it,—I believe the dear old lady would be disappointed in us both if we dodged our—well,—" he finished with emphasis,—"our responsibilities."

And after that, somehow, the evening on the porch went as well as the breakfast and dinner and supper had gone.

It was the second day of their housekeeping that Betty Jo noticed smoke coming from the stone chimney of the clubhouse up the river. She reported her observation to Brian when he came in from his work for dinner. During the afternoon, they both saw boats on the quiet waters of The Bend, and at supper told each other what they had seen. And in the evening they together watched the twinkling lights of the clubhouse windows, and once they heard voices and laughter from somewhere on the river as though a boating party were making merry.

Two days later, Brian and Betty Jo were just finishing dinner when a step sounded on the porch, and a man appeared in the open doorway.

The stranger was dressed in the weird and flashy costume considered by his class to be the proper thing for an outing in the country, and his face betrayed the sad fact that, while he was mentally, spiritually, and physically greatly in need of a change from the unclean atmosphere that had made him what he was, he was incapable of benefiting by more wholesome conditions of living. He was, in fact, a perfect specimen of that type of clubman who, in order to enjoy fully the beautiful life of God's unspoiled world, must needs take with him all of the sordid and vicious life of that world wherein he is most at home.

With no word of greeting, he said, with that superior air which so many city folk assume when addressing those who live in the country: "Have you people any fresh vegetables or eggs to sell?"

Brian and Betty Jo arose, and Brian, stepping forward, said, with a smile: "No, we have nothing to sell here; but I think our neighbor, Mr. Warden, just over the hill, would be glad to supply you. Won't you come in?"

The man stared at Brian, turned an appraising eye on Betty Jo; then looked curiously about the room.

"I beg your pardon," he said, removing his cap, "I thought, when I spoke, that you were natives. My name is Green,—Harry Green. There is a party of us stopping at the clubhouse, up the river, there;— just out for a bit of a good time, you know. We are from St. Louis,—first time any of us were ever in the Ozarks,—friends of mine own the clubhouse."

"My name is Burns," returned Brian. "We noticed your boats on the river. You are enjoying your outing, are you?"

Again the man looked curiously from Brian to Betty Jo. "Oh, yes; we can stand it for awhile," he answered. "We're a pretty jolly bunch, you see;—

266

know how to keep things going. It would kill me if I had to live here in this lonesome hole very long, though. Don't you find it rather slow, Mrs. Burns?"

Poor Betty Jo's face turned fairly crimson. She could neither answer the stranger nor meet his gaze, but stood with downcast eyes;—then looked at Brian appealingly.

But Brian was as embarrassed as Betty Jo; while the stranger, as he regarded them, smiled with an expression of insolent understanding.

"I guess I have made another mistake," he said, with a meaning laugh.

"You have," returned Brian, sharply, stepping forward as he spoke; for the man's manner was unmistakable. "Be careful, sir, that you do not make another."

Mr. Green spoke quickly, with an airy wave of his hand: "No offense; no offense, I assure you." Then as he moved toward the door, he added, still with thinly veiled insolence: "I beg your pardon for intruding. I understand, perfectly. Good-afternoon, Mr. Burns! Good-afternoon, miss!"

Brian followed him out to the porch; and the caller, as he went down the steps, turned back with another understanding laugh: "I say, Burns, you are a lucky devil. Don't worry about me, old man. I envy you, by Jove! Charming little nest. Come over to the club some evening. Bring the little girl along, and help us to have a good time. So-long!"

Mr. Harry Green probably never knew how narrowly he escaped being manhandled by the enraged but helpless Brian.

Brian remained on the porch until he saw the man, in his boat, leave the eddy at the foot of the garden and row away up the river.

In the house, again, the two faced each other in dismay.

Betty Jo was first to recover: "I am sure that it is quite time for Auntie Sue to come home and take charge of her own household again. Don't you think so, Mr. Burns?"

And Brian Kent most heartily agreed.

CHAPTER XXI.

THE WOMAN AT THE WINDOW.

THE members of the clubhouse party were amusing themselves that afternoon in the various ways peculiar to their kind.

At one end of the wide veranda overlooking the river a group sat at a card table. At the other end of the roomy lounging place, men and women, lying at careless ease in steamer-chairs and hammocks, were smoking and chatting about such things as are of interest only to that strange class who are educated to make idleness the chief aim and end of their existence. On the broad steps leading down to the tree-shaded lawn, which sloped gently to the boat landing at the river's edge, still other members of the company were scattered in characteristic attitudes. Across the river, in the shade of the cottonwoods that overhang the bank, a man and a woman in a boat were ostensibly fishing. In a hammock strung between two trees, a little way from the veranda, lay a woman, reading.

Now and then a burst of shrill laughter broke the quiet of the surrounding forest. A man on the steps called a loud suggestive jest to the pair in the boat, and the woman waved her handkerchief in answer. The card-players argued and laughed over a point in their game. Some one shouted into the house for Jim, and a negro man in white jacket appeared. When the people on the veranda had expressed their individual tastes, the one who had summoned the servant called to the woman in the hammock under the tree, "What is yours, Martha?"

Without looking up from her book, the woman waved her hand, and answered, "I am not drinking this time. Thanks."

A chorus of derisive shouts and laughter came from the veranda. But the woman went on reading. "Oh, let her alone!" protested some one, good-naturedly. "She was going a little strong, last night. She'll be all right by and by, when she gets started again."

The negro, Jim, had returned with his loaded tray, and was passing among the members of the company with his assortment of glasses, when some one called attention to Harry Green, who was just pulling his boat up to the landing after his visit to the little log house down the river.

A boisterous chorus greeted the boatman: "Hello, Harry! Did you find anything? You're just in time. What'll you have?"

With a wave of greeting, the man fastened his boat to the landing, and started up the slope.

"He'll have a Scotch, of course!" said some one. "Did anybody ever know him to take anything else? Go and get it, Jim. He'll be nearly dead for a drink after rowing all that distance."

The woman in the hammock lowered her book, and lay watching the man as he came up the path toward the steps.

Harry Green, who, apparently, was a person of importance among them, seated himself in an easy chair on the veranda, and accepted the glass proffered by Jim.

"Did you find any eggs, Harry?" demanded one.

The man first refreshed himself with a long drink; then looked around with a grin of amused appreciation: "I didn't get any eggs," he said; "but I found the nest all right."

A shout of laughter greeted the reply.

"What sort of nest, Harry? Duck? Turkey? Hen? Dove? Or rooster?" came from different members of the chorus.

Raising his glass as though offering a toast, he answered: "Love! my children; love!"

A yell of delight came from the company, accompanied by a volley of: "A love-nest! Well, what do you know about that! Good boy, Harry! Takes Harry to find a love-nest! He's the boy to send for eggs! I should say, yes! Martha will like that! Oh, won't she!"

This last remark turned their attention toward the woman in the hammock, and they called to her: "Martha! Oh, Martha! Come here! You better look after Harry! Harry has found a love-nest! Told you something would happen if you let him go away alone!"

Putting aside her book, the woman came to join the company on the veranda.

She was rather a handsome woman, but with a suggestion of coarseness in form and features, though her face, in spite of its too-evident signs of dissipa tion, was not a bad face.

Seating herself on the top step, with her back

against the post in an attitude of careless abandonment, she looked up at the negro who stood grinning in the doorway. "Bring me a highball, Jim: you know my kind." Then to the company: "Somebody give me a cigarette."

Harry tossed a silver case in her lap. Another man, who sat near, leaned over her with a lighted match.

Expelling a generous cloud of smoke from her shapely lips, she demanded: "What is this you are all shouting about Harry having another love-nest?"

During the answering chorus of boisterous laughter and jesting remarks, she drank the liquor which the negro brought.

Then Harry, pointing out Auntie Sue's house, which was easily visible from where they sat, related his experience. And among the many conjectures, and questions, and comments offered, no one suggested even that the man and the woman living in that little log house by the river might be entirely innocent of the implied charge. For those who are themselves guilty, to assume the guilt of others is very natural and altogether human.

In the moment's quiet which followed the arrival

of a fresh supply of drinks, the woman called Martha said: "But what is the man like, Harry? You have enthused quite enough about the girl. Suppose you tell us about the man in the case."

Harry gave a very good description of Brian Kent.

"Oh, damn!" suddenly cried Martha, shaking her skirt vigorously. She had spilled some of the liquor from her glass.

A woman on the outer edge of the circle whispered to her nearest neighbor, and a hush fell over the group.

"Well," said Martha, drinking the liquor remaining in her glass, "why the devil don't we find out who they are, if we are so curious?"

"Find out! How? We'll find out a lot! What would you do,—ask them their names and where they are from?" came from the company.

"It is easy enough," retorted Martha. "There is that native girl that Molly picked up the day we landed here to help her in the kitchen. She must belong in this neighborhood somewhere. I'll bet she can tell us something. What is her name?"

"Judy,—Judy Taylor. Great idea! Good! Send her out here, Jim," responded the others.

THE RE-CREATION OF BRIAN KENT

When the deformed mountain girl appeared before them, she looked from face to face with such a frightened and excited expression on her sallow, old-young features, and such a wild light in her black beady eyes, that they regarded her with silent interest.

Judy spoke first, and her shrill monotone emphasized her excited state of mind: "That there nigger said as how Missus Kent was a-wantin' ter see me. Be ary one of youuns sure 'nough Missus Kent?"

The group drew apart a little, and every face was turned from Judy to the woman sitting on the top step of the veranda with her back against the post.

Judy went slowly toward the woman, her beady eyes fixed and staring as though at some ghostly vision. The woman rose to her feet as Judy paused before her.

"Be you-all Brian Kent's woman?" demanded Judy.

The excited exclamation from the company and the manner of the woman suddenly aroused the mountain girl to a realization of what she had done in speaking Brian Kent's name. With an expression of frightened dismay, she turned to escape; but the

275

group of intensely interested spectators drew closer. Every one waited for Martha to speak.

"Yes," she said, slowly, watching the mountain girl; "I am Mrs. Brian Kent. Do you know my husband?"

Judy's black beady eyes shifted slyly from one face to another, and her twisted body moved uneasily.

"No, ma'm; I ain't a-sayin' I knows him exactly. I done heard tell 'bout him nigh 'bout a year ago, when there was some men from the city come through here a-huntin' him. Everybody 'lows as how he was drowned at Elbow Rock."

"The body was never found, though," murmured one of the men in the group.

"Who lives in that little log house over there, Judy?" Harry Green asked suddenly, pointing.

"There? Oh, that there's Auntie Sue's place. I 'lowed everybody knowed that," returned the girl.

"Who is Auntie Sue?" came the next question.

One of the women answered, before Judy could speak: "Auntie Sue is that old-maid school-teacher they told us about. Don't you remember, Harry?"

'Is Auntie Sue at home now, girl?'' asked Mrs. Kent.

Judy's gaze was fixed on the ground as she replied: "I don't know, ma'm. I ain't got no truck with anybody on yon side the river."

"Is there any one living with Auntie Sue?" asked some one; and in the same breath from another came the question, "Who is Mr. Burns?"

Judy jerked her twisted shoulders and threw up her head with an impatient defiance, as she returned shrilly: "I'm a-tellin' youuns I don't know nothin' 'bout nobody. Hit ain't no sort er use for youuns ter pester me. I don't know nothin' 'bout hit, an' I wouldn't tell youuns nothin' if I did."

And with this, the mountain girl escaped into the house.

While her friends on the veranda were looking at each other in questioning silence, Mrs. Kent, without a word, turned and walked away into the woods.

As she disappeared among the trees, one of the men said, in a low tone: "You better go after her, Harry. She is on, all right, that it's Brian Kent. She never did believe that story about his death, you know. There is no knowing what she'll do when she gets to thinking it all over."

"It is a darned shame," exclaimed one of the women, "to have our party spoiled like this!"

"Spoiled nothing!" answered another. "Martha is too good a sport to spoil anything. Go on, Harry. Cheer her up. Bring her back here. We'll all help get her good and drunk to-night, and she'll be all right."

There was a laugh at this, and some one said: "A little something wouldn't hurt any of us just now, I'm thinking. Here, Jim!"

Harry Green found Mrs. Kent sitting on the river-bank some distance above the boat landing.

She looked up at the sound of his approach, but did not speak. Dropping down beside her, the man said: "I'm damned sorry about this, Martha. I never dreamed I was starting anything, or I would have kept my mouth shut."

"It is Brian, all right, Harry," she answered, slowly. "It is funny, but he has been on my mind all day. I never dreamed that it was this part of the country where he was supposed to have been drowned, or I wouldn't have come here."

"Well, what does it matter, anyway?" returned the man. "I don't see that it can make any difference. We don't need to go down there where he is, and it is damned certain that they won't call on us."

Looking out over the river, the woman spoke as if thinking aloud: "This is just the sort of place he would love, Harry—the river and hills and woods. He never cared for the city—always wanted to get away into the country somewhere. Tell me, what is she really like? Does she look like—like—well,—like any of our crowd?"

One by one, the man picked a number of pebbles from among the dead leaves and the short grass within reach of his hand, as he answered: "Oh, I was just kidding when I raved about her to the bunch." One by one, he flipped the bits of stone into the water. "She really doesn't amount to much. Honestly, I hardly noticed her."

The woman continued speaking as though thinking her thoughts aloud: "Brian was a good man, Harry. That bank affair was really my fault. He never would have done such a thing if I hadn't devilled him all the time for more money, and made such a fuss about his wasting so much time in his everlasting writing. I'd hate to have him caught and sent to the 'pen' now."

"You're a good sport, Martha," he returned heartily. "I know just how you feel about it. And I can promise you that there is not one of our crowd that will ever whisper a thing. They are not that kind, and you know how they all like you. Come, dear. Don't bother your head about it any more. I don't like to see you like this. Let us go up to the house, and show them how game you are,—shall we?"

He put his arm about her, but the woman gently pushed him away. "Don't do that, now, Harry. Let me think."

"That is just what you must not do," he retorted, with a laugh. "Thinking can't help matters. Come, let us go get a drink. That is what you need."

She looked at him some time before she answered; then, with a quick movement, she sprang to her feet: "All right! You're on!" she cried, with a reckless laugh. "But you'll go some if you keep up with me to-night."

And so, that evening, while Brian Kent and Betty Jo from the porch of the little log house by the river watched the twinkling lights of the clubhouse windows, the party with mad merriment tried to help a woman to forget.

But save for the unnatural brightness of her eyes and the heightened color in her face, drink seemed to have little effect on Martha Kent that night. When at a late hour the other members of the wild company, in various flushed and dishevelled stages of intoxication, finally retired to their rooms, Martha, in her apartment, seated herself at the window to look away over the calm waters of The Bend to a single light that showed against the dark mountainside. The woman did not know that the light she saw was in Brian Kent's room.

Long after Betty Jo had said good-night, Brian walked the floor in uneasy wakefulness. The meeting with the man Green and his too-evident thoughts as to the relations of the man and woman who were living together in the log house by the river filled Brian with alarm; while the very presence of the man from the city awoke old apprehensions that in his months of undisturbed quiet in Auntie Sue's backwoods home had almost ceased to be. Through Auntie Sue's teaching and influence; his work on his book; the growing companionship of Betty Jo and their love, Brian had almost ceased to think of that absconding bank clerk who had so recklessly launched himself on a voyage to the unknown in the darkness of that dreadful night. But, now, it all came back to him with menacing strength.

The man, Green, would talk to his companions of his visit to the log house that afternoon. He would tell what he had discovered. Curiosity would lead others of the clubhouse party to call. Some one might remember the story of the bank clerk, who was supposed to have lost his life in that neighborhood, but whose body was never found. There might even be one in the party who knew the former clerk. Through them the story would go back to the outside world. There would be investigations by those whose business it was never to forget a criminal who had escaped the law.

Brian felt his Re-Creation to be fully established; but what if his identity should be discovered before the restitution he would make should be also accomplished? And always, as he paced to and fro in his little room in the log house, there was, like a deep undercurrent in the flow of his troubled thought, his love for Betty Jo.

It is little wonder that, to Brian Kent, that night, the voices of the river were filled with fearful doubt and sullen, dreadful threatenings.

And what of the woman who watched the tiny spot of light that marked the window of the room where the re-created Brian Kent kept his lonely vigil? Did she, too, hear the voices of the river? Did she feel the presence of that stream which poured its dark flood so mysteriously through the night between herself and the man yonder?

Away back, somewhere in the past, the currents of their lives in the onward flow of the river had drawn together. For a period of time, their life-currents had mingled, and, with the stream, had swept onward as one. Other influences—swirls and eddies and counter-currents of other lives—had touched and intermingled until the current that was the man and the current that was the woman had drawn apart. For months, they had not touched; and, now, they were drawing nearer to each other again. Would they touch? Would they again mingle and become one? What was this mysterious, unseen, unknown, but always-felt, power of the river that sets the ways of its countless currents as it sweeps ever onward in its unceasing flow?

The door of her room opened. Harry Green entered as one assured of a welcome. The woman at the window turned her head, but did not move. Going to her, the man, with an endearing word, offered a caress; but she put him aside. "Please, Harry,— please let me be alone to-night?"

"Why, Martha, dear! What is wrong?" he protested, again attempting to draw her to him.

Resisting more vigorously, she answered: "Everything is wrong! You are wrong! I am wrong! All life is wrong! Can't you understand? Please leave me."

The man drew back, and spoke roughly in a tone of disgust: "Hell! I believe you love that bank clerk as much as you ever did!"

"Well, and suppose that were true, Harry?" she answered, wearily. "Suppose it were true,—that I did still love my husband? Could that make any difference now? Can anything ever make any difference now? You will tire of me before long, just as you have grown tired of the others who were before me. Don't you suppose I know? You and our friends have taught me many things, Harry. I know, now, that Brian's dreams were right. That his dreams could never be realized, does not make them foolish nor wrong. His dreams that seemed so foolish—such impossible ideals—were more real, after all, than this life that we think so real. *We* are the dreamers,—we and our kind,—and our awakening is as sure to come as that river out there is sure of reaching the sea."

The man laughed harshly: "You are quite poetical, to-night. I believe I like you better, though, when you talk sense."

"I am sorry, Harry," she returned. "Please don't be cross with me! Go now,—please go!"

And something forced the man to silence. Slowly, he left the room. The woman locked the door. Returning to the window, she fell on her knees, and stretched her hands imploringly toward the tiny spot of light that still shone against the dark shadow of the mountain-side.

Between the mighty walls of tree-clad hills that lifted their solemn crests into the midnight sky, the dark river poured the sombre strength of its innumerable currents,—terrible in its awful power; dreadful in its mysterious and unseen forces; irresistible in its ceaseless, onward rush to the sea of its final and infinite purpose!

And here and there on the restless, ever-moving surface of the shadowy, never-ending flood twinkled the reflection of a star.

CHAPTER XXII.

AT THE EMPIRE CONSOLIDATED SAVINGS BANK.

THE President of the Empire Consolidated Savings Bank looked up from the papers on his desk as his secretary entered from the adjoining room and stood before him.

"Well, George?"

The secretary smiled as he spoke: "Mr. Ward, there is an old lady out here who insists that you will see her. The boys passed her on to me, because, —well, she is not the kind of woman that can be refused. She has no card, but her name is Wakefield. She—"

The dignified President of the Empire Consolidated Savings Bank electrified his secretary by springing from his chair like a schoolboy from his seat at the tap of the teacher's dismissing bell. "Auntie Sue! I should say she couldn't be refused! Where is she?" And before the secretary could collect his startled thoughts to answer, Homer T. Ward was out of the room.

When the smiling secretary, the stenographers, and other attending employees had witnessed a meeting between their dignified chief and the lovely old lady, which strengthened their conviction that the great financier was genuinely human, President Ward and Auntie Sue disappeared into the private office.

"George," said Mr. Ward, as he closed the door of that sacred inner sanctuary of the Empire Consolidated Savings Bank, "remember I am not in to any one;—from the Secretary of the Treasury to the Sheriff, I am not in."

"I understand, sir," returned the still smiling George. And from that moment until Homer T. Ward should open the door, nothing short of a regiment could have interrupted the interview between Auntie Sue and her old pupil.

Placing the dear old lady tenderly in a deep, leather-upholstered chair, Mr. Ward stood before her as though trying to convince himself that she was real; while his teacher of those long-ago, boyhood days gazed smilingly up at him.

"What in the name of all that is unexpected are you doing here, Auntie Sue?" he demanded; "and why is not Betty Jo with you? Isn't the girl ever coming home? There is nothing the matter with her, is there? Of course not, or you would have wired me."

It was not at all like the bank president to ask so many questions all at once.

Auntie Sue looked around the private office curiously, then smilingly back to the face of the financier.

"Do you know, Homer," she said with her chuckling little laugh, "I—I—am almost afraid of you in here. Everything is so grand and rich-looking; and there were so many men out there who tried to tell me you would not see me. I—I am glad I didn't know it would be like this, or I fear I never could have found the courage to come."

Homer T. Ward laughed, and then—rather full-waisted as he was—went down on one knee at the arm of her chair so as to bring his face level with her eyes.

"Look at me, Auntie Sue," he said; "look straight through me, just as you used to do years and years ago, and tell me what you see."

And the dear old lady, with one thin soft hand on his heavy shoulder, answered, as she looked:

"Why, I see a rather naughty boy, whom I ought to spank for throwing spitballs at the old schoolroom ceiling," she retorted. "And I am not a bit afraid to do it either. So sit right over there, sir, and listen to me."

They laughed together then; and if Auntie Sue wiped her eyes as the schoolboy obediently took his seat in the big chair at the banker's desk, Homer T. Ward's eyes were not without a suspicious moisture.

"Tell me about Betty Jo first," the man insisted. "You know, Auntie Sue, the girl grows dearer to me every year."

"Betty Jo is that kind of a girl, Homer," Auntie Sue answered.

"I suppose it is because she is all I have to love," he said, "but, you know, ever since Sister Grace died and left the fatherless little kid to me, it seems like all my plans have centered around her; and now that she has finished her school; has travelled abroad, and gone through with that business-college course, I am beginning to feel like we should sort of settle down together. I am glad for her to be with you this summer, though, for the finishing touches; and when she comes home to stay, you are coming with her."

Auntie Sue shook her head, smiling: "Now, Homer, you know that is settled: I will never leave my little log house by the river until I have watched the last sunset. You know, my dear boy, that I would be miserable in the city."

It was an old point often argued by them, and the man dismissed it, now, with a brief: "We'll see about that when the time comes. But, why didn't you bring Betty Jo with you?"

"Because," Auntie Sue answered, "I came away hurriedly, on a very important trip, for only a day, and it is necessary for her to stay and keep house while I am gone. The child must learn to cook, Homer, even if she is to inherit all your money."

"I know," answered the banker;—"the same as you make me work when I visit you. But your coming to me sounds rather serious, Auntie Sue. What is your trouble?"

The dear old lady laughed, nervously; for, to tell the truth, she did not quite know how she was going to manage to present Brian Kent's case to Homer T. Ward without presenting more than she was at this time ready to reveal.

"Why, you see, Homer," she began, "it is not

really my trouble as much as it is yours, and it is not yours as much as it is—"

"Betty Jo's?" he asked quickly, when she hesitated.

"No! no!" she cried. "The child doesn't even know why I am here. Just try to forget her for a few minutes, Homer."

"All right," he said; "but you had me worried for a minute."

Auntie Sue might have answered that she was somewhat worried herself; but, instead, she plunged with desperate courage: "I came to see you about Brian Kent, Homer."

It is not enough to say that the President of the Empire Consolidated Savings Bank was astonished. "Brian Kent?" he said at last. "Why, Auntie Sue, I wrote you nearly a year ago that Brian Kent was dead."

"Yes, I know; but he was not—that is, he is not. But the Brian Kent your detectives were hunting was—I mean—is."

Homer T. Ward looked at his old teacher as though he feared she had suddenly lost her mind.

"It is like this, Homer," Auntie Sue explained: "A

few days after your detective, Mr. Ross, called on me, this stranger appeared in the neighborhood. No one dreamed that he was Brian Kent, because, you see, he was not a bit like the description."

"Full beard, I suppose?" commented the banker, grimly.

"Yes: and every other way," continued Auntie Sue. "And he has been working so hard all winter; and everybody in the country respects and loves him so; and he is one of the best and truest men I ever knew; and he is planning and working to pay back every cent he took; and I cannot—I will not—let you send him to prison now."

The lovely old eyes were fixed on the banker's face with sweet anxiety.

Homer T. Ward was puzzled. Strange human problems are often presented to men in his position; but, certainly, this was the strangest;—his old teacher pleading for his absconding clerk who was supposed to be dead.

At last he said, with gentle kindness: "But, why did you come to tell me about him, Auntie Sue? He is safe enough if no one knows who he is."

"That is it!" she cried. "Some one found out

about him, and is coming here to tell you, for the reward."

The banker whistled softly. "And you—you—grabbed a train, and beat 'em to it!" he exclaimed. "Well, if that doesn't—"

Auntie Sue clasped her thin hands to her breast, and her sweet voice trembled with anxious fear: "You won't send that poor boy to prison, now, will you, Homer? It—it—would kill me if such a terrible thing were to happen now. Won't you let him go free, so that he can do his work,—won't you, Homer? I—I—" The strain of her anxiety was almost too much for the dear old gentlewoman's physical strength, and as her voice failed, the tears streamed down the soft cheeks unheeded.

In an instant the bank president was again on his knees beside her chair.

"Don't, Auntie Sue: don't, dear! Why, you know I would do anything in the world you asked, even if I wanted to send the fellow up; but I don't. I wouldn't touch him for the world. It is a thousand times better to let him go if he is proving himself an honest man. Please, dear, don't feel so. Why, I will be glad to let him off. I'll help him, Auntie

Sue. I—I—am as glad as you are that we didn't
get him. Please don't feel so about it. There, there,
—it is all right, now."

So he comforted and reassured her until she was
able to smile through her tears. "I knew I could
depend on you, Homer."

A few minutes later, she said: "And what about
that man who is coming to claim the reward,
Homer?"

"Never you mind him!" cried the banker; "I'll
fix that. But, tell me, Auntie Sue, where is young
Kent now?"

"He is working in the neighborhood," she returned.

He looked at her shrewdly. "You have seen a lot
of him, have you?"

"I have seen him occasionally," she answered.

Homer T. Ward nodded his head, as if well pleased
with himself. "You don't need to tell me any more.
I understand, now, exactly. It is very clear what has
reformed Brian Kent; you have been up to your old
tricks. It is a wonder you haven't taken him into
your house to live with you,—to save him from associating with bad people."

295

He laughed, and when Auntie Sue only smiled, as though humoring him in his little joke, he added: "By the way, has Betty Jo seen this latest patient of yours? What does she think of his chances for complete recovery?"

"Yes," Auntie Sue returned, calmly; "Betty Jo has seen him. But, really, Homer, I have never asked her what she thought of him."

"Do you know, Auntie Sue," said the banker, reflectively, "I never did believe that Brian Kent was a criminal at heart."

"I know he is not," she returned stoutly. "But, tell me, Homer, how did it ever happen?"

"Well, you see," he answered, "young Kent had a wife who couldn't somehow seem to fit into his life. Ross never went into the details with me, fully, because that, of course, had no real bearing on the fact that he stole the money from the bank. But it seems that the youngster was rather ambitious,— studied a lot outside of business hours and that sort of thing. I know he made his own way through business college before he came to us. The wife didn't receive the attention she thought she should have, I suppose. Perhaps she was right at that. Anyway, she wanted a good time;—wanted him to take her out more, instead of spending his spare time digging away at his books. And so it went the usual way,— she found other company. Rather a gay set, I fancy; at least it led to her needing more money than he was earning, and so he helped out his salary, thinking to pay it back before he was caught, I suppose. Then the crash came,—some other man, you know,— and Brian skipped, which, of course, put us next to his stealing. I don't know what has become of the woman. The last Ross knew of her she was living in St. Louis, and running with a pretty wild bunch, —glad to get rid of Brian, I expect. She couldn't have really cared so very much for him.

"Do you know, Auntie Sue, I have seen so many cases like this one. I have been glad, many times, that I never married. And then, again, sometimes, I have seen homes that have made me sorry I never took the chance. I am glad you saved the boy, Auntie Sue: I am mighty glad."

"You have made me very happy, Homer," Auntie Sue returned. "But are you sure you can fix it

about that reward? The man who is coming to claim
it will make trouble, won't he, if he is not paid,
somehow?"

"Yes, I expect he would," returned the president,
thoughtfully. "And my directors might have something to say. And there are the Burns people and
the Bankers' Association and all. Hum-m-m!"

Homer T. Ward considered the matter a few moments, then he laughed. "I'll tell you what we will
do, Auntie Sue; we will let Brian Kent pay the reward himself. That would be fair, wouldn't it?"

Auntie Sue was sure that Brian would agree that
it was a fair enough arrangement; but she did not
see how it was to be managed.

Then her old pupil explained that he would pay the
reward-money to the man who was coming to claim
it, and thus satisfy him, and that the bank would
hold the amount as a part of the debt which Brian
was expected to pay.

Auntie Sue never knew that President Ward himself paid to the bank the full amount of the money
stolen by Brian Kent in addition to the reward-
money which he personally paid to Jap Taylor, in
order to quiet him, and thus saved Brian from the

publicity that surely would have followed any other course.

It should also be said here that Judy's father never again appeared in the Ozarks; at least, not in the Elbow Rock neighborhood. It might be that Jap Taylor was shrewd enough to know that his reputation would not permit him to show any considerable sum of money, where he was known, without starting an investigation; and for men of his type investigations are never to be desired.

Or it is not unlikely that the combination of money and the city proved the undoing of the moonshiner, and that he came to his legitimate and logical end among the dives and haunts of his kind, to which he would surely gravitate.

CHAPTER XXIII.

IN THE ELBOW ROCK RAPIDS.

HE day following that night of Brian Kent's uneasy wakefulness was a hard day for the man and the woman in the little log house by the river.

For Brian, the morning dawned with a sense of impending disaster. He left his room while the sky was still gray behind the eastern mountains, and the mist that veiled the brightness of the hills seemed to hide in its ghostly depths legions of shadowy spirits that from his past had assembled to haunt him. The sombre aisles and caverns of the dimly lighted forest were peopled with shadowy memories of that life which he had hoped would never again for him awake. And the river swept through its gray world to the crashing turmoil at Elbow Rock like a thing doomed to seek forever in its own irresistible might the destruction of its ever-living self.

As one moving in a world of dreams, he went about his morning's work. "Old Prince" whinnied his usual greeting, but received no answer. "Bess" met him at the barnyard gate, but he did not speak. The sun leaped above the mountain-tops, and the world was filled with the beauty of its golden glory. From tree and bush and swaying weed, from forest and pasture, and garden and willow-fringed river-bank, the birds voiced their happy greetings to the new day. But the man neither saw nor heard.

When he went to the house with his full milk-pail, and Betty Jo met him at the kitchen-door with her cheery "Good-morning!" he tried resolutely to free himself from the mood which possessed him, but only partially succeeded. Several times, as the two faced each other across the breakfast table, Brian saw the gray eyes filled with questioning anxiety, as though Betty Jo, also, felt the presence of some forbidding spectre at the meal.

After several vain attempts to find something they could talk about, Betty Jo boldly acknowledged the situation by saying: "What in the world is the matter with us, this morning, Mr. Burns? I am possessed with the feeling that there is some one or something behind me. I want to look over my shoulder every minute."

At her words, Brian involuntarily turned his head for a quick backward glance.

"There!" cried Betty Jo, with a nervous laugh, not at all like her normal, well-poised self. "You feel it, too!"

Brian forced a laugh in return: "It is the weather, I guess." He tried to speak with casual ease. "The atmosphere is full of electricity this morning. We'll have a thunder-storm before night, probably."

"And was it the electricity in the air that kept you tramping up and down your room last night until almost morning?" she demanded abruptly, with her characteristic opposition to any evasion of the question at issue.

Brian retorted with a smile: "And how do you know that I tramped up and down my room last night?"

The color in Betty Jo's cheeks deepened as she answered, "I did not sleep very well either."

"But, I surely did not make noise enough for you to hear in your room?" persisted Brian.

The color deepened still more in Betty Jo's cheeks, as she answered honestly: "I was not in my room when I heard you." She paused, and when he only looked at her expectantly, but did not speak, continued, in a hesitating manner quite unlike her matter-of-fact self: "When I could not sleep, and felt so as though there were somebody or something in the house that had no business here, I became afraid, and opened my door so I would not feel so much alone; and then I saw the light under the door of your room, and,—" she hesitated, but finished with a little air of defiance,—"and I went and listened outside your door to see if you were up."

"Yes?" said Brian Kent, gently.

"And when I heard you walking up and down, I wanted to call to you; but I thought I better not. It made me feel better, though, just to know that you were there; and so, pretty soon, I went back to my room again."

"And then?" said Brian.

"And then," confessed Betty Jo, "whatever it was that was keeping me awake came back, and went on keeping me awake until I was simply forced to go to you for help again."

Poor Betty Jo! She knew very well that she

ought not to be saying those things to the man who, while he listened, could not hide the love that shone in his eyes.

And Brian Kent, as he thought of this woman, whom he loved with all the strength of his best self, creeping to the door of his room for comfort in the lonely night, scarcely dared trust himself to speak. At last, when their silence was becoming unbearable, he said, gently: "You poor child! Why didn't you call to me?"

And Betty Jo, hearing in his voice that which told her how near he was to the surrender that would bring disaster to them both, was aroused to the defense. The gray eyes never wavered as she answered, bravely: "I was afraid of that, too."

And so Betty Jo confessed her love that answered so to his need; but, in her very confession, saved their love from themselves. If she had lowered her eyes—

Brian Kent, in reverent acknowledgment, bowed his head before her. Then, rising, he walked to the window, where he stood for some time looking out, but seeing nothing.

"It was that horrid man coming yesterday that has

so upset us," said Betty Jo, at last. "We were getting on so beautifully, too. I wish he had gone somewhere else for his vegetables and eggs and things!"

Brian was able to smile at this as he turned to face her again, and they both knew that,—for that time, at least,—the danger-point was safely past.

"I wish so, too," he agreed; "but never mind; Auntie Sue will be home in a day or two, and then everything will be all right again."

But when he had taken his hat and was starting out for the day's work, Betty Jo asked, "What are you doing to-day?"

"I was going to work on the fence around the clearing," he answered. "Why?"

"I—I—wish you could find something to do nearer the house," came the slow answer. "Couldn't you work in the garden, perhaps?"

"I should say I could!" he returned heartily.

All that forenoon, as Betty Jo went about her household duties she felt the presence of the thing that filled her so with fear and dread. With vigorous determination she scolded herself for being so foolish, and argued with herself that it was all a nervous fancy born of her restless night. But, the next moment, she would start with a sudden fear and turn quickly as if to face some one whose presence she felt behind her. And Brian, too, as he worked in the garden, caught himself often in the act of pausing to look about with nervous apprehension.

During the noonday meal they made a determined effort to laugh at themselves, and by the time dinner was over had almost succeeded. But when Brian, as he pushed back his chair, said, jestingly, "Well, am I to work in the garden again this afternoon?" Betty Jo answered, emphatically, "Indeed you are! I will not stay another minute in this house alone. Goodness knows what I will do to-night!"

There was no jest in the man's voice as he answered: "I'll tell you what you will do to-night,— you will go to bed and you will go to sleep. You will leave the door to your room wide-open, and I shall lie right there on that couch, so near that a whisper from you will reach me. We will have no more of this midnight prowling, I promise you. If any ghost dares appear, we—"

The reassuring words died on Brian Kent's lips.

His eyes, looking over Betty Jo's shoulders, were fixed and staring, and the look on his face sent a chill of horror to the girl's heart. She dared not move nor look around as he sat like a man turned to stone.

A woman's laugh broke the dead silence.

With a scream, Betty Jo sprung to her feet and whirled about.

As one in a trance, Brian Kent arose and stood beside her.

The woman, who stood in the open doorway, laughed again.

Martha Kent's heavy drinking the night before, when her clubhouse friends in a wild debauch had tried to help her to forget, was the climax of many months of like excesses. The mood in which she had sent the man Green from her room was the last despairing flicker of her better instincts. Moved by her memories of better things,—of a better love and dreams and ideals,—she had spent a little hour or two in sentimental regret for that which she had so recklessly cast aside. And then, because there was within her no foundation of abiding principle for her sentiment, she had again put on the character which had so separated her from the life of the man to whom she was married, indeed, but with whom she was never one. With the burning consciousness of what she might have been and of what she was ever tormenting her, she sank, as the hours passed, deeper and deeper into the quicksands of physical indulgence until, in her mad determination to destroy utterly her ability to feel remorse, she lost all mental control of herself, and responded to every insane whim of her drink-disordered brain.

As she stood there, now, in the doorway of that little log house by the river,—face to face with the man and the woman who, though they were united in their love, were yet separated by the very fact of her existence,—she was, in all her hideous, but pitiful, repulsiveness, the legitimate creation of those life-forces which she so fitly personified.

Betty Jo instinctively drew closer to Brian's side.

"Hello, Brian, dear!" said the woman, with a drunken leer. "Thought I'd call to see you in your charming love-nest that Harry Green raved so about. Can't you introduce me to your little sweetheart?"

"No?" she continued, and laughed again. Then coming an unsteady step toward them, she added, thickly: "Very well, Brian, old sport; you won't introduce me,—I'll have to introduce myself." She grinned with malicious triumph at Betty Jo: "Don't be frightened, my dear. It's all right. I'm nobody of importance,—just his wife,—that's all,—just his wife."

Betty Jo, with a little cry, turned to the man who stood as if stricken dumb with horror. "Brian?" she said. "Oh, Brian?"

It was the first time she had ever addressed him by his given name, and Brian Kent, as he looked, saw in those gray eyes no hint of doubt or censure, but only the truest love and sympathy. Betty Jo had not failed in the moment of her supreme testing.

"It's true, all right, isn't it, Brian?" said Martha Kent. "I'm his wife fast enough, my dear. But you don't need to worry,—you two. I'm a good sport,—I am. I've had my fun. No kick coming from me. Just called to pay my respects,—that's all. So-long, Brian, old sport! Good-bye, my dear!"

With an uncertain wave of her hand, she staggered through the doorway and passed from their sight.

In the little log house by the river the two who had kept the fineness of their love stood face to face.

For Betty Jo, the barrier which Brian Kent had maintained between them to protect her from his love was no longer a thing unknown. But the revelation, coming as it did, had brought no shadow of distrust or doubt of the man to whom she had so fully entrusted herself. It had, indeed, only strengthened her faith in him and deepened her love.

For one glorious triumphal moment the very soul of the man exulted in the truth which Betty Jo made known to him. Then he turned slowly away, for he dared not trust himself to look at her a moment longer.

With bowed head he paced up and down the room. He went to the table which held Auntie Sue's sewing-basket, and fingered the trifles there. Then, slowly, he passed through the open door to the porch, where Betty Jo, through the window, near which she stood, saw him look away over the river and the mountains.

310

Suddenly, she saw him start, and stare intently at some nearer object that had caught his attention. As Betty Jo watched, he moved to the edge of the porch, and, stooping, grasped the railing with his hands;— his head and shoulders were thrust forward; his lips were parted; his whole attitude was that of the most intense and excited interest. Then, straightening up, he threw back his head, and laughed aloud. But his laughter alarmed the girl, who ran to the door, crying, "What is it, Brian?"

"Look!" he shouted, madly, and pointed toward the river. "Look, Betty Jo!"

Martha Kent, alone in one of the clubhouse boats, was rowing with drunken clumsiness toward the head of the Elbow Rock rapids.

The woman's friends had missed her, and, guessing, from some remark she had made, where she had gone, had sent four men of the party after her; for they realized that she was in no condition to be alone in a boat on the river, particularly on that part of the stream near Auntie Sue's place. After leaving Brian and Betty Jo, she had gone back to her boat in the eddy at the foot of the garden, and was pulling out into the stream when she saw her friends approaching. With a drunken laugh, she waved her hand, and began rowing from them directly toward the swift water. The men shouted for her to stop, and pulled with all their strength. But the woman, taking their calls as a challenge, rowed the harder, while every awkward pull of the oars carried her nearer the deadly grip of the current.

Betty Jo, as she reached Brian's side, and saw what was happening on the river, grasped the man's arm appealingly, with a cry: "Brian! Brian! She is going into the rapids! She will be carried down to Elbow Rock!"

But Brian Kent, for the moment, was beside himself. All that he had suffered,—all that the woman out there on the river had cost him in anguish of soul,—all that she had taken from him of happiness, —came before him with blinding vividness; and now,—now,—in her drunkenness, she was making her own way to her own destruction.

"Of course she is!" he shouted, in answer to Betty Jo. "Her friends yonder are driving her to it! Could anything be more fitting?"

As though grasped by powerful unseen hands beneath the surface, the boat shot forward. The woman, feeling the sudden pull of the current, stopped rowing, and looked about as if wondering what had happened. Her friends, not daring to follow closer to the dangerous water, were pulling madly for the landing at the foot of the garden. The boat in the middle of the river moved faster.

"Look, Betty Jo, look!" shouted the man on the porch, madly. "It's got her now—the river has got her—look!"

With a scream of fear, the woman in the boat dropped her oars, and grasped the gunwale of the little craft.

Brian Kent laughed.

Betty Jo shrank back from him, her eyes, big with horror, fixed upon his face. Then, with a quick movement, she sprang toward him again, and, catching his arm, shook him with all her strength and struck him again and again with her fist.

"Brian! Brian!" she cried. "You are insane!"

The man looked down at her for an instant with an expression of bewildered astonishment on his face, as one awakened from a dream. He raised his hand and drew it across his forehead and eyes.

The boat with the helpless woman was already past the front of the house.

Betty Jo cried again as if calling the man she loved from a distance: "Brian! Brian!"

With a sudden movement, the man jerked away from her. The next instant, he had leaped over the railing of the porch to the ground below and was running with all his might toward the river, at an angle which would put him opposite or a little below the boat when he reached the bank.

With a sob, Betty Jo followed as fast as she could.

As Brian Kent raced toward the river's edge, the powerful current drew the boat with the woman into the first rough water of the rapids, and, as the skiff was shaken and tossed by the force that was sweeping it with ever-increasing speed toward the wild turmoil at Elbow Rock, the woman screamed again and again for help.

The warring forces of the stream whirled the little craft about, and she saw the man who was nearing the bank. She rose to her feet in the rocking boat, and stretched out her arms,—calling his name, "Brian! Brian! Brian!" Then the impact of the boat against a larger wave of the rapids brought her

314

to her knees, and she clung to the thwarts with piteous cries.

Betty Jo and the clubhouse men, who had overtaken her, saw Brian as he reached the river opposite the boat. For a little way he raced the tumbling waters until he had gained a short distance ahead of the skiff; then they saw him, without an instant's pause, leap from the high bank far out into the boiling stream.

Running along the bank, the helpless watchers saw the man fighting his way toward the boat. One moment, he disappeared from sight, dragged beneath the surface by the powerful currents with which he wrestled. The next instant, the boiling waters would toss him high on the crest of a rolling wave, only to drag him down again a second later. But, always, he drew nearer and nearer the object of his struggle, while the rapids swept both the helpless woman and the tossing boat and the swimming man onward toward the towering cliff, and the thunder-roar of the mad waters below grew louder and louder.

The splendid strength of arms and shoulders which Brian Kent had acquired by his months of work with his ax on the timbered mountain-side sustained him now in his need. With tremendous energy, he breasted the might of the furious river. To the watchers it seemed at times that it was beyond the power of human muscles to endure the terrific strain. Then he gained the boat, and they saw him striving with desperate energy to drag it toward the opposite shore and so into the currents that would carry it past the menacing point of the cliff and perhaps to the safety of the quiet water below.

All that human strength could do in that terrible situation, Brian Kent did. But the task was beyond the power of mortal man.

For an instant the breathless watchers on the bank thought there was a chance; but the waters with mad fury dragged their victims back, and, with terrific power, hurled them forward toward the frowning rocks.

It was quickly over.

In that wild turmoil of the boiling, leaping, seething, lashing, hammering waves, the boat, with the woman who crouched on her knees on the bottom, and the man who clung to the side of the craft, appeared for a second lifted high in the air. The next instant, the crash of breaking wood sounded above the thundering roaring of the waters. The man and the woman disappeared. The wreck of the boat was flung again and again against the cliff, until, battered and broken, it was swept away around the point.

Against the dark wall of rock Brian Kent's head and shoulders appeared for an instant, and they saw that he held the woman in his arms. The furious waters closed over them. For the fraction of a second, the man's hand and arm appeared again above the surface, and was gone.

Betty Jo sank to the ground with a low cry of anguish, and hid her face.

Another moment, and she was aroused by a loud shout from one of the men who had caught a glimpse of the river's victims farther out at the point of the rocky cliff.

Springing to her feet, Betty Jo started madly up the trail that leads over the bluff. The men followed.

Immediately below Elbow Rock there is a deep hole formed by the waters that pour around the point of the cliff, and below this hole a wide gravelly bar pushing out from the Elbow Rock side of the stream forces the main volume of the river to the opposite bank. In the shallow water against the upper side of the bar they found them.

With the last flicker of his consciousness, Brian Kent had felt his feet touch the bottom where the water shoals against the bar, and, with his last remaining strength, had dragged himself and the body of the woman into the shallows.

Betty Jo was no hysterical weakling to spend the priceless seconds of such a time in senseless ravings. The first-aid training which she had received at school gave her the necessary knowledge which her native strength of character and practical common sense enabled her to apply. Under her direction, the men from the clubhouse worked as they probably never had worked before in all their useless lives.

But the man and the woman whose life-currents had touched and mingled,—drawn apart to flow apparently far from each other, but drawn together again to once more touch, and, as one, to endure the testing of the rapids,—the man and the woman had not brought to the terrible ordeal the same strength.

One was drawn into the Elbow Rock rapids by the careless indifference and the reckless spirit that was born of the life she had chosen; by her immediate

318

associates and environment; and by the circumstances that were, at the last analysis, of her own making.

The other braved the same dangers, strong in the splendid spirit that had set him against such terrible odds to attempt the woman's rescue. From his work on the timbered mountain-side, from his life in the clean atmosphere of the hills, and from the spiritual and mental companionship of that little log house by the river, he had brought to his testing the splendid strength which enabled him to endure.

Somewhere in that terrible conflict with the wild waters at Elbow Rock, while the man whose life she had so nearly ruined by her wantonness was fighting to save her, the soul of Martha Kent went from the bruised and battered body which Brian drew at last from the vicious grasp of the currents.

But the man lived.

CHAPTER XXIV.

JUDY'S RETURN.

IN the early evening twilight of the day following the tragedy at Elbow Rock, Betty Jo was sitting on the porch, to rest for a few minutes in the fresh air, after long hours of watching beside Brian's bed.

A neighbor woman had come to help, but Betty Jo would not leave the side of the man she loved as he fought his way slowly out of the dark shadow of the death that had so nearly conquered him. Nor, indeed, would Brian let her go, for even in those moments when he appeared most unconscious of the life about him, he seemed to feel her presence. All through the long, long hours of that anxious night and day she had watched and waited the final issue; —feeling the dark messenger very close at times, but gaining hope as the hours passed and her lover won his way nearer and nearer to the light;—courageous always;—giving him the best of her strength, so

320

far as it was possible to give him anything;—making him feel the steady, enduring fullness of her love.

At last, they felt that the victory was won. The doctor, satisfied that the crisis was safely past, went his way to visit other patients. By evening, Brian was resting so easily that the girl had stolen away for a few minutes, leaving the neighbor to call her if he should waken.

Betty Jo had been on the porch but a short time when a step sounded on the gravel walk that led from the porch steps around the corner of the house. A moment more, and Judy appeared.

The mountain girl stopped when she saw Betty Jo, and the latter went to the top of the steps.

"Good-evening, Judy!" said Betty Jo, quietly. "Won't you come in?"

Slowly, with her black beady eyes fixed on Betty Jo's face, Judy went up the steps.

As the mountain girl reached the level of the porch-floor, Betty Jo drew a little back toward the door.

Judy stopped instantly, and stood still. Then, in a low tone, she said: "You-all ain't got no call ter be afeared, Miss Betty Jo. You hain't never goin' ter have no call ter be scared of me again, never."

"I am so glad for you to say that, Judy," returned Betty Jo, smiling. "I don't want to be afraid of you, and I am not really; but—"

"Ain't you-all plumb a-hatin' me for what I done?" asked Judy, wonderingly.

"No, no; Judy, dear, I don't hate you at all, and you must know that Auntie Sue loves you."

"Yes," Judy nodded her head, thoughtfully. "Auntie Sue just naturally loves everybody. Hit wouldn't be no more'n nature, though, for you-all ter hate me. I sure have been poison-mean."

"But that is all past now, Judy," said Betty Jo, heartily. "Come and sit down?" She started toward the chairs.

But the mountain girl did not move, except to shake her head in refusal of the hospitable invitation.

"I ain't a-goin' ter put my foot inside this house, nor set with you-all, nor nothin' 'til I've said what I done come ter say."

Betty Jo turned back to her again: "What is it, Judy?"

"Auntie Sue done told me not ter let you-all er Mr. Burns see me 'til she come back. But I can't help hit, an' if I don't talk 'bout that none, I reckon she ain't a-goin' ter mind so much. You-all don't know that I seed Auntie Sue that night 'fore she went away, an' that hit was me took her ter the station with 'Old Prince,' an' brung him back, did you ?"

"No," said Betty Jo, "I did not know; and if Auntie Sue told you not to tell us about it, I would rather you did not, Judy."

"I ain't aimin' ter," Judy returned; "but Auntie Sue don't know nothin' 'bout what's happened since she went away, an' hit's that what's a-makin' me come ter you-all."

Betty Jo, seeing that the poor girl was laboring under some intense emotional stress, said, gently: "What is it that you wish to tell me, Judy? I am sure Auntie Sue will not mind, if you feel so about it."

The mountain girl's eyes filled and the tears streamed down her sallow cheeks, while her twisted shoulders shook with the grief she could not suppress, as she faltered: "My God-A'mighty! Miss

Betty Jo, I—I—didn't aim ter do hit! I sure didn't!
'Fore God, I'd er let 'em kill me first, if I'd only
had time ter think. But hit—hit—was me what told
that there woman how Mr. Burns was Brian Kent.
Hit's—hit's—me what's ter blame for gittin' her
killed in the river an' him so nigh drowned. O
God! O God! If he'll only git well!

"An' I ain't a-feelin' toward you-all like I did,
Miss Betty Jo. I can't no more. I done left them
clubhouse folks, after I knowed what has happened,
an' all day I been hangin' 'round here in the bresh.
An' Lucy Warden she done told me, this afternoon,
'bout how you-all was takin' care of Mr. Burns, an'
how you just naturally wouldn't let him die. An'—
an'—I kin see, now, what hit is that makes Auntie
Sue and him an' you-all so different from that there
clubhouse gang an' pap an' me. An' I ain't a-wantin'
ter be like I been, no more, ever. I'd a heap rather
jump inter the river an' drown myself. 'Fore God,
I would! An' I want ter come back an' help you-all
take care of him; an' live with Auntie Sue; an'—an'
—be a little might like youuns, if I kin. Will you
let me, Miss Betty Jo? Will you? I most know
Auntie Sue would, if she was here."

Before the mountain girl had finished speaking, Betty Jo's arm was around the poor twisted shoulders, and Betty Jo's eyes were answering Judy's pleading.

And so, when Auntie Sue came home, it was Judy who met her at the station, with "Old Prince" and the buggy; and as they drove down the winding road to the little log house by the river, the mountain girl told the old gentlewoman all that had happened in her absence.

CHAPTER XXV.

THE RIVER.

RIAN KENT recovered quickly from the effects of his experience in the Elbow Rock rapids, and was soon able again to take up his work on the little farm. Every day he labored in the garden, or in the clearing, or at some task which did not rightly fall to those who rented the major part of Auntie Sue's tillable acreage.

Auntie Sue had told him about her visit to the President of the Empire Consolidated Savings Bank, and of the arrangement made by the banker—as she understood it—for Brian's protection. But while the dear old lady explained that Homer T. Ward was one of her pupils, she did not reveal the relation between Brian's former chief and Betty Jo. Neither Auntie Sue nor Betty Jo, for several very good reasons, was ready for Brian to know the whole truth about his stenographer. It was quite enough, they reasoned, for him to love his stenographer, and for

326

his stenographer to love him, without raising any more obstacles in the pathway of their happiness.

As the busy weeks passed, several letters came from the publishers of Brian's book,—letters which made the three in the little log house by the river very happy. Already, in the first reception of this new writer's work, those who had undertaken to present it to the public saw many promises of the fulfillment of their prophecies as to its success. When the third letter came, a statement of the sales to date was enclosed, and, that afternoon, Betty Jo went to Brian where he was at work in the clearing.

When they were comfortably, not to say cozily, seated on a log in the shade at the edge of the forest, she announced that she had come for a very serious talk.

"Yes?" he returned; but he really looked altogether too happy to be exceedingly serious.

"Yes," she continued, "I have. As your accredited business agent and—" she favored him with a Betty Jo smile—"shall I say manager?"

"Why not managing owner?" he retorted.

"I am glad you confirm my promotion so readily,"

she returned, with a charming touch of color in her cheeks, "because that, you see, helps me to present what I have to say for the good of the firm."

"I am listening, Betty Jo."

"Very well; tell me, first, Brian, just exactly how much do you owe that bank, reward-money and all, and Auntie Sue, interest and everything?"

Brian went to his coat, which lay on a near-by stump, and returned with a small pocket account-book.

"I have it all here," he said, as he seated himself close beside her again. And, opening the book, he showed her how he had kept a careful record of the various sums he had taken from the bank, with the dates.

"Oh, Brian, Brian!" she said with a little cry of delight, "I am so glad,—so glad you have this! It is exactly what I want for my wedding present. It was so thoughtful of you to fix it for me."

Thus by a characteristic, Betty Jo turn she made the little book of painful memories a book of joyous promise.

When they again returned to the consideration of

business matters, Brian gave her the figures which answered her questions as to his total indebtedness.

Again Betty Jo exclaimed with delight: "Brian, do you see? Take your pencil and figure quick your royalties on the number of books sold as given in the publishers' statement."

Brian laughed. "I have figured it."

"And your book has already earned more than enough to pay everything," said Betty Jo. "Isn't that simply grand, Brian?"

"It is pretty 'grand,' all right," he agreed. "The only trouble is, I must wait so long before the money is due me from the publishers."

"That is exactly what I came to talk about," she returned quickly. "I tried to have it different when I made the arrangements with them, but the terms of payment in the contract are the very best I could get; and so I have planned a little plan whereby you —that is, we—won't need to wait for your freedom until the date of settlement with the publishers."

"You have a plan which will do that?" Brian questioned, doubtfully.

She nodded vigorously, with another Betty Jo

smile. "This is the plan, and you are not to interrupt until I have finished everything: I happen to have some money of my very, very own, which is doing nothing but earning interest—"

At the look on Brian's face, she stopped suddenly; but, when he started to speak, she put her hand quickly over his mouth, saying: "You were not to say a single word until I have finished. Play fair, Brian, dear; please!"

When he signified that he would not speak, she continued in her most matter-of-fact and businesslike tone: "There is every reason in the world, Brian, why you should pay off your debt to the bank and to Auntie Sue at the earliest possible moment. You can think of several reasons yourself. There is me, for instance.

"Very well. You have the money to your credit with the publishers; but you can't use it yet. I have money that you can just as well use. You will make an assignment of your royalties to me, all in proper form, to cover the amount you need. You will pay me the same interest my money is now earning where it is.

"I will arrange for the money to be sent to you in

the form of a cashier's cheque, payable to the banker, Homer T. Ward, so the name Brian Kent does not appear before we are ready, you see. You will make believe to Auntie Sue that the money is from the publishers. You will send the cheque to Mr. Bank President personally, with a statement of your indebtedness to him properly itemized, interest figured on everything. You will instruct him to open an account for you with the balance. And then—then, Brian, you will give dear Auntie Sue a cheque for what you owe her, with interest of course. And we will all be so happy! And—and—don't you think I am a very good managing owner? You do, don't you?"

When he hesitated, she added: "And the final and biggest reason of all is, that I want you to do as I have planned more than I ever wanted anything in the world, except you, and I want this so because I want you. You can't really refuse, now, can you?"

How, indeed, could he refuse?

So they worked it out together as Betty Jo had planned; and when the time came for the last and best part of the plan, and Brian confessed to Auntie Sue how he had robbed her, and had known for so

331

long that she was aware of his crime against her, and finished his confession by giving her the cheque, it is safe to say that there was nowhere in all the world more happiness than in the little log house by the river.

"God-A'mighty sure helped me to do one good turn, anyway, when I jumped inter the river after that there book when Mr. Burns done throw'd hit away," commented the delighted Judy.

And while they laughed together, Betty Jo hugged the deformed mountain girl, and answered: "God Almighty was sure good to us all that day, Judy, dear!"

It was only a day later when Auntie Sue received a letter from Homer T. Ward which sent the dear old lady in great excitement to Betty Jo. The banker was coming for his long-deferred vacation to the log house by the river.

There was in his letter a kindly word for his former clerk, Brian Kent, should Auntie Sue chance to see him; much love for his old teacher and for the dearest girl in the world, his Betty Jo.

But that part of Homer T. Ward's letter which most excited Auntie Sue and caused Betty Jo to laugh until she cried was this: The great financier, who, even in his busy life of large responsibilities, found time for some good reading, had discovered a great book, by a new and heretofore unknown writer. The book was great because every page of it, Homer T. Ward declared, reminded him of Auntie Sue. If the writer had known her for years, he could not have drawn a truer picture of her character, nor presented her philosophy of life more clearly. It was a remarkable piece of work. It was most emphatically the sort of writing that the world needed. This new author was a genius of the rarest and best sort. Mr. Ward predicted boldly that this new star in the literary firmament was destined to rank among those of the first magnitude. Already, among the banker's closest book friends, the new book was being discussed, and praised. He would bring a copy for Auntie Sue and Betty Jo to read. It was not only the book of the year;—it was, in Homer T. Ward's opinion, one of the really big books of the century.

"Well," commented Betty Jo, when they had read and reread that part of the letter, "dear old Uncle Homer may be a very conservative banker, but he certainly is more than liberal when he touches on the question of this new author. Won't we have fun, Auntie Sue! Oh, won't we!"

Then they planned the whole thing, and proceeded to carry out their plan.

Brian was told only that Mr. Ward was coming to visit Auntie Sue, and that he must be busy somewhere away from the house when the banker arrived, and not come until he was sent for, because Auntie Sue must make a full confession to her old pupil of the part she had played in the Re-Creation of Brian Kent before Homer T. Ward should meet his former clerk.

Brian, never dreaming that there were other confessions to be made, smilingly agreed to do exactly as he was told.

When the momentous day arrived, Betty Jo met her uncle in Thompsonville, and all the way home she talked so continuously of her school, and asked so many questions about his conduct and life and their many Chicago friends, that the helpless bank president had no chance whatever of asking her a single embarrassing question. But, when dinner was over (Brian had taken his lunch with him to the clearing), Homer T. Ward wanted to know things.

"Was Brian Kent still working in the neighborhood?"

Auntie Sue informed him that Brian was still working in the neighborhood.

"Betty Jo had seen the bank clerk?" Betty Jo's uncle supposed. "What did she think of the fellow?"

Betty Jo thought Brian Kent was a rather nice fellow.

"And how had Betty Jo been amusing herself while her old uncle was slaving in the city?"

Betty Jo had been doing a number of things: Helping Auntie Sue with her housework; learning to cook; keeping up her stenographic work; reading.

"Reading?" That reminded him, and forthwith Mr. Ward went to his room, and returned with the book.

And then those two blessed women listened and admired while he introduced them to the new genius, and read certain favorite passages from the great book, and grew enthusiastic on the new author, saying all that he had written in his letter and many things more, until Betty Jo could restrain herself no longer, but ran to him, and took the book from his hands, and, with her arms around his neck, told him that he was the dearest uncle in the world, because she was going to marry the man who wrote the book he so admired.

There were long explanations after that: How the book so highly valued by Banker Ward had actually been written in that very log house by the river; how Auntie Sue had sent for Betty Jo to assist the author with her typewriting; how the author, not knowing who Betty Jo was, had fallen in love with his stenographer, and, finally, how Betty Jo's author-lover was even then waiting to meet her guardian, still not knowing that her guardian was the banker Homer T. Ward.

"You see, uncle, dear," explained Betty Jo, "Auntie Sue and I were obliged to conspire this little conspiracy against my man, because, you know, authors are funny folk, and you never can tell exactly what they are going to do. After giving your heart to a genius as wonderful as you yourself know this one to be, it would be terrible to have him refuse you just because you were the only living relative of a rich old banker;—it would, wouldn't it, uncle, dear?"

And, really, Homer T. Ward could find reason in Betty Jo's argument, which ended with that fatal trick question.

Taking his agreement for granted, Betty Jo continued: "And, you see, Auntie Sue and I were simply forced to conspire a little against you, uncle, dear, because you know perfectly well that, much as I needed the advantage of associating with such an author-man in the actual writing of his book, you would never, never have permitted me to fall in love with him before you had discovered for yourself what a great man he really is, and I simply had to fall in love with him because God made me to take care of a genius of some sort. And if you don't believe that, you can ask Judy. Judy has found out a lot about God lately.

"You won't think I am talking nonsense, or am belittling the occasion will you, uncle, dear?" she added anxiously. "I am not,—truly, I am not,— I am very serious. But I can't help being a little excited, can I? Because it is terrible to love a banker-uncle, as I love you, and at the same time to love a genius-man, as I love my man, and—and—not know what you two dearest men in the world are going to do to each other."

And, at this, the girl's arms were about his neck again, and the girl's head went down on his shoulder; and he felt her cheek hot with blushes against his and a very suspicious drop of moisture slipped down inside his collar.

When he had held Betty Jo very close for a while, and had whispered comforting things in her ear, and had smiled over her shoulder at his old teacher, the banker sent the girl to find her lover while he should have a serious talk with Auntie Sue.

The long shadows of the late afternoon were on the mountain-side when Brian Kent and Betty Jo came down the hill to the little log house by the river.

The girl had said to him simply, "You are to come, now, Brian;—Auntie Sue and Mr. Ward sent me to tell you."

She was very serious, and as they walked together clung closely to his arm. And the man, too, seeming to feel the uselessness of words for such an occasion, was silent. When he helped her over the rail-fence at the lower edge of the clearing, he held her in his arms for a little; then they went on.

They saw the beautiful, tree-clad hills lying softly outlined in the shadows like folds of green and time-worn velvet, extending ridge on ridge into the blue. They saw the river, their river, making its gleaming way with many a curve and bend to the mighty sea, that was hidden somewhere far beyond the distant sky-line of their vision; and between them and the river, at the foot of the hill, they saw the little log house with Auntie Sue and Homer T. Ward waiting in the doorway.

When the banker saw the man at Betty Jo's side, his mind was far from the clerk whom he had known more than a year before in the city. His thoughts were on the author, the scholar, the genius, whose book had so compelled his respect and admiration. This tall fellow, with the athletic shoulders and deeply tanned face, who was dressed in the rude garb of the backwoodsman, with his coat over his arm, his ax on his shoulder, and his dinner-pail in his hand,—who was he? And why was Betty Jo so familiar with this stranger,—Betty Jo, who was usually so reserved, with her air of competent self-possession? Homer T. Ward turned to look inquiringly at Auntie Sue.

His old teacher smiled back at him without speaking.

Then, Betty Jo and Brian Kent were standing before him.

"Here he is, Uncle Homer," said the girl.

Brian, hearing her speak those two revealing words, and seeing her go to the bank president, who put his arm around her with the loving intimacy of a father, stood speechless with amazement, looking from Homer T. Ward and Betty Jo to Auntie Sue and back to the banker and the girl.

Mr. Ward, still not remembering the bank clerk in this re-created Brian Kent, was holding out his hand with a genial smile.

As the bewildered Brian mechanically took the hand so cordially extended, the older man said: "It is an honor, sir, to meet a man who can do the work you have done in writing that book. It is impossible to estimate the value of such a service as you have rendered the race. You have a rare and wonderful gift, Mr. Burns, and I predict for you a life of remarkable usefulness."

Brian, still confused, but realizing that Mr. Ward had not recognized him, looked appealingly at Betty Jo and then to Auntie Sue.

Auntie Sue spoke: "Mr. Ward is the uncle and guardian of Betty Jo, Brian."

" 'Brian'!" ejaculated the banker.

Auntie Sue continued: "Homer, dear, Betty Jo has presented *her* author, Mr. Burns;—permit me to introduce *my* Brian Kent!"

And Judy remarked that evening, when, after supper, they were all on the porch watching the sunset: "Hit sure is dad burned funny how all tangled an' snarled up everythin' kin git 'fore a body kin think most, an', then, if a body'll just keep a-goin' right along, all ter onct hit's all straightened out as purty as anythin'."

They laughed happily at the mountain girl's words, and the dear old teacher's sweet voice answered: "Yes, Judy; it is all just like the river, don't you see?"

"Meanin' as how the water gits all tangled an'

mixed up when hit's a-boilin' an' a-roarin' like mad down there at Elbow Rock, an' then all ter onct gits all smooth an' calm like again," returned Judy.

"Meaning just that, Judy," returned Auntie Sue. "No matter how tangled and confused life seems to be, it will all come straight at the last, if, like the river, we only keep going on."

And when the dreamy Indian-summer days were come and the blue haze of autumn lay softly over the brown and gold of the beautiful Ozark hills, the mountain folk of the Elbow Rock neighborhood gathered one day at the little log house by the river.

It was a simple ceremony that made the man and the woman, who were so dear to Auntie Sue, husband and wife. But the backwoods minister was not wanting in dignity, though his dress was rude and his words plain; and the service lacked nothing of beauty and meaning, though the guests were but humble mountaineers; for love was there, and sincerity, and strength, and rugged kindliness.

And when the simple wedding feast was over, they all went down to the river-bank, at the lower corner of the garden, where, at the eddy landing, a staunch John-boat waited, equipped and ready.

THE RE-CREATION OF BRIAN KENT

When the last good-byes were spoken, and Brian and Betty Jo put out from the little harbor into the stream, Auntie Sue, with Judy and Homer T. Ward, went back to the porch of the little log house, there to watch the beginning of the voyage.

With Brian at the oars, the boat crossed the stream to the safer waters close to the other shore, and then, with Betty Jo waving her handkerchief, and the neighbor men and boys running shouting along the bank, swept down the river, past the roaring turmoil of the Elbow Rock rapids into the quiet reaches below, and away on its winding course between the tree-clad hills.

"I am so glad," said Auntie Sue, her dear old face glowing with love, and her sweet voice tremulous with feeling, "I am so glad they chose the river for their wedding journey."

THE END.

Note.—This biographical sketch of Harold Bell Wright will give the reader a knowledge and understanding of the life-work, aims and purposes of the author as expressed through his books. It is reprinted on these pages in response to popular demand.—The Publishers.

HAROLD BELL WRIGHT

A Biography

By Elsbery W. Reynolds

The biography of a man is of importance and interest to other men just to the degree that his life and work touches and influences the life of his time and the lives of individuals.

Only in a feeble way, at best, can the life story of any man be told on the printed page. The story is better as it is written on the hearts of men and women and the man himself does the writing.

He lives longest who lives best. He who carves deepest against corroding time is he who touches with surest hand the greatest number of human hearts.

He may or may not be a prodigy of physical strength. He may or may not be a tower of mental energy. But so long as this old world stands the man with an overpowering desire for all that is best for the race to be in the race, whose life is in tune with the divine and with the good that is within us all, whether he be orator, writer, artist or artisan, is a giant among men.

That which we read makes a deeper and more lasting impression on our lives than that which we see or hear. An author with millions of readers must be a great central power of thought and influence, at least, in his own day and generation. We can understand the truth of this through a study of the aims and life purposes of Harold Bell Wright as expressed through his books and the circumstances under which they were written.

The wonderful popularity of this author is well estimated by the millions of copies of his books that have been sold. This is also the greatest testimonial that can be given to the merit of his work. The great heart of the reading public is an unprejudiced critic. "Is not the greatest voice the one to which the greatest number of hearts listen with pleasure?"

When a man has attained to great eminence under adverse circumstances we sometimes wonder to what heights he might have climbed under conditions more favorable. Who can tell? It is just as easy to say what the young man of twenty will be when a matured man of forty. The boy of poverty makes a man of power while the boy nursed in the lap of luxury makes a man of uneventful life, and, again, a life started with a handicap remains so through its possible three score years and ten and the life begun with advantages multiplies its talents ten and a hundred fold.

So, after all, is not the heart of man the real man and is it not the guiding star of his ambition, his will, his determination, his conscience?

Harold Bell Wright, the second of four sons, was born May 4, 1872, in Rome, Oneida County, New York. From an earlier biographer we quote the following:

"Some essential facts must be dug from out the past where they lie embedded in the detrital chronicles of the race. Say, then, that away back in 1640 a ship load of Anglo-Saxon freedom landed in New England. After a brief period some of the more venturesome spirits emigrated to the far west and settled amid the undulations of the Mohawk valley in central New York. Protestant France also sent westward some Gallic chivalry hungering for freedom. The fringe of this garment of civilization spread out and reached also into the same valley. English determination and Huguenot aspiration touched elbows in the war for political and religious freedom, and touched hearts and hands in the struggle for economic freedom. Their generations were a genuine aristocracy. Mutual struggles after mutual aims cemented casual acquaintance into enduring friendship. William Wright met, loved and married Alma T. Watson. To them four sons were born. A carpenter contractor, a man who builds, contrives and constructs, is joined to a woman into whose soul of wholesome refinement come images of dainty beauty, where they glow and grow radiant. With lavish unrestraint the life of this French woman pours itself into her sons. The third child died in infancy. The eldest survived his mother by some thirteen years. The youngest is a constructive mechanical engineer. The second son is Harold Bell Wright.

"During ten years this mother and this son live in rare intimacy. The boy's first enduring impression of this life is the vision of the mother bending affectionately over him while criticising the water color sketch his unpracticed fingers had just made. Crude blendings and faulty lines were pointed out, then touched into harmony and more accurate perspective by her quick skill. Together their eyes watched shades dance on sunny slopes, cloud shadows race among the hills or lie lazily in the valley below.

"Exuberant Nature and ebullient boy loved each other from the first. Alone, enravished, he often wandered far in sheer joy of living. He brings, one day, from his rambles a bunch of immortelles which mother graciously receives. Twenty years later the boy, man-grown, bows reverently over a box of withered flowers —the same bouquet the mother took that day and laid away as a precious memento of his boyish love. Such was the first decade.

"A ten-year-old boy, motherless, steals from harsh labor and yet harsher surroundings, runs to the home of sacred memories, clambers to the attic, and spends the night in anguished solitude. This was his first Gethsemane. For ten years buffeted and beaten, battling with adversity, sometimes losing but never lost, snatching learning here and there, hating sham, loving passionately, misunderstood, misapprehended, too stubbornly proud to ask apologies or make useless explanations, fighting poverty in the depths of privation, wrestling existence from toil he loathed, befriending many and also befriended much, but always face to face with the grim tragedy which has held part of the stage since Eden.

"Such was the second decade. The first was spent on hill sides where shadows only made the light more buoyant as they fled

346

away. The second was passed in the valley where the shadow hung lazily till the cloud grew very black and drenched the soil.

"Lured to college, he undertook to acquire academic culture. As is well known, college life with its professorial anecdotes and jokes, its student pranks and grind, is routine drudgery and cobwebbery prose. Bookish professors and conventional students rarely have just such an animate problem of French artistry and Bohemian experience to solve. They did nobly, to be sure, but here was a mind which threw over them all the glamour of romance."

Mr. Wright entered the Preparatory Department of Hiram College at the age of twenty, having previously accepted the faith and identified himself with the Christian Church in the little quarry town of Grafton, Ohio. He continued active in the different departments of work in his church all during his school years with the ultimate result of his entering the ministry.

Having no financial means, while in school he made his way by doing odd jobs about town, house painting and decorating, sketching, etc. After two years of school life, while laboring to gain funds in order that he might continue his schooling, he contracted from overwork and out-door exposure a severe case of pneumonia that left his eyesight badly impaired and his constitution in such condition that, to the present day, he has never fully recovered.

Air castles were tumbled and hopes blasted when his physician advised him that it would be fatal to re-enter school for, at least, another year. Whereupon, seeking health and a means of existence, starting from a point on the Mahoning river, he canoed with sketch and note book, but alone, down stream a distance of more than five hundred miles. From this point, by train, he embarked for the Ozark mountains in southwest Missouri. Here, for some months, while gradually regaining his strength, he secured employment at farm work, sketching and painting at intervals.

Once more, he found himself on bed-rock, taking his last cent to pay express charges back to Ohio on some finished pictures, but, this time, fortune smiled promptly with a good check by return mail.

It was while in the Ozarks that Harold Bell Wright preached his first sermon. Being a regular attendant at the services, held in the little mountain log school house, he was asked to talk to the people, one Sunday, when the regular preacher had failed to appear.

From this Sunday morning talk, that could hardly be called a sermon, and others that followed, he came to feel that he could do more good in the ministry than he could in any other field of labor, and soon thereafter accepted a regular pastorate at Pierce City, Missouri, at a yearly salary of four hundred dollars. True to a resolve, that his work should be that through which he could help the most people, he had now chosen the ministry. A further resolve that he would give up this ministry, chosen with such earnest conviction, should another field of labor offer more extensive measures for reaching mankind, took him, in later years, into the field of literature. He left the ministry with many regrets but with the same earnest conviction with which he had earlier chosen it.

Following the publication of "The Shepherd of the Hills" hi publishers assured him that he could secure greater results from his pen rather than his pulpit and prevailed upon him to hence forth make literature his life work. This was in every way consistent with his teaching that every man's ministry is that work through which he can accomplish the greatest good.

In the battle of life there is always the higher ground that th many covet but few attain. In reaching this height Mr. Wrigh has given to a multitude, his time, strength and substance, tha they, too, might further advance. He is companionable, lovin and loyal to his friends. He hates sham and hypocrisy and an attempt to glorify one's self by means other than the fruits o one's own labor.

This boy, who, from the death of his mother, was driven int a hand to hand struggle with life for a bare existence, was neces sarily forced into contact with much that was vicious and corrupt But he in no way became a part of it. That same inherent lov for mental cleanliness and spiritual truths that has so distin guished the works of the man kept the boy unstained in his unfor tunate environment.

Mr. Wright resigned his charge at Pierce City for the larger work at Pittsburg, Kansas. In the second year of his pastorate— 1899—he married Frances E. Long in Buffalo, New York. Thi union of love had its beginning back in the school days at Hiram Unto them have been born three sons, Gilbert Munger, 1901, Pau Williams, 1902, and Norman Hall, 1910.

In Pittsburg, Mr. Wright received enthusiastic support from his church people. Finances were soon in a satisfactory condi- tion, and church attendance reached the capacity of the building but still the young pastor was not satisfied. Pittsburg was a mining town, a young men's town. A little city with saloons and brothels doing business on every hand. His soul was on fire for his church to do a larger work and, with the hope of arousing his people, he conceived the idea of writing "That Printer of Udell's," planning to read the story, by installments, on special evenings of successive weeks, to his congregation.

Pittsburg was made the principal scene and the church of the story was the kind of church he wanted his Pittsburg charge to be. The teachings set forth, through the preacher of the story, in the latter half of the book, are the identical things the author was preaching. The first chapters of the story are very largely colored by Mr. Wright's early life, but they are by no means auto- biographical.

"That Printer of Udell's" was written without thought or inten- tion of offering it for publication. During the author's ministry he made some of the warmest and most abiding friendships of his life, and it was through certain of these friends that he was per- suaded from reading the story, as intended, but to offer it for publication, giving it, thus, a wider usefulness.

Having a leave of absence of several weeks from his church during the winter of 1901-2 he accepted an invitation from the pastor of a Chicago church to hold a special meeting, and it was during this meeting that the author and his publisher met for the first time. Mr. Wright delivered a sermon entitled "Sculptors of Life" that was so impressive that I sought him out with entreaties to repeat his sermon as a lecture to a certain company of young people.

The acquaintance thus begun very quickly became one of friendship, without any knowledge or thought that it would in time lead to a co-operative life work, and when the author later offered his book for publication it was without request or thought of financial remuneration. Mr. Wright, however, was given a contract paying him the highest royalty that was being paid for any author's first book.

"That Printer of Udell's" was written almost entirely in the late hours of the night and the very early hours of the morning. Great demands were being made on the author's time in the way of requests for officiating and speaking at public and civic functions in addition to the now heavy requirements of his church. His aggressive activities, backed by his splendid spirit, fearlessness and courage in combating the evils of his little city made for him a host of admirers, alike, among his enemies and friends. When he left to accept a pastorate in Kansas City, Missouri, his resignation was not accepted.

After one year in Kansas City he found that he was not physically able to carry out the great city work as he had dreamed it and planned it, on a scale that would satisfy his longings for service, and it made him seriously consider whether there was not some other way that would more equally measure with his strength. He went again to the Ozarks, this time for rest and meditation, and while there began writing "The Shepherd of the Hills." This story has a peculiar significance for the author. He feels toward it as he can not feel for any of his other books. "The Shepherd of the Hills" was written as a test. The strength of the message he was able to put into the story and the response it should find in the hearts of men and women was to decide for him his ministry henceforth, whether he would teach the precepts of the Man of Galilee by voice or pen. It was a testing time that bore fruit not only in this simple, sweet story, that to quote an eminent divine, "is one of the greatest sermons of our day," but resulted as well in the splendid volumes that have followed.

"The Shepherd of the Hills" was finished during the year of his pastorate at Lebanon, Missouri, and but for the sympathy, encouragement and helpful understanding of his church officers and membership, it is doubtful if the story could ever have been completed. When Mr. Wright delivered the manuscript to his publishers the first of the year, 1907, for publication the next fall, he had accepted the pastorate of the Christian Church in Redlands, California, hoping this land of sunshine would give him a larger measure of health.

Some months later, resigning his Redlands pastorate, he went to the Imperial Valley and there, the following year, wrote "The Calling of Dan Matthews." The church and its problems were weighing on the author and affecting his life no less than when he was in the ministry and it was only natural that he should give to the world "a picture that is true to the four corners of the earth." Every incident in the story has its counterpart in real life and,

349

with but few exceptions, came under the author's personal observation. He did not get the real pleasure out of writing "The Calling of Dan Matthews" that he did the story which preceded it. But he could not, try as he would, escape it.

The publication of "The Calling of Dan Matthews" in the fall of 1909 was just two years after the publication of "The Shepherd of the Hills."

"The Winning of Barbara Worth" required more time and effort in the collecting of material than any book the author had written, but probably gave him, at least, as much pleasure. He is very careful with regard to descriptive detail, and even while writing "The Calling of Dan Matthews" he was making a study of the desert and this great reclamation project. Before sending his manuscript for publication he had it checked over by the best engineers on the Pacific coast for inaccuracies in any of his descriptions that involved engineering or reclamation problems.

"The Winning of Barbara Worth" bears the distinction, without doubt, of being the only book ever published that called its publisher and illustrator from a distance of two and three thousand miles, into the heart of a great desert, for a consultation with its author. This story of the Imperial Valley and its reclamation was written in the same study as was "The Calling of Dan Matthews." A study of rude construction, about eighteen by thirty-five feet, with thatched roof and outside covering of native arrow-weed and built entirely by the author himself.

When Mr. Wright finished "The Winning of Barbara Worth"—so named in honor of Ruth Barbara Reynolds—he was a sick man. He often worked the night through, overtaxing his nerve and strength. For several months he virtually dwelt within the four walls of his study and for a time it was feared he would not live to finish the book. He wrote the last chapters while confined to his bed, after which he was taken by easy stages, through the kindness of friends, to that part of Northern Arizona that is so delightful to all lovers of the out-of-doors. In this bracing mile-high atmosphere he soon grew well and strong, almost to ruggedness, and on the day his book was published he was riding in a wild-horse chase over a country wild and rough where the writer of this sketch would only care to go, carefully picking his way, on foot. So it was weeks after publication before the author saw the first bound copy of his book. During these summer and fall months, while regaining his strength, he was busy with sketch and note book collecting material, for this part of Arizona is the scene of his novel "When a Man's a Man."

"Their Yesterdays" was written in Tucson, Arizona, and was published in the fall of 1912, just one year after the publication of "The Winning of Barbara Worth." In order to write this story, with the least possible strain on his nerves and vitality, Mr. Wright secluded himself in a little cottage purchased especially for this work. His material was collected from the observations of his thoughtful years and his intimate knowledge of human hearts. This book is, perhaps, more representative of the real Harold Bell Wright than anything he has done. It is the true presentation of his views on life, love and religion. I once asked Mr. Wright, in behalf of the faculty, to deliver an address to a graduating class of some twenty-odd young men of the Morgan Park Academy (Chicago). He was very busy and I suggested that without special effort he make the commonplace remarks that one so often hears on like occasions. For the first time that I remember he somewhat impatiently resented a suggestion from me, saying, "These young men are on the threshold of life and the very best that is within me is due to them. I can give to them only such a message as I would, were I to stand before judgment on the morrow." It was with just this spirit that the author wrote "Their Yesterdays."

Following "Their Yesterdays" the next book in order of publication was "The Eyes of the World," published in the fall of 1914. It was written in the same arrow-weed study on Tecolote Rancho in the Imperial Valley where he wrote "The Calling of Dan Matthews" and "The Winning of Barbara Worth." Being fully in sympathy with the author's purpose in writing this story, the campaign of advertising was of such educational character and so eventful in many ways, that it will long be remembered by authors, publishers and reading public, and, we trust, make for cleaner books and pictures.

As it was in the writing of "The Calling of Dan Matthews" so it was in the writing of "The Eyes of the World," the sense of duty stood highest. The modern trend in books and music and art and drama had so incensed the author that "The Eyes of the World" was the result of his all impelling desire for cleaner living and thinking. As is true of all writers, there are sometimes those who fail to catch the message in Mr. Wright's books. He is occasionally misunderstood, and that was especially true with "The Eyes of the World." To the great majority of people, clean living and thinking, the message was not to be misinterpreted and to them the book is blessed. To that small minority it was convicting and, from a few such, it brought forth condemnation which, in a fellow author here and there, was pronounced and emphasized by envy and jealousy. To critics of this class Mr. Wright makes no reply and is not in the least disturbed.

"The Uncrowned King," a small volume—an allegory—published in 1910, to me, is one of the most delightful of Mr. Wright's books. Possibly, it has an added charm because of certain peculiar conditions. It was written in Redlands, California, during the winter of 1909-10, although the notion for the little volume occurred to the author while living in Kansas City. It was one of those times when the longing and will to do a work greater than the physical would permit seemed almost overpowering when, unconsciously coming to his aid, a young woman talking to a company of Christian Endeavorers chanced to remark, "After all, the real kings of earth are seldom crowned." All through the evening service thoughts that this inspired kept running through the author's mind and late that same night he wrote the outline which was only completed some years later and given to his publishers to enrich the world.

His first four novels in order of publication have been dramatized and enjoyed by thousands from before the footlights and it has been a delight to renew acquaintances with old friends in this way. It remained for "The Eyes of the World" to be the first of his books to be presented in a feature production of motion pictures.

The likes and dislikes of Harold Bell Wright are quite pronounced. He is unpretending, cares not for the lime-light and avoids interviews for the public press. Loud, boisterous conversation is but little less offensive to him than vulgarity in speech or action. His friends are strong, clean-minded men who are doing things in the world and are as necessary to his being as the air to his existence, and his generosity to them is no less marked than his caring and providing for his family, which is almost a passion. He is extremely fond of most forms of out-door life. The desert with its vast expanse, fierce solitude and varied colors is no less attractive to him than the peaceful quiet of wooded dells, the beauty of flowering meadows or the rugged mountains with their roaring trout streams that furnish him hours of sport with rod and line. He enjoys hunting, horse-back riding or long tramps afoot. But when there is work to be done it is the one thing that bulks largest and all else must wait.

After finishing "The Eyes of the World," Mr. Wright embarked on the building of a home in the Santa Monica mountains near Hollywood, California. So in the summer of 1915 the little family of five began making their residence in the new canyon home, one of nature's delightful spots.

Then again, the author went into camp in the Arizona desert while writing "When a Man's a Man." For he finds it very helpful to live in the atmosphere of his story while doing the actual writing and he also avoids frequent interruption. I think he got more real enjoyment out of this story than any he has previously done. It is a story of the out-of-doors in this great unfenced land where a man must be a man. I suppose, too, he enjoyed writing this work so much, partly, because it comes so easy for him to just tell a story without the intervention of some nerve racking problem. The only book he has heretofore written that is purely a story is "The Shepherd of the Hills," and I sometimes wonder to what proportion of his readers does this Ozark story hold first place. For all such, I am sure, "When a Man's a Man" will find a reception of special heartiness because it is just a fine, big, wholesome novel of simple sweetness and virile strength.

I have written this sketch of Harold Bell Wright that you may know him as intimately, if possible, as if you had met him in person. But should you have the opportunity of making his acquaintance do not deny yourself the pleasure. If you are a lover of his books I am sure you are just the kind of person that the author himself delights to meet.

"Relay Heights," February 15, 1916.